OBSESSED

JANE HEAFIELD

BLOODHOUND
— BOOKS —

www.bloodhoundbooks.com

Print ISBN: 978-1-5040-8245-7

ALSO BY JANE HEAFIELD

CHAPTER ONE

I was supposed to be dead, but the nightmare was far from over. My scream of pain would bring running feet. I had to escape. So I wiped blood from my eyes and crawled away from the stream.

With the blood removed, my eyes took in the night. The trees were a thick, vast wall surrounding me, and I was thankful for their presence. I paused to listen for noises, barely breathing, and only dared to move onwards after a lengthy period without stir or sound from the gloom beyond.

My whole body was numb and I felt no pain, but I was aware of my knee catching something hard. It was my mobile phone. I snatched it up. The screen was a spiderweb of cracks. The clock said 7.41pm. The last thing I remembered was moving quickly through the woods, towards my target, because the party had already started – and that was at 7.27.

In the following fourteen minutes I reached my destination and got half killed, and I remembered none of it. Except fighting for my life and knowing it was a lost battle. Even if the events themselves never resurfaced, I'd never forget that molten feeling that I was going to die in the cold and the dark.

What if I hadn't stopped for petrol? If I'd had a shower instead of a bath? If I had paused to eat before setting off? With just a single, insignificant change to the night's events, I could have avoided the vicious attack that changed my life.

I cut these thoughts. I needed to leave. If my attacker had heard my scream of pain, he would know I still clung to life and would return to finish off his prey. I managed to stand with the aid of a thick tree and the sensation in my body began to return. It started with a chill that soon became fiery pain. My head, my hand, my shoulder – all started throbbing.

The agony seemed to wake me up. I remembered that I followed the stream to get here, so I could trek alongside to escape – provided I took the correct direction.

As I stumbled through the trees, I heard voices off to the left. It sounded like giggling from a male and a female, perhaps new lovers out for a romantic stroll. Bizarrely, I thought it unfair to force them to swap their joy for shock. Unfair of me to ruin their night by seeking help. The park might be full of cool memories for them, the place where they met, shared their first kiss, and I cannot fracture their enchantment.

Even worse, perhaps they wouldn't sympathise: I chose to come here alone, so provoking the assault on me. I brought this upon myself and don't deserve aid.

So on I stumbled, and soon their voices were behind me, faded. Lost in the cold January breeze.

The trees ended at a road on which the far side was the car park. I recalled being alone when I pulled up, but there was now a second car. I watched for a few moments to make sure it was empty. Perhaps it belonged to the laughing lovers strolling in the woods.

This close to my car, to escape, I should have been elated, but it was quite the opposite. The empty road seemed like a boundary between safety and danger. Here, nestled between high trees, I was hidden, invisible, but out there I would be exposed and pinned under lights, marked out for whatever human monster was watching from their own secret spot.

But the journey had to be made. As best a shambling stagger as I could manage, I ran for my car. I blipped the central locking and the vehicle flashed at me. The noise was terrifying, surely loud enough to draw my attacker from even a mile away. I threw myself in so fast that every injured place turned to fire. I locked the doors and started the engine.

But didn't move. The sun visor was down and I saw myself in the mirror. Above my right eye was a large gash leaking blood and with hair embedded in it. I flicked on the interior light to survey the rest of the damage.

My jeans were soaking wet, but my jumper was dry, although blood from my face had stained it. My left shoulder ached as if I'd fallen on it. My right hand also throbbed and it was hard to bend the fingers. I had an image of my hand and phone getting busted at the same time, but the how eluded me. It all eluded me. I tried to picture the face of my attacker, but all I had was a shimmering blur, as if glimpsed through rippling water.

This was the second time I'd suffered such a memory blackout. The first time was ten years ago, at age nineteen, when I nearly died following a drugs overdose.

I didn't seek professional help, but consulted the internet. I already knew, from seeing it happen around me, that substance abuse could cause such blackouts, but I'd never known anyone to lose more than slices of a night. I lost a whole night and it worried me.

But the internet research comforted me. I learned about

'dissociative amnesia' and how the brain could repress memory of trauma. It sounded scary, but I lightened the load by imagining my brain as the type of good friend who would refuse to remind you of an embarrassing drunken dance at a works Christmas party.

In addition, I was heartened by stories of people whose memory loss was no barrier to coping as normal thereafter. So I chalked the event down to a wake-up call about the state of my life, and vowed to better myself for the future.

I accomplished that mission. I never touched drugs again, moved cities to be away from bad influences, and got a loving husband and a child and a job. I never looked back – literally: I pushed that missing night and near-death experience into a dusty mental cupboard. It became a positive, for without it there might have been a subsequent overdose or foolish endeavour, and one I never walked away from.

The memories of that decade-old ordeal had never returned. There was a chance I would never recall the events of tonight either.

Perhaps that would turn out to be a blessing.

CHAPTER TWO

I knew I wouldn't make the 7.30 start time for the party, but this was beyond fashionably late. People had already left messages and voicemails, especially my sister and husband. Nobody would be panicking yet, but I knew I should really call ahead. However, I couldn't bring myself to. This was a story that had to be told face to face.

I was certain I'd be unable to drive in such a state and would probably arrive at the pub in the back of a police car, but I took it slow and made it to the Blue Orb without incident. That's when something vital that I've overlooked hit me. I'd hoped to brush off the attack as a minor incident, perhaps even an accident, and treat it like a funny little story to tell people – but look at the state of me.

My coat was in the car – it was new and I hadn't wanted to ruin it on sharp undergrowth in the woods – so I could cover my bloodied jumper, but I couldn't hide my face. I was clearly a terrible mess and none of my friends or family was going to be able to continue partying. A lot of time and effort had gone into my sister's birthday bash, and she might never forgive me for ruining it.

I sat in the car park and watched the main window in the lounge area. The coloured lights of the children's disco flashed across the closed blinds, like a form of Morse code telling me how much fun everyone was having because they'd been smart enough not to go hunting in the dark woods. I wondered if the light of the disco would hide my facial injuries.

I was debating whether to go in or call my sister with a lie about a broken-down car, but the choice was snatched from me.

Maud came out of the main doors. I watched her raise her phone, probably to call me, and then lower it again as she spotted my car. She started to come down the stairs. I figured this was the best scenario for me. I could explain to Maud without onlookers. And the car park was dim enough that my injuries wouldn't glow like neon. I got out to meet my older sister. I had my coat on, zipped fully up to hide my bloodied jumper.

Maud was a big lady and her bad knees meant she moved slowly, so I should have at least met her halfway. Instead, I waited by my car and let her come to me. I wasn't going to enjoy what happened next and couldn't bring myself to drag the moment closer.

Ten feet out, Maud stopped and said, 'So what happened?' Her tone was only part curiosity. The other part was accusatory. I spend a lot of time alone in remote places, and she was always on my back about the risks I was taking. I certainly had no defence now, did I?

'I'm sorry I'm late,' was my weak response.

She pointed at my lower half. 'Why are your jeans wet? And what's with the shoe covers?'

I looked down, noticing I still wore plastic shoe covers over my trainers. I forgot to take them off before driving here. 'They're so I don't contaminate the woods. And the jeans... I had to run through a stream.'

'Had to? Lisa, what's... Look at me, Lisa.'

I realised my head had been bowed and my long brown hair hid the damage on my face. When I looked up and swept that hair aside to expose it all, Maud gasped. She rushed closer and grabbed my shoulders. I winced at the pain in my left arm. 'My God. Lisa. What happened to you?'

In the car, I'd planned a story about a fall; I'd even considered muddying my hands for realism. But here, now, with my big sister wracked with worry, I couldn't lie. 'I was attacked,' I say immediately. 'A big teenaged girl. In the woods. She attacked me.'

She pulled me into a hug, which I returned with force. 'Christ, Christ, Christ,' she moaned, again and again.

She led me into my car. At first I thought it was for privacy, but I knew otherwise when she put the interior lights on. With her face close to mine, she stared at my damage, and ran fingers softly across the cuts and bruises, like a blind man reading braille. I said nothing, but Maud spoke in contradictions, as if suffering a strange form of Tourette's.

'I warned you about doing this treasure-hunting lark alone. Can people not walk this world in safety anymore? Did you do something to provoke this? How can someone attack someone for no reason like this?'

She grabbed my left hand. That one wasn't injured, but it had suffered worst of all. 'Where's your wedding ring?'

I looked at my hand. I turned it this way and that. I even rubbed at my third finger in case of illusion. But the ring was definitely missing. 'She took it. I don't remember. But she must have taken it.'

'Does Ted know?'

'No. I came straight here and told you. I don't know how to tell him. Or where. Not here, for sure. I can't ruin the party.'

'You need to tell him as soon as he gets back. I'll stand with you if that makes it easier. Okay?'

It took me a moment to understand. 'When he gets back? Is he not here?'

'He went out for cigarettes. He'll be back soon.'

Ted hadn't said anything about being short of cigarettes when we'd arrived at the pub, only minutes before I'd headed out. But that was beside the point: he'd be back soon and I didn't want to face them both out here. My sister and husband shared a belief that my hobby was perilous. They had often warned me of the dangers, and that was back when I'd never been attacked late in the woods. This was fuel for the fire. They would corner and reprimand me.

'I'll get him to rush back,' Maud said, pulling out her phone. I snatched it off her, but before she could react, the car was filled with light. A car pulled in behind us. I knew it was Ted.

Maud got out. I didn't. In the rear-view, I watched her scuttle to Ted's vehicle. She began talking before he'd even gotten out of the car. I caught snippets of it:

'... robbed... never listened... battered face... waste of time... treasure-hunting silliness...'

I should explain this 'treasure-hunting silliness'. Don't picture Lara Croft or Indiana Jones: I am a geocacher. The dictionary describes geocaching as *an outdoor sport involving searching for hidden items using Global Positioning System coordinates online.*

The sport was invented in the early 2000s and today there are myriad websites dedicated to it, hosting millions of geocaches around the world. I'd been a geocacher for ten years, since just after I got married. Anyone with a smartphone could play: you joined a website, picked a geocache, and followed the GPS coordinates to find it. You could also create your own caches, called 'hides'.

'Treasure' is a misleading word, however. A standard cache was just a container with a logbook, which hunters signed. Then they logged the visit on the website, perhaps with a photo. On my Topgeocaching.net profile page, it said I had thirteen hides, all in South Yorkshire, and 134 finds across the country. I had never hunted geocaches abroad, but some of the veterans had been across the planet.

As Ted and Maud approached my car, I climbed out. But not to talk to them. Without even a glance back at them, I headed briskly for the pub, declaring, 'We'll do this inside. I'm going for a drink.'

Ted collared me at the bar. After holding my hair aside for a long, close look at my face, he said, 'You get the registration plate?'

Ted hid his emotions well and often his sarcasm was hard to read; it could mean he was angry, but equally it could indicate a good mood. I couldn't fathom if he was having a go or trying to relax me.

'I'm okay,' I said. 'An idiot in the woods, that's all.'

'Did she rob you?'

Had my sister already mentioned the wedding ring? Did Ted want to see what I'd say about it? I showed him the plain finger. It took taken him a moment to realise.

'She stole your ring? Why did you let...?'

He quickly realised the error of finishing that question, but too late. 'Let them? I'm not some karate master. I didn't let anyone do anything. I was attacked by a big teenage girl and she did what she wanted. Look at my face. What could I have done?'

My outburst didn't go down well. 'How about not going out into the woods on your own so late? Could you have done that?'

My drink arrived. After I paid, and while I gulped down half a pint in one go, Ted said, 'This girl left your handbag, I see. Just my two grand ring she took then.'

I wanted to slam the pint glass down, but refrained. 'That was in the car. I'm in pain here, Ted. Some sympathy?'

He put his arm around me, and was about to apologise, when his hand hit my bad shoulder and made me groan. That set him off again. 'Jesus, you're in a bad way. Is it not just your face? What else did they do? We need to get you to a hospital.'

'No. I just need a drink and some rest, and I'll be fine tomorrow. Where's Dan?'

'You can't let him see your face. I mean, not tonight. The kids are all in the cinema.'

'I'm going to go see him.'

'Well... tell him you fell over or something.'

'Maybe that's what happened,' I said, then went to find my son.

Dan was diagnosed with autism five years ago, when he was three. The condition is known as a spectrum because symptoms vary between children. The TV might typically portray autistic kids as silent and withdrawn, but Dan was quite the opposite. Although he sometimes needed his own time, he was generally outgoing and loud; he didn't mind noise in moderation and could handle crowds and fuss for short periods.

The only obvious outward indication of his disability was a constant need to touch things, especially hair. To help, we gave him a wig that he would play with when stress was overtaking him. As he got older, a mobile phone worked just as well to divert his attention.

He was on his phone when I found him. The pub had a side room made out like a home cinema and the kids at the party had been shunted here to watch cartoons and give the adults some peace. Ten of them were sitting cross-legged, watching *Peppa Pig*; Dan was at the back, facing away from the screen and jabbing at his mobile. He ran to me when I opened the door.

Outside, in the quiet hallway, I gave him a clear look at Mummy's damaged face. I'd figured it was best to get his shock out there and over and done with.

'Did someone beat you up?' he asked. He started to fiddle with my hair and I figured he was upset. Best not to add to that stress, so I lied. I told him I hit the brake too hard in my car and headbutted the steering wheel.

Using his fingers, Dan combed my hair in such a way that it fell over my forehead and bad eye. That seemed to comfort him. He asked me to sit with him for the cartoons and I was happy to: my own anxiety levels were skyrocketing.

We sat at the back and Dan, comforted by my presence, was able to concentrate on the screen. I was thankful because this allowed me to hide the tears falling down my cheeks. So far I'd done a mighty job of feigning indifference to my attack, but the mask was beginning to crumble.

CHAPTER THREE

On Sunday, the 23rd, I woke at just before midday, still dressed in dirty clothing and lying atop the bed quilt. My head felt ready to pop. Ted was absent.

I rushed into the bathroom to check my injuries. Given how much worse my right hand and left shoulder felt, I almost daren't look at my face. And with good reason: the laceration above my right eye was a ragged line, although two plasters held the wound closed. I didn't recall self-surgery so could only imagine someone else had provided aid. My entire forehead looked like pounded beef. The backs of all four fingers on my right hand were bruised and stiff. I still had no memory of how each injury was caused.

I did, though, remember being a little abrupt with Ted. Understandable, given what I'd been through, but Ted had had his wife attacked and then been given grief off her. So I headed downstairs to find and apologise to him.

Halfway down the stairs, a memory resurfaced. Not of the attack, but an event after we'd gotten home. In my drunken state, Ted had tried to have sex with me. I recalled his hands, fumbling to lift my shirt. I recalled slapping those hands away.

Over the last few months, I hadn't felt very sexy and we'd been intimate only a handful of times. To make things worse, on each of those occasions I had submitted only because it had been Ted's desire. If the choice had been mine, we wouldn't have had sex in almost a year.

For certain my own insecurities had played a role, but Ted's social life hadn't helped. He'd been out a lot in the evenings, learning Brazilian jiu-jitsu, a grappling and submissions martial art. The last time we'd been out as a couple was a fading piece of history. But it was possible he'd boosted his social life because he felt his wife was distant.

Ted was in the living room, standing by the window and staring out. I couldn't see our son, but his bedroom was empty. 'Where's Dan?'

Ted shook his head. 'I told you you were drinking too much. Remember anything at all?'

My headache was indication of how much I'd drunk last night. 'Where is he?'

'Maud's house. We were both drunk, so she took him. He'll be back in a bit.'

I was intrigued as to what could be holding his attention outside. I looked out the living-room window. Nothing doing, but I did note both our cars outside. 'Tell me we didn't drive back?'

His snort of a laugh was as good as another claim that I overdid the booze last night. I walked into the kitchen for water.

'Donald and his mate drove us home in the cars last night,' Ted called out from the living room.

Donald was my sister's husband. 'We should thank them.'

'I did. I wasn't out cold drunk by then. You remember getting attacked in the woods, right?'

Unlike with the beer last night, this time I slammed my drink down to emphasise my frustration. 'Don't be a twat, Ted.

Yes, I remember that. I remember losing my wedding ring. And I remember you being a twat about that too.'

'It was two grand.'

'And you think I threw it away because I was pissed at you.'

'I never said that. But it is puzzling how someone could get a ring off your finger. I mean, if you just keep your fist closed...'

I suddenly remembered the same claim from last night, in the same condescending tone. And my response: *Try that heroic crap when someone will keep kicking until they get what they want.*

This time I said, 'I don't want to have talk about this again.'

Then I heard Ted crossing the living room. He appeared in the doorway. 'You're going to have to. They're here. You didn't want to do this last night, but now we have to. Come on.'

'What? Who's here?'

But I already had a suspicion, based on another returned fragment of last night: Ted saying, *You got robbed and assaulted, Lisa, and we can't just let it lie.*

And to confirm it, Ted now said, 'The police.'

My heart started to thud. The truth was that I lied last night. I lied to my sister and my husband about who attacked me, and why. I was hoping they would quickly skip past the whole event and store it in the history files. But they hadn't, and now I would be forced to repeat that fallacy to police officers.

I joined Ted at the living-room window, where we watched two officers, one female, one male, exit a patrol car parked behind Ted's. They looked up and down the street, as if seeking a criminal to nab before dealing with the woman who got robbed.

'It was just some altercation in the woods,' I said. 'Why did you call the police?'

He looked at me as if I had two heads. 'Just write off a violent robbery? Leave that thieving bastard roaming free to do it again? Besides, two grand ring, remember? We might get it back. You can wear it in court when this bozo goes down for five years.'

This sarcasm was easy to read: Ted was still pissed at me for going out late and alone... and losing the wedding ring. I have to admit he was right about reporting the crime, but it didn't alter my annoyance. 'Might this be the real reason my sister took Dan overnight? So he's not here to see this?'

The officers open the gate, then stop. They straighten their clothing, like job interviewees about to walk into a prospective boss's office.

'Hold nothing back,' Ted said, ignoring my question. 'Something about your story doesn't add up, Lisa. So make sure the maths is correct when you tell these two.'

I nodded. There was no way out of this now. I took an armchair so nobody could sit next to me, and there I waited while Ted went to answer the knock on the door. I took deep breaths and tried to tell my nerves to stop jangling. I was acting as if I was a criminal about to be arrested.

Moments before the police entered the living room with Ted, I leaped up to grab an ornament off the fireplace so my hands would have something to fiddle with. Was this level of stress how Dan felt so often? I even thought about hunting out sunglasses to hide my bruised eye, but of course, the police would want to have a long, close look at the damage.

Even before they were all in the room, Ted was telling my story for me. He managed to mention geocaching, my injured face, and the stolen ring before the male officer told him to take a breath, slow down.

And then they're here, all staring at me. The female officer was younger than the male by about ten years, much shorter, and pretty, yet she had an air of experience. Conversely, her big, hard-faced partner seemed to ooze inexperience. I would have rather dealt with the male for this reason, but I didn't get my wish.

The female turned to Ted. 'Mr Holten, why don't you pop into the kitchen to talk to my partner and I'll have a word with Lisa?'

Mere moments later the boys were absent, all doors were shut, and I was alone in a box with the woman. She ruined my plan to have her sit five feet away on the sofa, by kneeling right before me. 'Let me see your face.'

I'd let my hair fall over my eye again. I swept it aside to expose the damage. 'I was attacked but it wasn't that bad.'

'Have you been to the hospital? You had a bad head injury, your husband said. He said you can't remember much.'

I shook my head. 'It's the drink more than anything. The head injury isn't that bad. Looks worse than it is. But I really didn't have a chance to see much anyway. It was dark.'

'Run me through what happened. You were at a party, right?'

'Yes, for my sister. She got good news.'

I go over this 'good news' briefly. Maud ran a stall in the same shopping centre where I worked. For years she had rented the patch, but a couple of weeks back she signed up to buy it from the owner. The party was to celebrate. The early part of the function was a magic show for the kids in attendance, so I'd asked my sister if I could attend a little later: I wanted to finally visit a geocache nearby...

I realised I'd segued into the story of my attack, but didn't want to go down that road again. 'Ted, my husband, he's already told you the rest. I can't really offer more than I told him.'

She stared at me for a few seconds. She had big, sweet eyes and a touch of rouge on her face. I imagined that drunken louts wouldn't take her seriously on a Saturday night. But I could also see hardened criminals being hypnotised into losing their brashness in an interview room.

But then those eyes got serious. She glanced at the closed kitchen door, beyond which my husband and her partner were probably having the same conversation.

'Lisa, listen to me. You want to save some time here?'

I shrugged. 'I guess. I mean... what do you mean?'

'I'm supposed to pussyfoot around, lead you this way and that, throw in some sympathy and some trickery, and eventually get you to open up. We'll skip it. I'll just give you a promise. You ready?'

I nodded even though I didn't have the faintest clue what she was talking about.

'I promise that I'll arrest him right now, get him out of this house, and make sure he never hits you again. All you have to do is nod. Nod at me to show I'm right, and I'll end it.'

It struck me then. Why the officers had split Ted and me up. Why this lady needed me to tell my story even though Ted had imparted it already. 'You think my husband did this? You think he beats me up?'

She didn't answer, but said, 'Just a nod. One little nod.'

For a moment I shook my head. 'No, no way. Not Ted. What he told you was the truth. A girl attacked me in the woods. It wasn't even an attack, more of a fight that I lost. I lost my wedding ring. I got a cut and some bruises, but that's all.'

She didn't push it. But as she stood up, I grabbed her wrist, and for a moment we locked eyes. In hers I saw a flicker of hope, and in mine I know she witnessed a moment of consideration. Right then I was about to speak the truth – not the truth she expected, though, because Ted had never laid a hand on me.

No, she would hear a story that would turn this simple mugging investigation into something much bigger. It would be so easy to unload everything on someone with such comforting eyes. She was right before me, and it would only take a few words, and of course, it was the right thing to do.

But then the moment passed, and I let go of her wrist. 'I got in a fight with a girl. I don't want to press charges or make a statement. I just want to forget it and move on.'

CHAPTER FOUR

Sunday was usually a rest day, but inactivity would allow my mind to relive yesterday's nightmare. Instead, I set about doing chores. Once I'd fixed this, cleaned that, and binned the other, I turned to important duties.

Top of the list was Dan's diary. We were in the process of trying to get our son an Educational Health and Care Plan, a necessary step towards obtaining a place in a special school.

It was a long process to convince the council that a mainstream school couldn't provide the structure or atmosphere that Dan's educational needs required. I'd so far made dozens of phone calls, written just as many letters, and attended meeting after meeting with teachers, psychologists, and counsellors. Another vital element was to prove that Dan's struggles at school were affecting his home life. My job was to keep a diary of daily life.

Dan's SENCo (Special Educational Needs Coordinator), year 2 teacher Miss Haven, had told me to make notes of Dan's struggles, worries, and challenging behaviour, our own problems as parents of an autistic child – and, most important, to tie every negative to the simple fact that a mainstream school was no good for him. Usually Sunday was when I would take those daily diary scribblings and transfer them to a single document.

Once there was enough evidence that Dan needed special help, it would be sent to the council. After that it was a waiting game, but Miss Haven, the SENCo, had instructed me not to sit idly on my hands. The backlog of kids awaiting help was enormous and, unfortunately, not every plea would be successful. She wanted us to make sure the council knew we were eager and determined, and the best way: 'blitzkrieg', to quote her. An avalanche of emails. A blizzard of phone calls.

It seemed like queue jumping, but Miss Haven convinced me that many applications were for children with far fewer struggles than Dan; some were for kids who needed no help at all and whose parents simply wanted a certain special school because it was on their doorstep. It seemed to me to be a little like the old case of being given what you wanted just to shut you up. So be it. I fired off another *where-are-we-at-now?* email that evening.

Another job that Sunday was to go over our finances. Ted lost five hours at work last month because his employer, Premier Carpets, lowered its daily trading hours, and money was getting tight. Ted thought we could dip into Dan's child saver account, but I wouldn't have that. Yes, it already contained over £5,000, but the fund was to help our son with a car or a flat when he turned eighteen.

Taking money from it, even if it got replaced soon after, would feel like a desperate act. I didn't ever want to feel desperate.

Things would never get that bad, I promised Ted. If we had to lose a holiday this year, so be it. Even one of the cars – I needed mine for the school run, but Ted could bus to work. Two weeks ago we cancelled our cinema monthly membership. Last week I dumped the Amazon Prime account and tonight I excised the YouTube Premium subscription. Little manoeuvres like that could make a big difference. There was no need to panic.

Besides, I had other worries. Tomorrow I would have to venture out of the house, in stark daylight, and hiding my facial injuries would be impossible. A thick layer of make-up would help, but people would still notice, and they'd talk. Maybe, like the female police officer, some would assume my husband hit me.

In the late afternoon, Ted took Dan to a Fun Splatter swimming session in Rotherham and I watched YouTube videos of make-up for wounds. Before long I'd subconsciously gravitated to watching how heavily scarred people coped out in public. Some of these folk were strong and next to them, with my little cuts and bruises, I was being a wimp. It didn't help to alleviate my fears.

As night closed in, different demons paid a visit. Sleep wasn't something I looked forward to tonight, and I admit it was because I was sober. I don't drink often and rarely in the house, but tonight I was desperate for alcohol. I needed the liquid courage. Without it, how could I lie in bed and drift off, knowing that only thin doors protected me from the monsters roaming the dark?

Dan had a virtual reality headset that was a great tool for calming him down. He enjoyed the social games, where users from across the world could mingle as avatars in digital rooms and chat. The anonymity made it easier for him to interact and I knew he'd made three close friends, who I'd confirmed were kids like him and not seedy adults in disguise.

Both parents enjoyed the odd blast on the VR too. Ted liked the shoot-'em-up games, but I liked a piece of software that allowed the user to travel through Earth's most epic and tranquil zones. Dan was in bed by nine and Ted, with an early rise tomorrow, retired upstairs just two hours later. I remained downstairs, slipped on the VR headset, and chose to take a slow stroll across the Moon Crossing Bridge in the hills of Kyoto, Japan.

After soaking up the beauty of this spot for an hour, my eyelids started to get heavy, so I headed upstairs. Ted had fallen asleep but the TV was on and playing a YouTube jiu-jitsu training video. I left it alone, just for some light, but turned off the volume. I got in bed and let my heavy eyes shut.

But tiredness was an illusion; my mind was as awake as it had ever been. Sometimes Ted's snoring was bad because of his smoking, but tonight he barely made a noise and for the first time in what seemed like a long time, I was awash in silence.

I watched the silent grappling video for a while. I knew all sorts of terms because of Ted's interest, but had no idea what I was seeing. Was that a kneebar, triangle choke, worm guard? I turned the TV off when a man in a blue Gi snared his opponent in a choke from behind. Something about that unnerved me.

No longer assailed by noise or light, my mind dislodged something previously half-submerged, and it floated free. I say half-submerged because I'd always had a suspicion; it was why I told you that I'd lied to my sister, and the police, about who attacked me. Now, I was certain of the facts.

My attacker was a man, not a teenaged girl. A *man* tried to murder me that night. I remembered his arm. An arm that was impossibly hard, like iron, latching around my neck from behind. He had crept up on me, I now knew. I couldn't remember it visually, but I just knew.

I closed my eyes, trying to clear all thoughts and sights to allow a further seismic shift in my head. I wanted the face of my attacker to appear, but it didn't. At least, it didn't evolve beyond the haziness of before. It was still, like a reflection upon rippling water.

But... I saw a stone. A rock from the stream caused the laceration above my eye and the bruising on my forehead. But my hand and shoulder and phone... what happened to those?

I tried to sink deeper and unearth more. I wanted answers. I wanted everything. Why were my jeans wet, yet not my top? Did I run away through the stream? How did my phone get broken? Did he snatch my ring or did I lose it?

I sat up in bed, breathing heavily. The fog would not lift, I would get no more answers, and this was the most unsettling part of all. What could have happened to me that was so vile and traumatic that my brain saw fit to save my sanity and redact those memories?

I was drifting off when a yelp of pain stirred me. It was Ted, from the other room. I didn't move, figuring he'd tweaked a limb or finger while turning over in bed. So it was a surprise when he appeared in the bathroom doorway, naked, one hand behind his back and the other held up for me to see. A finger was indeed injured. I saw a trickle of blood. He didn't ask why I was in the bath at – according to a clock on the wall – just after 4am.

Then he showed me his other hand, which held a large carving knife. I just stared, still numb from the mental assault of the whole night, which was far from over yet.

'Are you really going to wait for me to ask?' he said. 'Okay. Why was this bloody *samurai sword* under your pillow? I just stabbed myself half to death. I tried to cuddle you in my sleep, I think.'

'I was... worried.'

He put the knife in the sink. 'Because of your attack?'

I nodded and returned my gaze to where it had been for

over an hour previously: the ceiling. 'It's probably hard for you to understand.'

He sat on the closed toilet lid. 'No. You were scared last night. But, Jesus, what was the plan here? Race downstairs with that knife if you heard a noise? I thought the standard thing was to wake the man of the house. I go down, see it's nothing, make some grunting and banging noises, then come upstairs and pretend I wrestled a burglar and booted him out of the house.'

I couldn't tell if he was angry or confused, or both or neither, but I didn't care. I was a little annoyed at his brush-off of my worry.

'Thanks for trying to cuddle me,' I said, just because I was expected to respond in some way.

'That was a shock though. I'm not sure weapons under pillows will help you get over this. If you need help, I mean.'

'Are you talking about a psychiatrist?' I feigned a laugh. 'I just need some time to adjust. It's fresh.'

He put his hand in my bathwater, which was lukewarm. He probably realised I'd spent a long time here. 'We'll see.'

'I'll get over it,' I repeated.

Ted grabbed the knife from the sink. 'Can I put this back? No one is coming in the house.'

I nodded.

'Are we okay, Lisa? Me and you?'

'Sure thing. I'll get over it, I promise.'

For the second time, Ted gave my claim no reply.

CHAPTER FIVE

I did manage to get some sleep, but wished I hadn't: I woke at five to nine in the morning.

Ted was already gone. I leaped out of bed and bounded to Dan's bedroom door. The little star was already dressed for school, which was a first because he normally waited for me to bring his uniform. I gave him a big hug and apologised for lying in.

'You were up late,' he said. 'I heard you downstairs. I didn't want to wake you.'

Heard me downstairs? My sleepy head allowed a moment of panic as I wondered if Dan had heard an intruder in the house, but then I remembered I'd been downstairs until past one in the morning.

'Couldn't sleep. But I'm okay. Come on, let's eat.'

Dan could prepare quickly if nudged correctly, but the key was to avoid letting on that we were late. Which could mess with his head. I gave him cereal, which he consumed quicker than his standard beans on toasted waffles, and I made his packed lunch while he ate. As he brushed his teeth, I hurriedly dressed, then ushered him out of the house.

The neighbour, a buff young builder called Mr Skewis, had yet again parked his car on the street in such a way that it blocked a small portion of my exit from the driveway. He did this so he could get his works van in and out of his own driveway. Careful manoeuvring cost us another half minute. I would make it up by clear ignorance of speed limits.

We were halfway to school before I realised I'd applied no make-up to cover my facial injuries. I used pauses at corners and junctions to sweep my hair this way and that to find the best pose for hiding my damaged eye as best I could. But I was still worried about what people might say.

We arrived at school at twenty past nine, which was five minutes after the inner gate had shut. Dan would not be happy. To get him there without worrying him, I said, 'Think you're fast, do you?'

I let him win the race, but he stopped halfway across the field as he spied the shut gate, the lack of teachers waiting by it. I was ready for some upset, but Dan said, 'It doesn't bother me. I know before I was mad. But it's no biggie. Shall I take the blame? I can say it was autism.'

I ruffled his hair, then rang the intercom on the gate. 'No. My fault. We always tell the truth, remember?'

Two teachers came to open the gate. As they crossed the yard, I worked my hair again to hide my busted right eye and bruised forehead. One was his class teacher, Mrs Cross, a young woman with a facial scar from an abusive father – according to the rumour mill.

The other was Miss Haven, the Special Educational Needs Coordinator. She was tall and quite muscular for a woman, with short dyed-white hair. And an unhappy expression. I knew that I'd messed up somehow, missed a phone call or email or something.

After I'd sent Dan on his way with his teacher, Miss Haven said, 'I sent you an email yesterday. Did you not get it?'

'I didn't check my emails,' I said. 'I didn't expect anything on a Sunday. I assumed our business would all be conducted during school times.'

'Oh, well, it was to confirm the appointment with the educational psychologist. She's pencilled us in for 10am, Friday the 4th of Feb. Two Fridays from now. Still a Teams meeting, if that's good for you. I know that's probably longer away than we hoped, but is that okay for you?'

I couldn't remember if I had plans or appointments on that day, but it didn't matter. Rescheduling the educational psychologist would only delay an already long-overdue conclusion.

After discussing a few more details about Dan's EHCP application, we parted ways. Although it had been almost half an hour since the school bell, plenty of parents were still on the street, some talking in groups, including a throng of about six women outside the nearby corner shop.

As I walked towards the throng of women, to head inside to grab something for my work lunch, I kept my head down and tilted to the left, so gravity would drag my hair across my right eye.

The façade failed. As I passed the chatting mothers, a large woman who seemed to be the centre of attention blatantly stared at me. She was about thirty-five, with curly bleach-blonde hair from the 1980s and too much make-up, and looked like she'd take no shit from anyone. I'd seen her many times at school, but her kid wasn't in Dan's year and we'd never spoken. We did now.

'Nasty mark there on your face,' she said.

I had to look up to acknowledge her. Everyone in the group had stopped talking and was staring.

'So clumsy at times,' I replied, and couldn't get into the shop quick enough.

———

I was the assistant manager at Heaven Homestore, a variety store located in Meadowhall, which is the largest indoor shopping centre in Yorkshire. Because of my school drop-off and pick-up commitments, I worked the hours of 10am to 2pm every weekday and rolling shifts on Saturday.

If the manager had been on duty today, I would have called in sick; but with him off, I was top dog and the administrative tasks fell to me. It meant I could lurk in the office all day and hide my face from everyone.

Because my sister, Maud, owned her cake stall in Meadowhall, she could dictate her hours and on certain days designed her workdays to coincide with mine. On Mondays, Thursdays and Saturdays we would drive in together, although she would find alternative transport home. Maud was waiting at the corner of her street when I arrived.

On the journey in, we talked about mundane things. She knew I wouldn't want to drag up my attack so left it well alone. Until we pulled up in one of the car parks. She took out her make-up bag, which was the first red flag because her face was already loaded.

'As my husband sometimes says, let me do your face.'

I laughed. A little. 'We're not allowed make-up at work.'

'I know, you said before. A silly rule. Look at me, and I work with food.'

'But you don't have a see-you-next-Tuesday for a boss.'

Maud laughs. 'Maybe my employees do. Now sit back. I reckon your boss would prefer you looked like a good-night girl than someone who said no to the wrong man. Besides, it's just concealer.'

I had to bite my lip here to keep my emotions in check. I wanted to cry, and I wanted to berate Maud for such a callous remark. But, of course, why wouldn't she crack a crude joke? After all, she thought her sister got mugged by a tearaway teenaged girl, nary a man in sight. I closed my eyes, tried to clear my mind, and let her do my face.

The bruises mostly vanished, but the laceration was going nowhere. I should have gone to hospital, but apparently I got angry at the very suggestion of it at the pub on Saturday and no one had dared mention it since. But now I took my first good close look at the gash above my right eye, and knew the damn thing would for sure scar if I left it to its own devices.

Nothing I could do about it right now. We entered the shopping centre and there split. My store was on the Lower High Street and Maud's stall was in Lower Park Lane. She asked if I wanted to do lunch in the Dining Quarter, but I didn't fancy it. I wanted to run to work, lock myself in the office, and sprint to my car at home time.

But I didn't run, for that would have garnered attention. The centre was heaving with shoppers but my single face amongst so many drew only a handful of looks, with the majority of eyes locked on either store windows or beautiful young people. Blending in pleased me, but it also turned my mind to my attacker.

Meadowhall was a magnet for people of all ages, from all across Yorkshire and beyond. The man who tried to murder me was a monster, but weren't monsters all human-shaped? And, on bloodlust downtime, didn't they have to buy groceries like everyone else? He could be one any of the fat or thin, young or old, ugly or beautiful men surrounding me.

CHAPTER SIX

I wanted to get the story out of the way, so once in the Heaven store I approached the first staff member I spotted. I showed him my face, even swept my hair aside so he'd get a proper look.

'I got punched by someone riding past on a bike, and I don't want to talk about it.'

I left him puzzled and speechless and found the next nearest staff member. She got the same one-line story. She tried to asked questions, but I repeated the latter part: *I don't want to talk about it.* There were five more staff members on the floor, and a minute later they all knew.

Not everyone started at 9am, the store's opening time, so I entered the staffroom, where I found someone else. Same tale. It brought my good friend, Carla, out from the kitchen annexe. As the other girl started to ask for more details, Carla said, 'Are you deaf, Mo? She just told you. Punching cyclist. Damn fools are everywhere. End of story. Come grab a tea, Lisa.'

I was literally dragged into the small kitchen, where Carla made a tea for me. I was ready to give Carla a little more –

probably the original mugging story – but she suddenly started talking about shop events from yesterday.

I loved Carla right then. To a viewer it might have seemed that she didn't care about my misfortune, but I knew better. She knew I would be uncomfortable telling my story, and was willing to wait until I was ready.

Carla was forty and, like me, had had a life-changing experience. I used to be a thuggish tearaway, but one weekend I don't remember turned me. Carla used to be a self-admitted snotty bitch, but thyroid cancer five years ago gave her a new outlook, especially after people in her previous workplace didn't seem to care that she might die.

She beat that cancer and got a new job here as the treasurer, and now you'd be hard-pressed to find someone with a bad word to say about her.

After tea and chat, I headed into the manager's office, which had a one-way window overlooking the till area. There was a blinking message-waiting light on the phone. I sat and played it.

'Hey, sexy, me again. I'm no better, I'm afraid. Won't be in today. Hopefully tomorrow.'

Alice, calling in sick yet again. Third shift on the trot, third period of sickness in the six months she'd worked here. She was twenty-one and a parkour athlete, and I seriously doubted she was that ill, but it wasn't fair to accuse anyone of lying. Alan, the manager, certainly wouldn't call her bluff if they were on such good terms that she could call him sexy.

Whatever. I didn't care. I called her back and left a voicemail saying the standard PC thing about hoping she got better soon.

I cared a minute later though. I had to call Alan to let him know Alice was off again. He grunted his displeasure – we'd lost another staff member to maternity leave just last week – and said he was coming in. Great: bang went my plan to hide in the office all shift.

He was there half an hour later. He gave me a brief glance, which became a double take as he clocked my face. Immediate annoyance. But he didn't ask what had happened to me. He threw his briefcase on the desk.

'Did you find the Treasure of Lima then?'

Some colleagues didn't understand the attraction of geocaching, but Alan was the only person who ridiculed it. This wasn't the first time he'd mentioned some famous historical artefact he should never have heard of. It was clear he did the odd bit of research just to wind me up. By sheer luck I remembered the Treasure of Lima from a website I visited a few months ago.

'That's thousands of miles away in Costa Rica. I was down the road in Grenoside.'

Countered, he moved quickly on: 'I had Alice down for the stockroom today. So you'll have to do that. And before you moan, that's me being nice. I'm sure you'll be happy to hide that face away. We're due an FC, in case you didn't know.'

I did know. An FC, or flash check, involved a head-office hitman visiting a store unannounced to see if the place was up to scratch. They were known for hating overstocked and messy stockrooms. Making the place spick and span would be gruelling, but at least, like he said, I could avoid showing my face on the floor. But I was under no illusion that Alan was doing me a favour; he didn't want me to sully the appearance of his store.

As I was walking out, he threw a parting shot, as per usual.

'We'll have a word about the fighting thing later, okay?'

I wanted to spit. Fighting? If only I had been able to fight back.

While heading through the shop floor to reach the stockroom, I came across Toby, who was rearranging a cereal display that didn't need doing. Toby was a skinny kid of twenty who'd worked here for two years, since dropping out of college.

At one time he'd been quite sweet, albeit eager to pull a girl, but it seemed that a constant trail of rejection had hardened his soul and all charm had gone, leaving behind a lecherous little sod. Unfortunately for me, he liked older women and brunettes.

He hadn't been on the floor when I hunted everyone down to tell my story, but I didn't care to tell this kid anything. But as I tried to walk quietly past, a box of cereal landed in my path – intentionally – and he was there a half-second later to pick it up. And block me.

'What happened to your face?' he said. He tried to reach up and touch my bruises, but I pulled my head away.

'Some drunk girl hit me. No big deal. I don't like to talk about it.'

I started to walk past. He said, 'You need to be careful on those treasure-hunt things. Dangerous people in the woods.'

'It was just some drunk in the street, and it was probably an accident. Let's not talk about it again.'

I thought that would be the end of it. I was wrong.

CHAPTER SEVEN

A text from Ted saying *Found my ring yet?* was the extra push I needed. At dinner time, I called my sister to back out of meeting for food and instead remained in the stockroom, eating my sandwiches and trying to convince myself it was a bad idea.

Where had the idea even come from? Did I hope to be cured by some kind of exposure therapy? Regardless, the desire was there and it was hard to push aside. And then Ted's text came.

I collared Alan after lunch and told a little white lie that Dan had a dentist appointment and I needed to leave at one o'clock. He wasn't happy, but he never was. Half an hour later, I skipped out and hustled to my car. A quick trip, in and out, and then off to collect Dan from school. Hopefully with my wedding ring back on my finger.

That's right. I was heading back to the scene of my attack.

Despite ten years of geocaching, I'd never before visited the cache titled Sword Dance, which was only two miles west of my house. I'd avoided a number of those close to my home in

Grenoside, preferring to visit more remote ones for a sense of adventure.

However, when I had turned up at the pub on that fateful Saturday the 22nd of January, and found few adults yet in attendance and a magic show taking care of the kids, I saw an opportunity I couldn't resist. The Sword Dance geocache was only half a mile away along this very same road.

That Saturday, I turn right out of the pub car park and drive north along Main Street, which soon disappears into trees. Being January, it has been dark for some time already, but the gloom in the woods is like something from a cave far below the earth. A short way along, I come across a car park on my right and turn in. I sit in my car and reopen Sword Dance's webpage.

Each cache listing has a description and this one mentions the Grenoside Sword Dance, a ritual that takes place on Boxing Day and dates back to the 1750s. There is a cryptic clue:

HOW MANY STEPS NORTH WOULD THE ROSE AND THE LILAC TAKE FROM THE TREE BENCH?

I have to cheat and look at a hint further down the page. So, the memoirs of someone called Lady Tweedsmuir is called The Lilac and the Rose. *She was married to a famous writer who penned an adventure novel in 1915. Still no wiser, I ask Google, and then I am ready.*

Now, I exited the car park and stared at the sign pointing to three different woods: Wheata, Wharncliffe and Greno. Sword Dance was in Wheata. I wished I'd sought a geocache in Wharncliffe instead.

Many larch trees are being removed in British woodlands because of Ramorum Disease, a water mould that causes great swathes of damage and death, so the woodland trusts want us to make sure we helped minimise the spread by cleaning soil and leaves off feet and car wheels before leaving the area. I have gone one better by slipping on disposable shoe covers.

Now, this safety measure didn't even enter my mind.

I follow the track past a picnic area with just one young couple seated, who don't even notice me stroll past. I follow my GPS north-west, deeper into Wheata Woods.

The woods, over 600 years old, are popular with tourists, who can walk the trails and see the historical sites like mediaeval pits and quarries and even bomb craters. But this late there is no one around.

The track soon meets a stream and they run parallel like train tracks for a short time before parting. I walk between them, until the fork. Sword Dance's description instructs people to follow the track to the tree bench, although it doesn't really matter because water and tarmac meet again at the vital spot. On this literal fork in the road of life, I choose badly. I follow the stream because I want to make my hunt a little harder.

The tree bench is exactly that: a wide tree trunk that someone shaped into a small bench. Once there, I will face north and count my steps, and somewhere within reach of the thirty-ninth will be the geocache container. I can't wait to sign the book, log the visit on the webpage, and add one to my list of finds.

I never got that far.

Twenty metres past the fork, there was a ten-feet gap between water and track. Fifty metres in, the gap was as wide as two coaches end to end. A hundred metres and I could no longer see the track. It was daytime and bright light poked through the canopy, but I felt hopeless and vulnerable and lost.

As I walked, my legs and thumping chest felt the land rising uphill, but my eyes told me the ground was flat. It was as if gravity was becoming more powerful with every step deeper in, closer to the place where I almost – *should have* – died. My breathing got faster, the pressure against my body increasing. If I believed in the paranormal, I might have thought some incorporeal being was pushing against me, trying to prevent my moving forward. To save me.

I couldn't believe I came here alone in the dark. The darkness was poison to undergrowth, but amber nectar to the bad people in the world. A visit log by someone called MAISIE99L had mentioned two hypodermic needles found in a clearing near the cache. ALBO-ALBO commented that he'd seen nefarious people drinking in the same area. A lot of users warned their fellow treasure hunters to avoid the clearing, even in the daytime.

Little did they know that the most dangerous spot in these woods was elsewhere. And I had walked right into it.

My gaze jerked left as I heard a couple of voices, giggling. This made me stiffen as I recalled the laughing lovers from Saturday night. Could it be the same people?

It didn't matter. I pushed on. The stream started to curve to the right, back towards the track, and I froze. Ahead, I thought I could make out the tree bench, perhaps fifty metres away. I realised I was close to the place where I was attacked. And then I saw it.

Twenty metres ahead, lying at an angle across the stream like a makeshift bridge, was a hollowed log perhaps five feet in length. My mind flashed back. That log... it had been beside the stream... I had sat on it to fix a loose shoe cover... and seconds after I'd stood up...

Someone had been to the geocache since Saturday. Unlike me, they probably came in daytime and kicked that log into the stream before moving on... totally unaware that a violent attack had occurred in that very spot.

I stopped. The wedding ring could go to hell. Even if I saw it right now, glinting over by that log, there was no way I was going one inch closer. I took a step backwards. Then another, and another, and with each the pressure in my chest eased.

My foot wobbled as it came down on something lumpy and solid. There, in the undergrowth and out of place, was a smooth rock the size of a large man's fist. Unsure why, I picked it up. As I turned it over, I saw the stain. Faint, almost invisible, but there.

Blood.

Another flashback. I saw this very rock, wet with my blood, sailing through the air. I touched the gash above my eye. It had started to throb again. I dropped the rock and it rolled into the stream and vanished.

A dog barked some distance behind me, and I turned to look–

but before my head even moves an inch, a thick iron pole whips across my throat. It pulls me back, sucking me against flesh and bone. Now I understand: not an iron pole at all, but an arm, an arm as thick and solid as the Terminator's. A man had grabbed me from behind. Because of the pressure constricting my throat, I can't yell for help. Hell, I can barely breathe…

I instinctively threw my left hand to my throat, as if to remove the arm that was no longer there. So violently did I do this, fingernails caught my chin hard enough to cause stabbing pain.

A hand grabs my left wrist, pulling it away from the arm around my neck, forcing it downwards, straightening my arm down by my side. Then back, behind me. His groin. He forces my hand into his groin. I resist with all my strength, and it hurts my arm.

I touched my still-tender left shoulder.

I waited, but no additional flashback occurred. Maybe proximity was the key to unlocking more memories, so I lifted my foot, meaning to take a step closer to the log–

and I am tripped to the ground. I break my fall with my right hand, which still clutches my phone because I have been following GPS coordinates. Did I try to call for help, or did my attacker thwart this plan before I even had it? Either way, his foot crashes down onto my hand. Even above the scream of white-hot agony, I hear the crunch of the screen shattering inside my crushed fist.

I looked at my hand, those bruised fingers. I wanted, needed more, so I took another step forward, towards that log. There's a flash in my mind, followed by another. Fragments, whizzing by like a movie scene with too many jump cuts.

... his fingers, undoing the zip on my jeans... lifting my jumper... my hands fighting his, but there's no strength... jeans tossed in the water, jumper discarded into the undergrowth... can't fight him, must submit... but he's displeased, I was too tense, no eye contact, legs not open wide enough... the rock, raised up high and ready to crash down...

'Please, no, I'm sorry.'

I dropped to my knees. I was unsure how much of what I remembered was accurate, how much was a traumatised mind filling in holes, but that terrible line I was dead certain of. *Please, no, I'm sorry.* A plea for mercy that fell on uncaring ears.

... the rock descending like a meteor toward my face... cracking hard against bone... a roar of rage as he tosses the rock into the woods... dazed, dragged into the stream... under the surface, no air... staring up at him through the water...

I pawed at the air before my face, as if I could touch his, just inches away.

... shimmering face contorted in anger... his hands around my throat... consciousness stepping aside, making way for death...

CHAPTER EIGHT

B ut I did not die, of course. I could only assume that I'd stopped struggling while my attacker held me under the water, and he'd figured I was dead and had run. Or he'd been spooked by someone, perhaps the laughing lovers walking nearby. Either way, I had survived. The question was: did he know this? And, more important, did he care? Had the violence satisfied him? Or was I still a target?

I rushed out of those woods and didn't relax until I was safe in my car, just like last time. I didn't know how to feel. Had I been raped? I didn't have any of the disgust I thought I would have felt at such a likelihood.

Was this because surviving a near murder gave me a sense of triumph that washed out everything else? Was it because days had passed and time had begun the healing process? Was it because, with no solid memory of the rape, it seemed like nothing more than a bad dream?

I'd left my phone in the car and only now realised it was almost four o'clock. Dan! I had missed calls from the school and from Ted. I called the school to get confirmation of what I suspected: when I was late and they couldn't get hold of me,

Ted had been called and had picked up Dan. I apologised, gave no excuse, and hung up.

I didn't call Ted, preferring not to have an argument on the phone. Besides, I wanted to get away from these woods.

At home, I found my boys eating dinner in the kitchen. Dan was using his VR headset and holding both a controller and piece of cutlery in each hand. Ted was in black trousers and a white shirt, meaning he hadn't had time to change after work.

He looked up when I appeared in the doorway. Dan was talking to himself, reciting lines from a cartoon or book. He was so engrossed that he didn't notice when his mother and father skipped upstairs to have a row. I hadn't even taken my jacket off.

'Tell me you were late because you were getting my ring back?' Ted snapped.

I doubt he truly believed that so I didn't answer the question. 'I'm sorry. How were the teachers about it?'

He got up and approached the cupboard where we kept medicines. 'They seemed fine with it. They have great poker faces. You know who doesn't? Some fat woman who looked like someone tipped a bowl of spaghetti over her head.'

'What? Who? A teacher?'

Ted had taken his cod liver oil and A–Z vitamins bottles from the cupboard. He swallowed a pair of tablets, then got out his phone. 'No. This daft sod...'

He showed me a video. He was in the street outside school, filming a woman who was walking away with a bunch of others. I recognised the main antagonist: it was the curly-haired woman who'd made a remark about my face earlier.

'What happened?'

'She was hanging around outside the shop, even though this was like forty minutes after school. When I came out with Dan, she laid into me. Right there in the street, shouting her wormy

41

head off. Apparently, I'm no man for hitting women and if it happens again I'll lie in hospital and regret it.'

I was shocked. 'So she thought you'd hit me?'

'It would seem so. You didn't say anything like that, did you?'

'No, of course not.'

'It's just that you lied about a mugging that turned out to be a fight.'

'That's different.'

'So what gave her that impression?'

'I don't know. Maybe she just assumed because of my bruises. She probably knew who you were because you came out with Dan.'

Ted moved to the window, to stare out. 'Well, it would be nice if you could have a word with Spaghetti Head tomorrow and set her straight.'

I hated the idea of doing such a thing, but agreed to.

'And perhaps wear a hat or something to hide those bruises. Because the next person to make the same assumption might be Jack Reacher.'

We fell silent as I heard Dan bounding upstairs. He used the bathroom and then scuttled into his room. Once his door was shut, Ted said, 'So where were you?'

'I had to see a friend. She... Look, I'm sorry. That won't happen again. Can we just move on?'

I moved behind him and wrapped my arms around his waist. Ted turned into me and we kissed. Perhaps because of the argument, or maybe the fault of recent revelations, but the kiss felt awkward. I broke it and asked if he wanted a cup of tea.

His response was to kiss me again. I let him, but immediately he put a hand on my lower back and slid his fingers down my trousers. I jerked away. My heart was thumping, but I forced a smile. 'Not now. I just got in and it's not the right time.'

'When is it ever for you?' Ted said, and stormed past me, out of the room. He slammed the door behind him.

I felt like someone who'd just found a lump in her breast. Sex hadn't interested me much over the last few months, but I'd put that down to money and school worries and always believed things would change soon. Now, I wasn't so sure. Had we just reached a plateau because of my attack?

Because of what had happened to me in the woods, would I never again find pleasure in sex? Would I always feel disgust at the touch of a man, even that of my own husband? Our marriage had been showing signs of turbulence recently; was it now on a downward spiral to a crash and burn?

Had that faceless monster done far more damage than he or I knew?

Another night not blind drunk, so another night without sleep.

Around 2am, I got sick of staring at the ceiling and trekked downstairs. I checked the doors and windows were all locked, then grabbed Dan's VR. However, tranquillity wasn't what I needed. I wanted noise, so I chose the TV. A few minutes into funny cat videos on YouTube, I sat up straight. On the screen, CCTV showed a cat taking a dump into the open sunroof of a car. I didn't see the climax because by then I was pacing the room.

If the monster was stalking me, perhaps he was on CCTV. He might have been captured by cameras at Meadowhall. Or cameras on this very street. I could ask the neighbours if they'd let me view their footage. A car registration would lead directly to the bastard!

Speaking of cars, I heard one outside. I ran upstairs to have a sneaky peek out the bedroom window.

Across the road and a few doors down, one of the writers had just gotten home. I watched him exit his car and retrieve his coat from the back seat, then head down the garden path. He had a cast on his wrist.

The duo were a married male couple who wrote Regency romance books together under a single pseudonym. Both guys were in their forties but seemed younger because they had spiky dyed blond hair and wore flashy shirts. Nobody knew too much about them, even though they were flamboyant and social. As I watched, the man over the road – Eric, I think – stopped at his door and kicked off his trainers before heading inside in socks.

Why had he removed his footwear? Suspicious, I sneaked into Dan's room and hunted out his purple kids' binoculars. They were cheap and pretty useless, but adequate to confirm that the trainers dumped on the doorstep over the road were stained with mud.

How had they gotten muddy? Why had he been out so late? And that cast on his wrist, which hadn't been there when I'd last seen him a few days ago – how had he gotten it? Could he have been the man who att–

'What's wrong?' a voice croaked. I turned from the curtains. Ted was still in bed, unmoving. Had he uttered that question in his sleep?

'You okay?' he said.

'Yes.'

I waited for him to ask what I was doing at the window, but he rolled onto his front and said, 'Are we okay? Me and you?'

'Like you said years ago, we have an *unbreakable bond.*'

Ted made no reply and was breathing heavily a few seconds later. I knelt by the window so I wouldn't be as visible and continued to watch the house across the road. And thought about an unbreakable bond.

I'd first met Ted in a supermarket. After that hellish

nightmare weekend I'd mentioned, when I'd almost died of an overdose, I had decided to get my life on track. I'd moved cities, found a new home and employment, and had never gone near drugs again. The final part of the healing process was to get a good man by my side.

A new friend from work had said that the best place wasn't a nightclub, where blokes were drunk and horny, and it wasn't a dating website full of liars and frauds.

'Supermarket,' she'd said. 'Ready meal aisle. Blokes there have no girl to cook for them. That's where you'll meet a goody two shoes.'

She'd been joking, but the next day I was shopping and visited the ready meal aisle, just to see if my friend's theory had weight. Sure enough, I spotted a lone man there. When I approached with a meal that served two and asked if he wanted to share, I had been expecting only a funny story to tell my friend. The next day, Ted and I were boyfriend and girlfriend.

It nearly wasn't to be. I'd had boyfriends before, but I'd always picked from the bad boys in our social circle and there had been an air of free love. I'd been ready for Ted to say thanks and now get lost, but he hadn't. He'd wanted to see me again. Puzzled, and dressing to leave his flat, I'd asked why.

'Well, we have a bond now. We had sex.'

'I know. I was there.'

He'd looked hurt. 'That didn't mean anything to you?'

I'd given him a long look to assess his sincerity. He barely knew me. 'You're serious? You want to see me again just because we had sex?'

'I love you.'

That had knocked me for six. To cut a long story short, I was Ted's first sexual encounter and his love was true. I guess I understood. Sex was a special thing to some people. To him, the intimacy we'd shared had created what he'd called an unbreakable bond. He would never forget me and I would never forget him.

I knew he was right. Our time in bed had meant more than just quenching lust; he wasn't just some drunken action of the kind I was used to with idiots I didn't give a shit about. I agreed to see him again. We were inseparable after that.

And therein lay my fear. My rape and attempted murder had been a terrifying, damaging ordeal – but only to me. What emotional rollercoaster had the faceless monster ridden? Did he feel that victim and perpetrator had shared a magical moment? Did his mind relive our so-called intimacy, and feed off it? Was he determined to repeat those emotions, and scheming to take me again?

After all, I would never forget him, and he would never forget me. We had an unbreakable bond.

CHAPTER NINE

I woke at a respectable time in the morning, aided by my phone alarm. Ted was already gone, but he'd left a message on the fridge using some of Dan's magnetic letters: CAR TAX. The X was pinning the renewal reminder to the door. It needed paying by the end of the month. Another damn bill we could barely afford.

I got Dan downstairs and in front of his waffles and beans breakfast, then headed upstairs to dress. Today I added sunglasses and a bobbly hat. I looked a little strange, but the damage to my face was obscured.

My builder neighbour, Mr Skewis, had again parked his car in such a way that I had to carefully feed my vehicle out of my own driveway. He came out of his house as I was pulling away and I thought about stopping to give him an earful. It got no further than a thought.

We'd run out of ham for Dan's packed lunch so I pulled up outside the local minimart to buy a sandwich. Dan waited in the car while I ran in. The place was run by Alphonse and his wife, both in their early sixties, who immigrated here in the early

1990s when their home country of Australia hit a recession. A couple of years later they had a son, Glenn.

A handsome kid, he was the face of the minimart now his parents were both a little infirm. He was usually okay for local gossip. Today I had no energy for it, but I would make small talk in order to find a chance to mention his minimart's CCTV, which I hoped to get a look at.

At the counter, I dumped my goods and he grinned and said, 'How's your day, Mrs Holten? Did you enjoy Saturday night?'

I stared at him in shock, all thoughts of CCTV gone. Did he know? How did he know? Had Ted been in here with his big mouth? 'What do you mean?'

He was taken aback by my abrupt words. 'Nothing. Just making conversation.'

'Why a conversation about Saturday? Why specifically Saturday night? I haven't been in here since Thursday, so why not ask about Friday night?'

He raised his hands in defence. 'No big deal. Heard you went to a party.'

'I've done parties before. I've had days out. But you never asked about those. And you didn't mention a party at first, you asked if I enjoyed Saturday night. Why?'

Now he looked annoyed. 'One pound eighty-nine for the chocolate.'

I literally threw a pair of pound coins onto the counter, one of which rolled off to land by his feet. When he bent to get it, I grabbed my purchases and fled.

Back in my car, I could barely find the ignition with the key, so badly were my hands shaking. Just making conversation? And that grin... as if we shared a secret.

No, couldn't be. Glenn had a wife, he ran a minimart, he liked model aeroplanes...

That meant nothing, I realised. The chest-beating, axe-waving psychopaths got netted and locked up pretty quickly. The clever ones knew how to hide their sick minds and blend in amongst us. They seemed normal because they lurked behind masks. They had wives and jobs and hobbies – and friends and neighbours who expressed shock when one of their own got plastered all over the news.

Could Glenn be the man who had raped and tried to murder me?

After dropping Dan at school, I followed the thuggish woman with spaghetti hair out of the grounds. As usual, she paused outside the corner shop to chat with other mothers. Ted had picked up Dan forty minutes after school's end yesterday and she'd still been with her group, so I couldn't spare the time to wait until she was alone. I approached the group. Spaghetti Head spotted me first, said something to her pals, and eight pairs of eyes settled on me.

'My husband didn't hit me,' I said. I wanted them all to know. 'I heard you shouted at him and I think that was nice of you, caring like that. But I promise he didn't do this. I just wanted to mention it. Can I have a private word and I'll tell you what happened?'

I figured she'd be eager for gossip and I was right. She pointed down the side of the shop and I followed her there. We were only five metres from her friends, but it would have to do.

'Okay, who smacked you about?' the woman asked.

Ever since Ted had told me to explain things to this woman, I'd intended to give her the same story everyone had gotten: a thug girl attacked me. So I surprised myself when something

49

entirely different came out. 'A different man did this. He sexually assaulted me.'

I felt an immediate release, as if I'd been waiting to tell someone the truth for days. Something felt acceptable about telling a stranger, even though I knew she'd blab to her pals before I'd even gotten back to my car.

The woman punched her own palm. 'Then he needs some disfigurement of his own. Who was it? I'll help sort this bastard out for you. My brothers are guys not to be messed with. Bashing lasses is bad enough, but perverts need wiping out.'

No mention of going to the police, I noted. 'I don't know who it was. It was dark. Just some man. I'm okay, no lasting damage. I just wanted you to know it wasn't my husband.'

'We could find him easy enough, if you wanted. My brothers know how. He might have form.'

I shook my head. 'I'm really okay. But thank you anyway. I need to get home now. Thanks again.'

Clearly this woman was talking about illegal activity and I wanted no part of it. My mission here had been to make sure she didn't spread lies about Ted, and I'd achieved that. All I wanted now was to get away from her.

She watched me leave as she returned to her friends, but I was forgotten soon afterwards. When I drove past the group, nobody even glanced at my car and they seemed to be talking about one of their number's coat. Good.

CHAPTER TEN

In a repeat of yesterday, I walked through the crowds at Meadowhall and wondered if my attacker was somewhere close. Before, I'd considered that he might be present simply because shopping centres were busy places. But things had changed.

Now, he could be watching me.

My eyes skipped from man to man, but what was I looking for? Devil horns? The monster was a master of disguise and it would be impossible to determine a rotten mind by outward appearance. I intermittently threw glances behind me, hoping to catch someone watching me, but everyone back there and moving in my direction seemed to be staring.

Occasionally a man would suddenly stop and look in a shop window, but here that was a far cry from suspicious and I had to ignore it after about the tenth moment of panic.

The most frightening moment, though, was when a man walking towards me did a double take. I literally stopped dead in my tracks, certain that his shock was because I was supposed to be decomposing in the woods.

Seconds later I felt stupid. The man waved; a second

brushed past me from behind and both shook hands and began jabbering like old friends. Yet another false alarm.

In the end, all I could do was tell myself that, stalked or not, I was safe. The monster liked to hunt lone females at night and wouldn't expose his inner beast in a busy shopping centre. If he had followed me since this morning, he could have rammed my car off the road, or grabbed me in the car park, or even snatched me when I was talking to Spaghetti Head down an alley.

It wasn't much of an argument, but it got me to work without a breakdown. Once there, my thoughts turned to another man.

Toby was working one of the tills, so I quickly made my way to the staffroom. It was empty apart from a young girl hired just last week. She seemed to favour those her age, while looking down her nose at older employees like me, and we exchanged not a word before she left.

Once alone, I found Toby's coat on a hook and, with shaking hands, squashed the pockets until I located his mobile phone. It opened without need for a password.

I quickly looked through his text messages and Messenger logs, and finally Facebook and Instagram. I found plenty of posts to girls, many of whom hadn't replied. But nothing about me. This didn't mean a thing though: he was hardly going to create a post about rape and attempted murder. I wondered if there was a way to view his device's location history.

The door burst open and the young female returned to put her earrings away. She saw me standing by Toby's coat and I knew I'd been rumbled. She said nothing, but thirty seconds after she left again, the door reopened and of course Toby stood there. I was caught red-handed.

'Aha. So, after my phone number, eh?'

I faced him. I was scared because he blocked the door, but I was also angry. I hid both emotions beneath a neutral expression. 'I'm sorry. I got a missed call from someone. I wanted to check everyone's phones. I should have just asked.'

'You think I did it, don't you?'

I held my composure, but couldn't look at him. 'What do you mean?'

'The missed call. Can't be me, can it? You didn't give me your number. Or add me on Facebook.'

I wanted to kick myself. Had I really just taken his line – *you think I did it, don't you?* – as an admission that he'd attacked me? This little twerp? How paranoid was I being? In fact, what the hell was I doing in here, snooping through his phone? Toby hadn't attacked me that night. He was a hundred pounds soaking wet and was probably scared of the dark.

Deep down, I'd never really suspected him. Knowing nothing about my attacker was becoming too much to bear and perhaps I'd needed to focus on a target just to avoid going insane.

'So, you want to rectify those problems? Give me your phone number?'

I snapped back to the moment and thrust his phone into his hand. 'I don't give it out to anyone, especially staff.'

'I quit,' he joked.

I walked past him. His parting words were, 'You still look cute with that bruise.'

I left the room and outside, on the shop floor, suddenly had to lean against a wall and take deep breaths. Despite writing off Toby just seconds before, I found his voice in my head, repeating a line from yesterday:

'You need to be careful on those treasure-hunt things. Dangerous people in the woods.'

How had Toby known I'd been on a geocache on Saturday night? How had he known I was attacked in the woods?

Before leaving Meadowhall to go pick up Dan from school, I stopped at Argos to buy a CCTV camera. I got a twin-pack for £79.99, but this took me into my overdraft. I decided I'd tell Ted that they were free spares from work. One would go out front, to hopefully capture the monster's car on our street; the other would watch for him lurking in the backyard or the field beyond. They'd go up tonight.

I sat in my car for ten minutes after work. I was looking for a man who got into a vehicle but didn't drive away. Nobody seemed to be waiting for me to leave. While driving, I scanned the rear-view mirror for vehicles I'd seen parked, but this was a bust too.

I parked past the school this time, so I wouldn't have to walk past the corner shop, just in case Spaghetti Head and her cronies were infesting the place when I came out with Dan. At the gate, I kept my distance and hung back while she collected her kid.

Dan was by his teacher's side and didn't bolt towards me when I was spotted, so I knew there had been a problem and that she needed a word. We stepped aside and she got straight to the point.

'Dan has a problem with people's personal space, as you well know,' she began. It already sounded like a conversation we'd had many times.

'Just tell me what he did.'

Dan had overheard one of the girls in his class talking to a friend about her cool new branded underwear. Intrigued, he'd approached and pulled up her skirt in front of everyone. 'He told me he thought she was giving him permission by speaking loudly enough for him to hear. So, a little reminder is needed.'

A little reminder. That was a common term his teacher

used, which I had started to interpret as *Get your damn kid in order*. I had my own oft-used term: *Sorry about that. I'll have a word with him, don't worry*.

'I understand the meeting with the psychologist to report her findings is on the 4th of Feb, is that right?' she asked. I nodded and bit my lip. Was she seeking confirmation that all was going ahead as planned and that Dan would be out of her hair soon?

That line from her, more than Dan's indiscretion, meant I was still worked up when we got back to the car. As soon as his door was shut, I snapped at him.

'What the hell were you playing at? You don't touch girls like that.'

Or was my anger for another reason?

Dan looked at his hands in his lap. He said nothing.

'We talked about bubbles, Dan. It's a game, remember? You remember game rules, don't you? Why can't you remember these rules?'

His father had invented a game called Alien Poo that he wanted Dan to play at school. He had to pretend he was covered in two-feet-long spikes and that the people at school wore balloons filled with alien poo – get too close, pop a balloon, and you got covered in nastiness. They'd practised the game at home with success; every time his father or I got close to Dan, he shifted position to keep a two-foot buffer.

Dan's head drooped. 'Maybe I can't ever change.'

'You can change, Dan.' I paused, unsure if I was taking the right step forward. 'I did.'

He looked at me, surprised. 'You were born bad and changed to good?'

'No one is born bad. And you're not bad. Your autism means you're misunderstood. I wasn't bad, and you're not bad. I made some wrong choices. But I did what you can do and changed my way of thinking. That was what we tried to teach you with Alien Poo.'

'What wrong choices?'

'This was back in Nottingham, where I was born. I was just a normal little girl. But I got in with the wrong people one day. Wrong people are the ones whose behaviour is likely to change who you are. Being surrounded by people like that can turn you the same as them. I made a bad decision and the next day woke up a changed person.'

'Will I wake up a changed person one day?'

I felt a little pang of shame here. I had airbrushed the tale. I had done the same years ago, when talking to my family, and later Ted. I had told them that in the week before I'd overdosed, I had fallen in with a section of the homeless community that found fun in vandalism and running rampant around the streets.

Instead of attending college, I was wasting days just lying around under bridges or in parks or in shopping precincts. Instead of talking politics with college friends, I was partying and taking drugs. Instead of sleeping at those nice friends' houses, I was killing nights in abandoned warehouses or cardboard cities.

However, they were, to this day, unaware that this lifestyle had endured for much longer than I'd claimed. I'd been a waster for over a year by the time of the blackout. I'd committed far more mundane crimes than admitted.

Most shameful of all, I hadn't 'fallen in' with the wrong people: I had chosen them. After I had left school, the thought of a routine existence of work and bills and towing the line had depressed me. I had taken college classes as camouflage.

It was true that I'd woken up one day with a new outlook on life. Losing two full days, and knowing I was lucky not to have died or woken in hospital, had terrified me. And just like that, I decided no more. Within a week, I had dumped drugs, moved north, to Sheffield, found a flat, found a job, found a man, and launched upon a new, law-abiding, happy life. People could change.

'Mum? Did you hear me? Will I wake up one day not autistic anymore?'

I'd heard. But I couldn't answer truthfully. It was foolish to compare Dan's situation with mine. He had a disability. I had been a damn naïve, idiotic, runaway train, who'd needed a near-death experience to realise how stupid she had been.

'No, Dan, you won't wake without autism. It's a lifelong condition – remember we told you that? But you're also a kid and you have typical kid behaviour as well. You will learn over time and change as you get older. You're special, and smart, and funny, and you're the reason I am a different person.'

Dan's face creased in frustration. 'But why can some people change and I can't? This is why you make me play Alien Poo, isn't it? I can't change my brain and I have to pretend. Who says everyone isn't just playing a game? How do you know you've changed and you're not just pretending?'

I didn't really have an adequate answer for that.

CHAPTER ELEVEN

T ed was all positives: 'At least he's into girls.'

My boy's sexual orientation didn't matter and wasn't what worried me. Dan had always had a problem with other people's personal space, but until now I hadn't really thought about how this could become a problem as he got older. He would sometimes sit too close to someone, touch their shoulder, drink from their water bottle – but the event with the girl's knickers signalled a possible scary change. If he started to touch girls inappropriately...

Ted went to his jiu-jitsu class after his shift at the carpet store, so I went online to do research and got sucked in. A stroll across websites became a hike deep into the internet. With the monster never silent in the back of my mind, I soon unwittingly veered from the intended track. Before I knew it, I was miles away from puberty and autism and in the world of obsession. And that was where I discovered a new word: erotomania.

The disorder involved a delusion that someone was in love with you. Sufferers were mostly women and the subject of the delusion was often an individual higher up the social ladder, like a movie star.

There was a famous case involving King George V; a woman was known to lurk outside Buckingham Palace, awaiting a signal from the monarch. Her delusional mind would see the movement of a curtain and believe that was the signal: by twitching the curtain, the King was declaring his love for her.

I got so wrapped up in this that seven o'clock rolled around and Dan knocked on my bedroom door, asking for his dinner. While frying his bacon, I paced the kitchen like a caged tiger, full of fret.

Until now I'd assumed that the monster had either happened upon me in the woods or had targeted me en route, or even earlier that day. Now, there was a much more terrifying prospect.

What if he was someone who'd obsessed over me from afar for much longer? Was he an erotomaniac who had mistaken some innocent action of mine as a proclamation of desire? If so, that action could have been anything, even years ago. I had found a story about a man who was fixated on a pop star and believed emojis in her tweets and Facebook posts were coded messages aimed at him. Horrific.

But who was this man? What had I done to warrant this obsession? My thoughts turned again to Eric, the author from across the road. I had waved at him a few times while he was smoking on the doorstep, and wondered if this might have ignited his delusion. But he was gay and I felt I could write him off.

But not others. Like Glenn at the minimart. I had never flirted with him, but of course, that didn't matter. He could have developed his freakish idea that I wanted him from the way I'd handed over money and brushed his hand. Or because I bought bananas. Or any of a thousand other reasons.

Could the beast be Toby from work? I had interviewed and given him the job at Heaven Homestore. I had given him a pen once. I hadn't quit work. Each of those things obviously meant I loved him, right?

But these were men I knew. What about those on the periphery of my life, who saw me often but had never shared an interaction? Fathers at Dan's school. Male shopkeepers in the same area of Meadowhall as Heaven. Regular customers at the store.

Even worse, many victims of erotomaniacs had had no known interaction with their stalkers whatsoever. I could have stopped for a man at a zebra crossing five years ago, yet it had sparked neurotic love. Someone passing Heaven Homestore could have fixated on me as I tweaked a window display. A delivery driver could have read a little too much into the note I sometimes left that requested parcels to be hidden in our cardboard bin.

But the most important question was: why had the monster attacked me instead of approaching with flowers? The tale of the man and the emoji messages was scary, but nothing compared to his reaction when he learned that the pop star had never heard of him. He accused her of leading him on and tried to torch her house.

Had the monster raped and attempted to murder me because he felt I'd rejected him? If so, what might happen next? Would he try to finish what he'd failed to do and kill me? Had he left me alive in order to continue his stalking? Both scenarios were cause for panic and—

'MUM!'

I jumped at Dan's yell, then quickly realised what had brought him to the kitchen doorway, fingers pinching his nose shut. The bacon was burnt to a crisp and the smell filled the kitchen. I tossed the frying pan in the sink and hugged my boy.

'I'm sorry, Dan, I got sidetracked. I can do waffles. That okay?'

He nodded. When he left, I opened the back door to release the smoke and leaned against the frame, energy spent.

My stalker could be anyone anywhere and planning another attack. He could kill me next time. He could hurt Dan and Ted as part of some freakish plan to make me free and single and all his. Sitting back and doing nothing while he lurked out there was dangerous.

If he was unknown to me, I could do little to prevent bloodshed. But if the bastard was someone within my social circle, finding and stopping him was possible. It was all I had to go on. I would eliminate suspects one by one, until hopefully the monster was exposed.

Because I don't often judge, many of my friends turn to me when they need an ear. Maybe they just need a sounding board, because I don't think my advice-giving abilities are all there. Regardless, they've come to me with all manner of things from period pains to car purchases. And cheating partners.

Yvette's husband, David, had an affair about eight months ago, which she found out about because of something you'd only imagine happened in movies. He spoke another woman's name during sex. He claimed that this 'Ellie' was a work colleague and she'd been on his mind because they'd argued that afternoon.

But Yvette found Ellie amongst his Facebook friends, and she didn't work with him. Yvette and David were in their thirties, but Ellie was twenty, and the thought of losing her man to a younger model was rending.

Since Ted had never cheated on me, I wasn't best placed to offer advice, but Yvette had sought my help back then and I called her now for an update.

'I think the knobhead is still at it,' Yvette snapped as soon as

I asked how things were. 'He went out on Saturday evening. He was supposed to go to the pub with friends, but wouldn't say which one when he got back in case I checked, and he had mud on his trousers. It'll be that same bitch.'

I almost dropped the phone. Saturday night. Mud. Alone, these facts wouldn't be cause for concern, but when you factored in something that had happened about three months ago...

It had been a Saturday evening and I'd visited Yvette to root through some of her nephew's old clothing to see if any would be suitable for Dan. When she'd gone upstairs to fetch the clothing and toys, I was left alone with David. He'd been out drinking that afternoon, was clearly the worse for it, and his eyes were all over me. As soon as his wife was gone, he moved onto the sofa, next to me.

'They're long,' he said, pointing at my fingernails. 'Janey can't grow hers.'

When I spread them to look, he took my hand. I tried to pull it away, but he kept hold. When I looked up at him, he wasn't watching my nails. He was staring at my face.

And then he leaned in and tried to kiss me.

I pulled away. 'You're married, David,' I said. Then I shook my head at my own idiocy. 'And I'm married, and Yvette's my friend, and I wouldn't go with you anyway. Please don't do that again.'

He looked puzzled rather than disheartened. 'You always wear those tight jeans. Every time you come round here. Why wear them if you weren't trying to give me a hint?'

What? He thought my wardrobe was to impress him? I pulled a cushion onto my lap. 'They're skinny jeans, and I... I just like them. I always wear them. It's not for you. Look, let's stop talking about this.'

The choice was out of his hands as Yvette thumped down

the stairs. He returned to his armchair as his wife entered. A few minutes later, as I was looking through a box of clothing, I made the mistake of glancing at him and he grinned and winked from behind his wife's back.

'... I mean, why wouldn't he tell me?' Yvette now said down the phone. 'He could have told a lie about the mud. But to just clam up like that was wrong...'

A simple pair of skinny jeans had convinced David that I was crying out for his attention, so he deserved to be investigated. I hadn't truly suspected him, but the news about his vanishing on Saturday night and returning muddied... Right then I thought I might have hit pay dirt with my first shot.

'... And he washed – did I not mention that? That night, he put his stuff in the washer and he got in the bath. David doesn't take baths at night, and I do all the laundry. So that's a red flag right there... Lisa? Did you hear? Do you think David could be cheating again?'

I snapped back to the moment. 'I'll come see you, Yvette. Are you at home? Alone?'

'Yes. David's out. But I could come there if it's easier–'

'No,' I cut in. I would be going to her. I needed to get in her house. I needed to find evidence that my good friend's husband had raped and tried to murder me.

CHAPTER TWELVE

The journey home from Yvette's house in Parson Cross involved taking Wordsworth Road, where there was a set of traffic lights outside an expensive-looking detached house with two BMWs in the drive. The male occupant was working in his garden, which was littered with lengths of wood and tools – it seemed he was a joiner – as I waited at the red light and tried to deal with conflicting emotions.

Once Ted had gotten home from jiu-jitsu, I'd skipped out and raced to Yvette's house. But my time there had instantly become a bust. I'd planned to ask to use the toilet and instead snoop around for clues, but within seconds of entering the house, Yvette had given me a snippet of information she'd earlier left out.

She had called David on Saturday night and, although secretive about his location, he had indeed had friends with him. She had heard them in the background as well as pub music. This phone call took place at 7.40pm – approximately the time I was attacked.

David wasn't my attacker, and this was the cause of my internal confusion. I was happy a friend I'd known for years wasn't married to a monster. I could continue to see Yvette. But it would have been nice to pinpoint the monster. Instead, he was still out there and targeting me.

I glanced again at the joiner working in his garden, but this time my eyes lingered. I'd used this road a number of times and had sat at these lights often. I must have seen that man working on three or four occasions.

Had he also seen me? I recalled one time when I took a photo of the house on my phone, to show Ted the kind of place I would love to call home. Could the joiner have watched me from a window and mistaken my interest in his home for obsession with him? Could he have followed me at some point? What if–

A horn startled me. The light was green. The joiner was staring at me. I hit the accelerator and got out of there. I didn't start breathing properly until I was home a couple of minutes later. I squeezed past the neighbour's car and, once in my driveway, sat to compose myself.

The joiner had stared at me, but he might have looked up at the sound of the horn. Still, he needed to be explored. Should I go back now and watch in secret?

The option was removed when Ted came to the door and called out to ask if I was okay. I realised I'd been sitting in the car, engine running, for almost five minutes. I'd pulled out my phone without realising it, but more alarming was that the dialler was onscreen with 999 already typed in. I cancelled it immediately. For some reason the idea of calling the police disgusted me.

I got out of the car, told myself to give this paranoid shit up, at least for the rest of tonight, and went inside the house.

When Dan was in his bath and Ted was watching TV downstairs, I got to researching. First up, I used an online people directory to locate the occupants of the address on Wandsworth. With a name, I searched social media.

The joiner was one Shane Gibbon, thirty-three, three kids and a wife and a Facebook post from the Saturday when I was attacked. The family had been at Go Ape in Sherwood Pines, forty miles south in Nottinghamshire.

It wasn't impossible that he could have watched his trio of young boys enjoy that day out, then returned home and ventured out again after dark to undertake some fun of his own. In fact, a busy day could be the optimum time because on face value it provided an alibi.

However, various posts I scanned gave the impression that Shane Gibbon was happily married. Again, proof of nothing, but I decided to eliminate the joiner.

While on Facebook, I made my profile private and deleted a number of friends that I either barely knew or hadn't seen in years. Next, I looked at my son's profile. Not a social media fan, Dan only had a handful of friends. That made the process of reviewing those kids' fathers and uncles easier, just in case my name or picture had done the rounds and piqued someone's interest. Nobody stood out.

Ted had a lot more friends. Like me, he'd added people willy-nilly when social media was a new and exciting toy. His profile was private, which I hadn't before realised. I went downstairs and told him I wanted to check through his friends list. I had a lie planned, but he didn't even ask my reason and got up to fetch his phone from his car.

'Why did you leave it out there?' I asked.

He shrugged. 'Just didn't bring it in.'

I followed him to the front door. The driveway gates were

shut, which puzzled him. He said, 'Yep, foiled those burglars. No way they could get over this.'

He then stepped over the gate with a smug look, as if to prove a point. I said nothing and waited for his phone.

'Did you do my car tax?' he asked.

'I forgot. I'll do it tonight.'

I really had forgot and I'd spent most of my available funds. I'd have to enter my overdraft again. I made a mental note and took his phone upstairs to run through his male friends, social and professional. Unfortunately, he had dozens and dozens. I took photos of his list so I could check out the profiles over the coming days. Anyone who made the shortlist I could talk to Ted about.

I also wanted to look at more people on this estate. I had various names; the unknowns I could find using the people directory. I would probably be analysing people for the next week.

I had another set of tasks to perform too. I fished out the old set of bedroom curtains from the attic; the pair currently hanging were thin and painted silhouettes for pedestrians to see. Above the front door was a wind chime and I tossed it in the bin. Like the open driveway gates, I considered the thin curtains and the musical wind chime to be details that a wretched mind might read as invitations.

Perhaps useless efforts, since the damage had already been done and I was already in the cross hairs. Besides, it was far more likely that I, not the house, had charmed the monster. I would work on 'me' tomorrow.

After Dan had bathed and retired to bed, I asked Ted to install our new CCTV cameras, claiming that neighbours had reported various thefts from vehicles. He bought this and got to work. I ran a bath for myself.

While soaking, I considered my endgame. The goal was to

find a name for the police, but keep mine a secret. I could not let the story out. My friends and neighbours would not learn about what really happened to me. I would not be known as Woman Raped. This city would not gossip about me. I would not be a target of ridicule by those believing I had somehow 'asked for it' or withdrawn consent after the fact.

But there was a problem. We weren't talking here about some bank robbery or house burglary. I couldn't just deliver a name and hide and watch the police arrest the monster and fling him into prison. With luck, his home would be searched and a horde of evidence found. But if not, and sans my story, my statement, the police would have nothing but an anonymous claim.

It was a worry, but one I vowed to tackle after I had the bastard's name. However, something was about to happen that would change everything.

CHAPTER THIRTEEN

For the first time since my attack, I felt able to submerge my head in the bath. I closed my eyes and the warm water coursed over my face. Instantly I flashed back to that night, and despite my eyelids saw the rippling water, a shimmering face beyond. But I held my nerve, reminded myself I was at home, safe, and the vision faded to black. The relief was massive.

But also short-lived.

The bathroom sat between the two main bedrooms and had no window. Also, the switch for the light was on the outside. And that light suddenly went off.

The shock made me take a breath, but of water. Coughing, terrified, I leapt out of the bath and bolted through the black. I grabbed the door and hauled it open.

'What the hell are you doing?'

Dan backed away, shocked. He wasn't used to my raised voice; I knew never to yell at him. But I was out of control.

'Dan, answer,' I shouted. 'Why did you do that?'

Crying, he scuttled away into his room and slammed the door. The bang instantly wiped aside my anger. What was I thinking? Dan didn't know about my fears, and shouldn't be blamed for them.

Ted came bounding up the stairs. 'What the heck is the shouting about?'

I waved him away without a word. He went in silence. Realising I was naked and wet, I grabbed a towel and opened Dan's door. He was on the bed and threw the cover over his head when I entered.

'I'm sorry, Dan. I overreacted. It was just a joke, wasn't it?'

I saw the quilt shift as he nodded his head.

'Did you want the toilet, was that it?'

Another nod.

'The joke was funny. I'm sorry I got angry. Can I hug you as an apology?'

A third nod. I slipped under his quilt and we hugged in the dark. Then I lay him down and adjusted the quilt and tucked him in. He grinned while I did this.

'I still need the toilet,' he said when I was done.

I threw the cover off him, smiling.

After he'd returned and been tucked in again, I headed into my bedroom and sat at my dressing table, staring at my face in the mirror. My shiver wasn't entirely from being wet. When that light had turned off and I had leapt out of the bath, it hadn't been to confront a jokester. It had been to bar the door. For a split second, I had thought my attacker was in the house. The monster had returned for me.

I had thought time would heal, but I'd just had a blunt rebuttal. The mental anguish would not lessen as the weeks and months skipped by, but might actually increase. Would I fear the dark, and water, and men, for years? Forever?

It was a new worry to add to the fear of attack. I could bolt up the house and carry a weapon and look over my shoulder, but there were no safety precautions against the real enemy – the inner me. My mind would decay if left to wallow in anxiety. I would lose my sanity, and my home and family. The monster's very existence would wreck my life; he didn't need to stand before me with a weapon.

I had to prevent that. I had to end this whole thing. I had to take action. But how? What could I do?

I did have one idea.

I sent an email before school on Wednesday morning. Now that I knew the monster had probably been stalking me since way before he attacked, it was plausible he could have followed me on Saturday night. Many people knew I was a geocacher, but how had he known which site I'd be visiting? Because he might have been watching the Blue Orb pub when I left?

If so, there was a good chance his vehicle might have been caught by a camera in the car park. So, the first email went to that establishment: could I view their CCTV footage?

While Dan ate his breakfast, I sorted through my clothing for old gear. I wanted dowdy tracksuit bottoms and a T-shirt, and a worn coat I knew I still had. My work shoes would go in a bag and I'd wear scuffed trainers. No make-up at all. I also planned to call my local salon to finalise my new look: the hair was going short.

I wanted a bland appearance in the hope that my unknown audience of one would lose interest. A long shot given that he was already fixated, but it was worth a try.

When I returned downstairs, Dan was on his VR. That got me thinking. The social game he played was full of people in masks; all anyone knew about their comrades was a username and whatever they were told. Was it possible that my stalker had learned about me from Dan? Had my son been careless and told the wrong person about his mum?

It seemed unlikely since I couldn't imagine how he'd share a picture of me or why he'd give our address, but it was for good reason that warnings about online information sharing existed. I couldn't take that risk. When Dan was in the car, I skipped back into the house and got the VR headset.

The water from my bath last night was still in the tub, so I dropped the expensive piece of kit in. I'd tell Dan it must have been lying on the side and gotten nudged. He'd be upset, but we'd buy another – at some point after my stalker had been captured.

After dropping Dan off, I followed Spaghetti Head. She split from another mother just outside the gates and I pounced while she was alone. 'Hi, sorry. What's your name?'

She turned at the sound of my voice and gave me a suspicious look. 'Lorraine. Why?'

'I need your help,' I said. 'I told you I was attacked by a man, remember? There must be people you know of like that.'

She folded her arms. 'Why do I have to know people like that? What you saying?'

'I'm sorry. I meant – well, you said you could find people.'

'Maybe. You mean famous people or rapist scum?'

'You remember what I told you?'

'Say it. Say what you want from me.'

Now I understood. She wanted to embarrass me, perhaps so there would be no confusion as to who was in charge here. 'I want to find a rapist scumbag. Can you do that?'

'Sure can. Got no name for the guy, have you?'

'No. But you said something about these people having "form". Are you talking about being known to the police? There's a sex offenders register, isn't there? Can you get the names off that?'

She'd been very stand-offish and now stared at me for a good number of seconds, not a word said. Then she stuck out her hand. 'The name's Joan, by the way.'

The hand, the sudden admission of her real name: had she decided she trusted me? Had she figured I might be a police officer trying to entrap her? I shook her hand to make sure she knew I was on the level. 'Lisa.'

'Already know. So let's get down to business. There's no way to get at that scum list unless you ask the fuzz. You don't want them sods around, right?' I shook my head. 'But there's other ways to find shit out, if you know the right people. People in the know. My brothers know people in the know. I can get you names. For a price.'

This woman had shown concern for me recently and I'd foolishly approached her in the belief that she'd help out of moral duty. I should have known better. My pause put a frown on her face.

'Listen, missus, I don't know you, so me and my people got no reason to give you our precious time. Time is money. It's two hundred quid. What you got on you right now as a deposit?'

My purse contained about thirty pounds. I started to count it out. Joan glanced around but otherwise didn't seem to care that we were doing this deal out in the open. The total was £25.90. She took the lot.

'We'll call this an even twenty-five. Go get the rest. See you at kicking-out time.'

And that was that. She left and I remained, still a little unsure about what the hell had just happened.

But soon I was heading back to my car and feeling elated. I hadn't really considered that my attacker could already be known to the police. If I managed to find him, his name alone might warrant a thorough police investigation. They might send a forensics team out to the area in the woods with the hollowed log and locate his DNA, perhaps on the rock he cracked me with.

He could be known to lurk in that area, or a scour of nearby CCTV could show his vehicle at the correct time. There might even be witnesses – the laughing lovers – who had no idea the man they'd seen had just tried to kill someone. But even if all of this came to nothing, the monster would know his secret was out and surely he'd abandon his interest in me.

I saw only positives ahead. My pain could be over very soon.

CHAPTER FOURTEEN

At lunch, I left the Heaven store and visited a cash machine to withdraw my wages. I had £210 available before I'd reach my overdraft. Work paid me on the final Friday of each month, so I had eight days to wait. Back at the store, I got some change from a till so I had the balance of £175 to pay the woman calling herself Joan. I had £35 spare to last over a week. The afternoon shift dragged by.

On the field outside the school's inner gates, I waited for Joan to spot me. We stepped aside to talk.

'I got three names,' she said. 'Local morons living within a few miles of here. All done for sex shit. Got some faces for you. If you've got the cash.'

I paid her. She gave me her phone. The 'faces' were pictures of three men, each with a name drawn at the bottom in handwriting. They looked like police mugshots. I stared at each for a long time.

As I was staring at the first, a fat man with thinning hair, Joan gave me some background. 'Albin Peters. He's thirty-five. Got nicked for fiddling with his twin sister when he was fifteen. Nicked again for messing with his neighbour's twelve-year-old.

About ten years ago, that. Got five years for it. Did three. Arseholes on the parole board let him go for good behaviour. Easy to behave when you're in solitary so you don't get your arse striped.'

My memory had only fragments of the attack on me. I'd hoped for some kind of eureka moment, but it didn't occur. All I had of the monster's face was a shimmering image, glimpsed from beneath water. I moved on to the next picture. A younger man, handsome. Not a face anyone would think could front a rotten mind.

'Dewy wanker Smith. Twenty-four. Nicked two years ago trying to hook up with a fifteen-year-old girl. He locked her in his car. Tosser never did prison time for it. Same for when he was about fourteen and he molested a ten-year-old. Charmed life, that one.'

Still no eureka moment. I moved on to the third picture.

'Sammy Cardle,' Joan said. 'Fifty-six. Seasoned bastard, this one. Rape conviction in 2005. Did fourteen years. You'll like this. He jumped a woman camping alone in the woods. Woods, right? Like you. He knocked her out with a Z-drug–'

'Which one?'

'Which what?'

'Which Z-drug?'

'Hell knows,' Joan said. She gave me a long look. 'You like him for it, right? He's the one?'

I wasn't sure. No eureka moment. But staring at his face gave me a slight chill. He'd attacked a woman in the woods...

My long stare at his face convinced Joan. 'Give me your phone,' she said. When I handed it over, she typed something and returned it. I saw a draft message to no one: the name Sammy Cardle and an address.

The school gates started to open. Joan snatched her phone

and started walking away. 'You've got what you wanted. Not sure what you gonna do with it.'

She had a point. I could send the police to the address, but how sincere would I sound if I wasn't certain Cardle had attacked me? I was still wondering about this when I had Dan by my side and we were in the car. I saw Joan and her kid coming. I got out and stood in the road by my open door when she was alongside.

'Can you help?' I said, careful not to broadcast the form of that help.

Joan told her kid to wait, then she approached the car. We spoke over the roof. 'You need to have a face-to-face. Safe environment. Me and my two brothers can do that.'

'We meet up?'

She laughed. 'No, I don't mean a nice chat in a public place. This scum would hardly agree to that. I mean I get you in front of him and you can see if he's the guy who shagged you.'

My wince was more down to her objective than her language. I could picture it: a pair of thugs as a barrier, me on one side, a convicted sex offender on the other. He could be held until the police came. It was a scary idea, but I couldn't let it go.

Joan seemed to sense that I wasn't totally averse to her plan. 'What's your phone number?'

I recited it. She typed it into her phone and called me, letting it ring just once before hanging up.

'Now you got my number. Call if you want this to happen, evenings only. Offer runs out in a few days. You want to stop the nightmares happening for the rest of your life? Then two hundred quid is a small price. Think hard.'

She grabbed her son and walked on. I got in the car. Dan didn't even query why I'd talked to someone. As I drove away, I watched the rear-view. I was all nerves, but Joan was with friends outside the shop, chatting and laughing as if she'd offered me nothing more substantial than to meet for a cup of tea.

When Ted got home from work, I went to the local minimart to clear my mind. The young son of the owners, Glenn, was on duty, so I rejected going inside and instead strolled once around the block.

Back home, Ted and Dan were playing chess in the kitchen. It reminded me that I'd soon have to tell my son his VR was busted. Ted said, 'Give the police a call. Someone might have handed in the ring. Two grand, that.'

He sounded as if he still blamed me. Annoyed, I gave a sharp response. 'Exactly, two grand, so no one is going to find it and just hand it to the police.'

I stormed upstairs to the bedroom. Ted came up a minute later. 'Sorry. Guess I was just reminding you. I hate that we're just doing nothing about it.'

I tapped my head wound. 'Can't forget.'

'Yeah, I know. I'm sorry. It's just... maybe the police will arrest that girl for some other mugging. They could get the ring back. I just don't like this idea of leaving it, forgetting it, just moving on.'

Forgetting it? If only he knew. I saw his point, though, and promised to call the police. 'I'll say I was chased and dropped the wedding ring. That way there's no crime as such and it will be easier for me. That sound okay?'

'I guess,' he said, but I could tell he wasn't happy with that plan. 'Me and Dan are going swimming. You want to come?'

I felt a jolt like a punch to the gut. If they were going out, I would have free time to... 'No. I was going to go see a work friend for a bit. Remember I mentioned Carla, who had cancer?'

'No. But whatever. We'll see you when we all get back.'

He turned to go, but I stopped him. 'Oh, Carla wants to borrow £500. I said we would. I know we're short, but she's promised to pay it back in a few weeks. I'm low because bills went out. Can you transfer some to me from the car account?'

We each had a personal bank account, and another that we paid regularly into for bills. I covered the utilities while Ted saved for emergencies like car parts. I knew there was at least a thousand pounds in the 'car account'. He said, 'Sure. Yeah. I'll go do it now.'

I thanked him. Ted didn't know Carla socially so there was no chance he'd learn of my lie from her. But he did know about her cancer struggles and that he'd look pretty mean if he refused to help.

The money was in my personal account mere minutes later. I felt my anxiety rise. I had the money and, with Ted and Dan going out, I had the time. And once I'd sent a text to Joan, the likely became the inevitable.

Tonight, let's do it.

CHAPTER FIFTEEN

By the time I'd returned from the cash machine, there was still no reply to my text. Half an hour after that, I was standing at the bedroom window, watching for Ted's car with my phone in my hand. The plan: abandon the whole idea if Ted and Dan returned before Joan replied to my text. I already had an 'abort message' typed and ready to send. And then a car pulled up outside.

But it wasn't Ted's.

The bedroom light was off, so I was able to see the hips and legs of whoever sat in the passenger seat. I saw long boots over jeans and recognised the outfit from earlier. It was Joan.

She was halfway down my driveway when I opened the front door. 'What are you doing here?' I said. 'How did you know where I lived?'

'Figured you needed more proof about my skill in finding people. Are you ready? Get in the car. And leave your phone.'

I didn't delay. I knew that any pause, to grab a coat or check the back door was locked or whatever, would kill the impetus. The money was in my pocket and my keys were in the other side of the front door. So I dumped the phone on a small shelf above the door, locked up, and walked to the car. I got straight in the back. Seconds later, Joan was seated in front of me and the car was pulling away.

The driver was a man in his late forties, bald head, fat, T-shirt and jeans. He looked like the sort who could queue jump and nobody would say a word. The guy in the back with me was closer to my age. He wore double denim and a black T-shirt and looked pretty buff beneath. He was handsome, with a Van Dyke beard and slicked-back medium-length hair.

Joan introduced him as John, which could have been his real name, and the bruiser as Buzz, which sure as hell wasn't. Buzz gave me a weak nod in the rear-view mirror, while John extended a hand. I shook it and he held on long enough to relay a message: he liked what he saw in me. Despite where we were, what we were about to do and who he was, I felt a little flattered.

A flat palm poked over the back of the front passenger seat. 'Cash up front,' Joan said. I laid down £175 in notes. No going back now.

'I'm not sure though,' I said. 'I didn't really see him. I don't want the wrong man to... get in trouble.'

'We'll make sure first,' Joan said, and that was the last thing spoken for the next three miles.

The car turned into a residential street with a row of lock-up garages on both sides at the end. We parked here for privacy. The houses ahead were detached and had long front gardens without fences or gates. All bar the first on the right seemed to be in good order. That house was beaten and worn. Trash littered the garden, there was a board over the front window, and the faint remains of graffiti were across the front door and part of the walls either side.

Joan pointed at that very house. 'As you can see, the

hardworking ordinaries around here are no fans of sex scum. You ready?'

'No,' I said. Now, here, moments from action, I wanted nothing more than to go home. I announced this to all occupants.

Joan gave me a look of disgust. 'You came this far. In for a penny, in for a hundred and seventy-five pounds.'

I stared at the house. Inside was a man. Possibly *the* man. But I couldn't move. I said nothing.

Joan grunted. 'Well, darling, we seem to have wasted our time. Boys, we should get Princess home. She looks like she's about to faint.'

'No need for sarcasm, sis,' John said from his place beside me. He gave me a smile when I looked at him. 'The poor lady's been through a lot.'

Joan laughed. The scorn was much clearer in her tone now. 'All the more reason to get her home to bed. Is that what you want, Princess? Shall we end this nightmare?'

I didn't even look at her. I took a deep breath. 'In for a penny,' I said.

Joan raised her eyebrows, and then a thumb. No more scorn. 'Good one. You got some dark shit inside you after all. Do it.'

Before I could figure out who she was talking to, her brothers exited the car. They casually walked past the final garage and turned out of sight. I knew they were heading round the back of the vandalised house. To break in.

'I can't go inside,' I said.

Joan gave me a withering stare. 'This bastard did some girl, now he's done you, and you want to let the scumbag just roam free and rape someone else? You can live with that?'

I said nothing and Joan took this as consent. We sat in silence, just watching the house. I didn't know what to expect, and heard no commotion, but about five minutes later the front door opened. John, the handsome one in denim, gave a thumbs up, then immediately shut the door again.

I had no clue what that meant. But Joan did: she opened her door. 'Let's go, darling.'

Sheepishly, I followed her. We walked down the side of the house, through a gate in a tall fence, and into a dim backyard also littered with trash. The back door was wide open. The rear faces of houses on a parallel street overlooked this yard, but all their windows were dark. Nobody was watching. My heart was pounding.

Joan put on a balaclava I didn't know she had and offered me one. My fingers closed around it, but I was consumed by the urge to end this right here. Before something bad happened. I had paid for Joan and her brothers, they were here to serve me, and if I wanted to I could turn and run and never look back.

Instead, I put on the balaclava.

I followed Joan into the living room. The whole of the downstairs was pretty clean, except for the sofa. An empty plastic bin lay nearby and all over that sofa, and the man sitting on it, was trash. Only an idiot could fail to read the scene.

Joan's brothers stood at either arm of the sofa and Sammy Cardle was in the centre, the safest spot. He wore a fluffy purple onesie that totally jarred with the terror on his face. Joan had said he was fifty-six, but the man before me looked ten years older.

As Joan and I entered, nobody said a thing and Cardle looked at we two women with what I could only describe as pleading eyes. Either he'd already been informed why his house had been crashed, or the way we came in after the boys was a blatant clue who was in charge.

Buzz, the heavy beast, slapped Cardle on top of his head, which made him yelp and cower. 'Look at this woman here,' Buzz said, pointing at me. 'Recognise her?'

Joan whipped off my balaclava. My fingers scrabbled for it, but she tossed it away. So I froze and waited. Cardle tried to shrink in his seat, hands to his face, eyes peeking through fingers. I saw his eyes on me.

'I don't know her,' he said. 'Please. I've done nothing wrong.'

Buzz raised a foot and pushed hard against Cardle's shoulder, knocking him sideways on the sofa. 'You know who else has done nothing, you piece of shit? That other woman you raped in the woods. Tried to kill herself way back. She's like forty now and never goes out, can't make friends, can't work.'

Cardle shook his head. 'I'm sorry. I thought she had a knife. I hit her and–'

'There was no knife, you sack of shit. How many girls we gonna find on your computer? How many little bodies buried in your garden?'

For the first time, John made an impact. 'Step back, Buzz, let's give this guy some air.' He helped the offender sit up, and then sat next to him. He patted the guy's knee, then pointed at Lisa. 'Keep calm, my friend. Take a look at the woman there. You jump this pretty thing in the woods last Saturday?'

As before, I'd remained motionless, hypnotised, just watching. But the spell was broken when all four people looked my way. I suddenly remembered where I was, and why.

'It's not him,' I said.

'Come closer,' Joan said. 'Get right up here, see if that radar thing goes off. Gotta be sure.'

And I wasn't, not really. I took a step closer. And another. It was like walking out of a freezer, because the chill left me. By the time I was just three feet from the sofa, staring down at Cardle, all my nerves seemed to have gone.

'Which one?' I said to him. 'Which Z-drug did you use? Zaleplon?'

The offender stared at me. His hands moved slowly away from his face. 'Zopiclone,' he said, barely audible. 'I was addicted. That girl... I thought she had a knife. Thought she came at me with it. I know now there was no knife. I was appalled to learn what I did.'

'That gave me blurred vision. Zaleplon wears off quicker. You should have thought about next-day dangers for the women you raped.'

Only when Joan spoke did I realise that all three siblings were staring at me in surprise. 'Girl, are you a connoisseur? There's a turn-up for the old books.'

I ignored her. I moved closer still to the offender, so I could smell him, and look into his eyes. But it was for naught. I got no sense of him one way or the other. I figured that meant he wasn't the monster. Surely my radar would have been screaming.

'It's not him. Let's go.'

Joan tutted at me. 'You need to ask–'

'That's not him,' I said again, louder. Fear had gone, but disgust was rampant. One more person now knew I'd been raped, and who knew how many he would tell? I turned and walked away. I was ready to run down the road and to forget everyone back there.

Before I could open the door and escape, Joan grabbed my arm. 'You can't just leave.'

'That wasn't him,' I said. 'This was a waste of time. Now I just want to go home.'

'Oh really? Your sixth sense intuition bullshit told you that? What if you're wrong?'

My silence must have told Joan she was on a roll. She continued: 'We're here now. We sort this guy out. Five minutes out of your life, and you might be able to live the rest of it without nightmares. In for a penny, in for a pound. I'm just trying to help you, darling.'

'Right, right. So I can have my money back?'

'No. In for a penny. Listen, we can't just let this guy go free and clear. Give the bastard something to remember you by. Something that's not the feel of your pussy.'

She made a gesture at John and, like a magician with a rabbit, he made a stick appear seemingly out of nowhere. It was a pitted rounders bat with tape on the handle. The weapon didn't suit his pretty face. He handed it to Joan, who tried to hand it to me. The offender watched this interaction with growing horror.

'No. You want me to hit this guy? No. I said it's not him. The man I want is... he's on an entirely different level.'

'But if you're wrong? If you let this guy go, and it's him all along, he's beat you. This ain't like court, where it's better to let ten guilty go free rather than convict one innocent. We do this guy, and the next, and the next, and that way you've definitely got him.'

'I only want the man who hurt me–'

'And the other women? The ones this bastard did and got away with, the ones people don't know about? What about the ones to come? He'll mess with more women. You think scum like this is going to stop? We can save those future women some pain.'

She tried again to offer me the rounders bat. 'Him or not, what you need is revenge. You ever heard about those freaks who kill women who look like their mothers? They pretend they're killing Mum for all her abuse. Treat it like that. Forget this guy's face. He represents all the scum. Every sicko pervert in the world, right here in this one body.'

She sighed, aware that her sales pitch had faltered. 'Look, this guy's getting hurt tonight. Duty to society. If you don't do it, the boys will. But if they do it, you won't feel satisfied. And, trust me, you need satisfaction and this will give it to you.'

The man before me had done time for his crimes. He had paid his debt. He wasn't my attacker, and he could be a rehabilitated man with nothing but good to offer society. He would have a mother and friends and maybe kids who needed him. I tried to tell myself these and other arguments, but while they sounded good, none did a single thing to shift my eyes from that rounders bat.

CHAPTER SIXTEEN

In bed later that night, while Ted watched grappling videos and I read, he stuck a finger in my ear. I laughed, thinking he was playing. I stopped when he showed me his fingertip, and the spot of blood on it.

'Oh, that's from an insect. I squished a little fly in my ear.'

'Nice,' he said. Under the cover, he put his hand on my thigh.

'Not tonight. I've had a long day.'

'A long few months, you mean.' He smiled, but I could see he knew he'd overstepped a line with his insult.

'I'm sorry. Just not tonight.'

He hadn't moved his hand and it now travelled north up my body, towards my hips. I put my own hand on top of his, with the quilt between them, but he didn't stop. I made a fist and slammed it onto his hidden forearm.

'What the hell?' he said, and withdrew his hand.

'I'm not in the mood. I told you.'

'There's not in the mood and going berserk.'

I didn't know what to say to that. Obviously my reaction was down to a rape just days ago. But Ted didn't know about that. 'Look, I'm sorry. Just not tonight.'

'It's been nearly two months. What's wrong with you?'

'I don't know,' I lied. 'I just need time. I need... I need to feel sexy again. And don't tell me I am, because it doesn't work like that. I just... time, Ted, that's all. Time. Don't rush me. But I promise we'll do it soon.'

'Okay, I understand,' he said. He didn't make a serious effort to sound convinced and backed it up by lying down and turning away from me. I didn't know how to respond, so said nothing. We'd discuss it tomorrow.

Ted was snoring within minutes. I doubted I'd get off anytime soon so headed downstairs. The plan, or so I thought, had been to watch some TV, but at the bottom of the stairs I didn't turn to the living-room door. Instead, I stared at the shoe cabinet at the end of the hallway.

The idea was preposterous. Silly. Worrying. But I couldn't shake it. *Just a quick look*, I told myself. *Just to confirm. Just so I can move past it, even though I know I'm being paranoid.*

I had to. I had to. I approached the shoe cabinet. Grabbed one of Ted's trainers, then a shoe, then one of his wellington boots.

I threw the wellington down as if it had become radioactive, and I backed away. The boot wasn't what had freaked me though: it was my own mind. I had really just done it, hadn't I? I had checked Ted's footwear for mud. For evidence that he had attacked me in the woods. I was horrified. Of course my own husband, father of my child, wasn't the man who had raped and almost killed me.

But he left the party, didn't he? Apparently he needed cigarettes and was gone at the very time you were attacked. He knew where you were going.

He wouldn't have forced it then and there. Not during a

party. He would have waited until we were home that night. I'd never known Ted to want sex in the early evening, at least not for a long, long time.

But you've denied him for ages. Don't some wives think they have a sexual duty to their husbands? Don't some husbands think they have a right to sex with a partner? Didn't you not five minutes ago just promise him? You've been reading up. You know spousal rape wasn't even a crime in the UK thirty years ago. You know that in some countries marriage means eternal consent. Is it so outrageous that Ted could have chosen to take what was his?

This time I had no counter to the enemy that was the inner me.

You feel you owe him. He feels you owe him. And he decided to take what was his. He followed you that night. He used one of his practised chokeholds to subdue you. He made you give him what you are supposed to. And then he snatched that ring off your finger because it was a declaration that you would offer your sex and you had broken that contract.

I managed to stifle that horrible voice, but the despair grew wings. I put my head in my hands and started crying. Suspecting my own husband? My God, what was happening to me? Was I going insane because of the evil actions of an unknown man? And where would this downward spiral end? Would it ever?

On Thursday morning, after I'd dropped off Dan, I saw Joan again hanging around with her friends outside the corner shop. She gave me a smirk that I reluctantly returned, but no words were exchanged as I walked past. I felt really awkward about last night.

I'd been a bit distant that morning and had left the house in slippers, so had to return home for my work shoes. As I drove past the corner minimart, I saw a forensics van outside. Nosiness got the better of me and I pulled up.

Glenn wasn't around. His dad, Alphonse, was behind the counter. He was a tall, skinny guy with faded forearm tattoos, possibly from a hellraiser youth. In order to start a chat, I grabbed a chocolate bar and headed to the counter. Behind Alphonse, I saw a woman in black moving about in the stockroom. It wasn't his wife.

'What's with the police?' I asked.

'Fools broke in last night,' he spat, clearly still angry about the fact. 'They took some spirits and cigarettes and scratch cards, the bastards. And then they went upstairs for more. They don't usually do that. Usually cowards that just rob the place.'

He went on to explain that two men had confronted him and his wife and son, bearing machetes. They grouped the trio in one bedroom, where one robber stayed to watch them while the second searched the other rooms. After the men had left, Alphonse went to check downstairs and left his son to catalogue what was missing from their home.

The bastards had stolen laptops, mobile phones and other electronics. They'd also trashed the place. The police were investigating and swabbing for prints and DNA.

'Fourth time in three years,' he said. I knew. I recalled having seen police cars outside on a few occasions. 'So we're getting a dog. I want the meanest bastard animal out there. They'll leave DNA next time for sure. All up the walls when the dog rips their balls off.'

'I'm so sorry. You're such nice people. This shouldn't have happened.'

I moved on. I picked up my sister and we drove to

Meadowhall. I agreed to meet Maud for lunch and we split to go to our separate workplaces.

At Heaven Homestore, the young new starter called Alice phoned in sick again. I took the call, wished her well, and hung up. I didn't mind that she was off; being busy would give me less time to fret and overthink. I also chose to work a till in order to surround myself with people. No more hiding in the stockroom. Shying away from everyone would only make things worse in the long run. I needed to stop worrying that this or that man was my stalker.

If he was out there, watching me, so be it. He was one guy and as soon as I gave a second man a suspicious look, one had to be a mistake. That constituted paranoia. Paranoia would eat me alive.

It seemed to work. After an hour on the tills, I was laughing and joking with customers. Even some of the males, although I have to admit it was only those I deemed highly improbable as sexual predators.

Foolish, really, since in downtime the monster would be wearing an innocent mask.

CHAPTER SEVENTEEN

O n the way back to school that afternoon, I stopped at a cash machine and withdrew £50 of the money Ted had transferred to me. Joan was waiting on the school field with other parents, but she saw me arrive and moved to an empty spot. I approached.

Without a care for who saw, she handed me a small brown paper bag. I negated her casual policy by hurriedly stuffing it into my pocket as if we'd done a drug deal. Actually, this was worse.

'I've got three orders for you,' she said. 'Listen up carefully.'

I did. After, she held out her hand. I filled it with cash. She went back to her friends without a word.

I moved ahead of her so I could get Dan and get to the car without coming across her again. As we drove away, I got his phone out of the glovebox. 'I need to make a quick stop somewhere before we go home. You okay with that?'

He took his phone and loaded a game. That meant he didn't mind a detour. I drove about five miles east of our house and stopped on an old stone bridge over a river. Order number one from Joan: 'Be miles away from home when you turn it on.'

Here, I extracted the three items from the bag. One phone, one battery, one SIM card. I put the device together and turned it on, and quickly started scrolling through messages and calls. Dan, captivated by his own phone, didn't even seem to notice.

Order number two: 'Use the phone just for a couple of minutes. No more.'

I found nothing on the phone that gave me cause for concern, which was great news. I turned the device off, split it into three parts again, and got out of the car. Dan came with me, eager to see the river. He started looking on the ground for little stones to chuck into the water. I gave him the SIM card.

Order number three: 'Get rid of this as soon as you're done with it. The police can trace it.'

Dan gleefully dropped the SIM card over the side of the bridge, watching in awe as it somersaulted, hit the water, sank. Next, I handed him the battery, and finally the handset itself.

'Was it broken?' he asked.

'It was an old one. No good.'

On the way home, I assessed my feelings. The phone had contained no evidence that its owner, Glenn, was my attacker. I was glad because his parents ran the local minimart and my family knew them well. But was this really good news? If I'd found messages about my attack, or a photo of me out cold by the stream, or something else that could be used to bring a monster to justice, the horror would have been over soon.

Instead, I had eliminated just one man out of thousands, even millions. To achieve this, I'd caused heartache for three other people. All I had wanted was Glenn's phone, but Joan had insisted that her brothers had to camouflage the theft by stealing other items. The ultimate result of my actions then? The shopkeepers would never forget the break-in. I was down another £50.

And my attacker was still out there.

After I dropped Dan at school on Friday, I saw a man looking at my car. Not just looking but staring. He was walking around it, up close, peering deep into every window, like a policeman who'd found an abandoned vehicle. But this guy was as far from law enforcement as you could get. It was John, Joan's younger brother.

The handsome man of before had departed. His hair, no longer gelled, was a bit of a mess, and he wore a tracksuit that had seen better days. He waved at me and, not wanting to upset him, I waved back. I hoped he was waiting for his sister, but realised that she had left the school grounds before me.

As I got close, he said, 'You look nice this morning. Kid get into school okay?'

'Yes. Fine. Thanks. I'm just in a rush to get home now. Good to see you again.'

I got in the car and started the engine. And then the passenger door opened. John squatted by it.

'Something wrong?' I asked. I prayed he wouldn't get in.

'No, no. Just passing, thought I'd say hello. Actually, I wanted to ask you something. I know you said you didn't want to talk about this, back in the car the other night, but I got curious. Those Z-drugs you mentioned. You took Zaleplon, right?'

'Yes. It's a sleeping tablet.'

He gave me a sly grin. 'Sure is. But that's not why you took it.'

I didn't want to get into my personal history, but neither did I want to drag this conversation out. 'No. I took it for foolish reasons. A long time ago.'

'I know a guy who's on it. In the right amount, it gives him a buzz. The odd hallucination. But sometimes he goes overboard and can't remember things the next day.'

'It can do that. I went overboard. A long time ago. I was a stupid teenager back then. Anyway, nice to see you again, but I really need to get going.'

John didn't move. 'Sure. It's just... I can get you some. As much Zaleplon as you want. Just say the word.'

'No. That was a long time ago and I had a bad... no, thank you. I don't do that anymore. Not for a long time. That was a different me. Now, I really do need to get going.'

Still he didn't move. His smile vanished. 'Actually, the real reason I'm here is that Joan asked me to ask you if she could borrow some cash. As a favour, since she did you some favours.'

I looked around to make sure no one was listening. Ahead, Joan and two friends had just exited the shop and stopped to talk. 'I paid. It wasn't exactly a favour.'

'Kinda was. But even if not, any chance of that loan? Just a bit to tide her over, get the kids some food and that. It's winter and the heating's gone off.'

Kids? She had more than one? I didn't care to ask, I just wanted to get away from here. I had £30 in my purse and held it out. John made it vanish. 'That's all I can afford. I've got bills of my own. So it's just that one loan, okay? Please don't ask for any more.'

'No probs. I just knew you'd be okay with it, what with the bond we've got after that thing, you know?'

'I just want to put all that stuff behind me. Let's not mention it again. And please don't wait for me again like this outside school. I'm usually in a rush.'

'No probs. Not sure when Joan will get the cash back to you, but sometime. Unless we can earn it with another favour?'

'No, it's fine. No rush to pay it back. Thanks. I have to go now.'

He saluted, stood, closed my door and walked away. I turned my car in the road so I wouldn't have to drive past Joan, in case she tried to flag me down. I drove away, quick.

And I thought about that word John had used. Bond. He'd said we had a *bond*.

CHAPTER EIGHTEEN

Integrating myself into crowds at work seemed to have worked on my high anxiety levels pretty well, so the weekend was geared towards the social. On Saturday, my sister, Maud, babysat Dan while Ted and I went to a restaurant with a close neighbour couple. The boys were big Ultimate Fighting Championship fans and talked at length about an event airing live that night. We girls talked about the news.

My attack wasn't mentioned. I don't know if they knew about it or had been instructed by Ted not to ask.

Later that evening, I went into the attic, where I kept all my mother's expensive jewellery. In the same box was my old engagement ring. Some women wear both upon marriage, but I chose not to and stored it. A wise choice, it now seemed, for I would have lost both when I was attacked. I also found Ted's 'management' ring.

I sat in the dark for a short while afterwards, thinking about how it had been exactly seven days. This time last week, I was left for dead.

Ted and Dan had gone swimming. I showed him when they returned, but he wasn't impressed. 'Still two grand down though. And it's not a wedding ring. Guys will come on to you, thinking you're not over the line yet and still swayable.'

At least he found room to joke, so he was getting over the loss of money. I put the engagement ring on. 'Wedding rings are about commitment. Engagement rings are about love and life. This means just as much to me.'

I put my arms around him, and pulled him into a kiss. Dan made a retching noise, which made us both laugh. We kissed again. I was dismayed to find, however, that I was relieved once the embrace broke.

On Sunday I drove to Crystal Peaks Retail Park for a nosey around some shops. I browsed in numerous stores but the only item I needed was magnetic photo frames from Boots that I'd seen an online advert for. However, I spotted something else while crossing the store. And it stopped me dead in my tracks.

A pregnancy test.

I'd never felt pain from down below after my attack. There had been no blood or semen in my underwear. I'd showered after the party and found nothing untoward in or around my vagina. I hadn't even thought about pregnancy after learning I was raped. But now, seeing the test kits lined up before me, some with smiling women on the front, put the notion indelibly in my mind. I knew I could not rest until I had an answer.

I picked a top-end product. Once out of the store, I rushed to the toilets and performed a test. Three minutes later, I had that answer I craved.

Negative.

But it meant nothing. I knew from giving birth to Dan that the body started to produce hCG – a pregnancy hormone detected by the tests – as early as seven days after fertilisation. I was raped eight days ago. However, the chances of a correct result at this early stage were very low and false negatives were likely. I really needed to wait until I missed a period, which should be in about another ten days or so.

I ran back to the store. Ten days was a long time to wait in fear. I grabbed as many boxes as I could hold, which turned out to be eleven. It cost me over £80. Despite knowing that the negative result held no weight, I had felt soothed. I wanted more of that feeling. The negative was a painkiller. I needed it, in fact. I would test myself every day, until I was certain.

I would need a good hiding place for a horde of pregnancy tests though. I could imagine Ted's face if he yanked open a drawer and found them. Not a conversation I wanted to have.

Although I already knew exactly what I'd tell him if he discovered the tests. *I've cheated on you.* I'd rather tell him I'd slept with his father than admit the truth.

Test number 2: negative.

I had obvious reasons for being put off sex, but Ted didn't, yet his libido seemed to have waned. He hadn't come on to me in days, not even attempting a kiss. Most partners might have assumed he was wary after I'd knocked him back so many times. My suspicious mind no longer worked like that.

That Monday night, he came back from work, didn't say a word, and went upstairs. He came back down with his jiu-jitsu bag and said, 'Tom's got a grading tonight and we should all be there for that. And Declan needs help with his leglocks. He likes to practise with me.'

'Okay,' I replied.

'Yeah, Danny's got a match coming up, leglock guy, and I need to show him how to escape.'

'Okay.'

'Cool. Back later.'

And with that, he left.

Some autistic children hate impromptu journeys, but Dan was always keen. So when I told him to grab his shoes and coat, he did so with a skip and a smile. We got outside just in time for me to see Ted's car turning right at the end of the street. The west end. The opposite direction to his jiu-jitsu gym.

For Ted to give me little notice of a grappling class was not uncommon. But he'd never before tried to sell me his reason. Something had made me suspicious and now I was convinced: there was no class tonight.

I was ready for a lengthy drive, but Ted didn't even leave the estate. Just a couple of turns later, he stopped. I laid up my vehicle about thirty metres back, behind a BT van. The houses here were all detached and a lot more expensive than ours.

Ted exited his car and walked up a sloping garden path to a wood-framed glass porch. Shelves at ankle and hip height were loaded with plants and I couldn't see inside. I wouldn't see who opened the door to Ted. I hoped he was picking up a classmate.

'Where are we, Mum?' Dan said.

'I'm just waiting to see if my friend comes out of her house.'

He looked disappointed. The last time I'd rushed him out of the house without telling him where we were going, we'd gone to a funfair. 'Which house?'

I pointed to a random property. Dan then asked various questions about my friend, and I was forced to invent a name and a backstory for her. I hated lying to him, but he couldn't know the truth.

Soon after, Dan got busy on his phone game and we sat in silence. As the minutes passed, it became clear that Ted wasn't collecting a fellow grappler. It was over an hour before he reappeared.

These were expensive properties and I could imagine a home cinema, a games room – but not a gym. Yet Ted exited the house in his Gi – which I liked to call his pyjamas. Another red flag right there: Ted had never returned from jiu-jitsu wearing his uniform. Was it to back up his story? To hide the fact that he'd been up to a different form of grappling?

Before getting in his car, he bent down at the bottom of the garden. A tiny fence hindered my view of whatever he did. The next strange action was after he'd gotten in his car: he opened the door, leaned out, and spat liquid into the gutter.

The street was a dead end, so Ted had to turn his car in the road. Thankfully, the BT van blocked his view of my car until just about alongside, and he was travelling fast enough to miss it as he raced by. Still, I told Dan to duck and did the same myself.

'Are we hiding from someone?' Dan said, bent over and grinning.

'Just one of your dinner ladies. Unless you want to chat to her?'

'Ugh, no, not if it's Mrs Henderson.'

'It is. Shall we drive away before she comes over?'

'Yes. Now. Quick.'

I turned the car and got out of there.

Ted's car was outside our house when we got back. I squeezed past the neighbour's vehicle to park in the driveway. 'Dan, don't tell your dad where we went. He doesn't like me seeing my friend. We went to the petrol station, okay?'

He winked, pleased by the idea of keeping a secret.

'Now go find your dad and tell him a joke.'

That would keep Ted busy while I did some investigating. His key was on the hook inside the door and I unlocked his vehicle. The first place I checked was the glovebox, and I hit the jackpot. Inside was a bottle of mouthwash.

I found Ted in the shower. Dan was sitting on our bed, waiting. Next to him was Ted's Gi, dumped in a heap but with one arm neatly stretched out. It had mud on it. On his bedside cabinet, next to his current library book, was a keto snack bar, which Ted always ate after a gym session. I was meant to see these things, I knew. I sent Dan downstairs to put his shoes away.

Ted emerged from the shower, a towel around his waist. He immediately picked up his keto bar and started chomping. He said, 'Where did you go?'

'Petrol station. How was the jiu-jitsu?'

'Good.'

'Was the gym busy?'

Here was his chance to set me right. He could say he'd been to collect a friend, and that they'd practised grappling at his home instead of the gym. A little extreme, but plausible. But he didn't. He said, 'So-so. The usual suspects.'

My heart sank. 'Anything memorable happen?'

He shrugged and turned away to start dressing. 'Just a normal session. I did fall in some mud by the car park though. Got it all up my arm. Will that wash off?'

He pointed at the Gi. I picked up the muddy arm. 'Wow. It should come out.'

I left him to get changed. Halfway down the stairs, I stopped and sat.

Strangely, the knowledge that Ted was having an affair didn't upset me. I'd heard of cheated partners accepting infidelity as long as they didn't get dumped, and I felt a little like that. I knew Ted needed more intimacy than I was offering. He was letting off steam. If an affair lightened his stress, and as long as he didn't abandon Dan and me for this other woman, I could live with it.

Harder to accept was *why* Ted had sought sex outside of marriage. It hurt to know he had been pushed into another woman's arms by his wife's spiralling craziness.

CHAPTER NINETEEN

Test 3: Negative.

Ever since my memory had returned a story of rape, I'd been voraciously reading about this awful offence. At first I sought out statistics, and while the numbers were shocking, they were just that: numbers. A list of facts did nothing to help me with my own mania. Seeking information about society's outlook on rape of women by men led me deeper into a black abyss, but rape culture was also off the mark.

What I wanted was personal tales. I wanted to read about women like me. How they'd been attacked. How they'd coped afterwards. What it was like to see an attacker exposed, see him in court; to have their stories told to the world. And to learn if the maelstrom of emotions in my head was par for the course. Maybe, selfishly, I also wanted to know I didn't suffer alone.

Woman after woman, rape after rape, here, there, everywhere. It was inevitable that I would find a story close to the bone. I had no idea that I was about to read something that would change my life.

Often I would consume an online story, then click on a link

to find another; this method could open up articles I might otherwise have never found through search engine results. The downside was that hopping across links like stepping stones could slowly veer me off track and into irrelevant territory.

It happened on Tuesday, the first day of the new month. Somehow I'd meandered onto a recent piece about transgender rapists, and was ready to give up for that day. I decided on one more story and clicked a link in the SEE ALSO section. It was in this next article that I saw a word that sucked the breath out of me.

The piece had been published way back in March of 2005. It was about a sexual attack on a woman from a small district in north-west Edinburgh. The article showed a picture of the victim sitting in a living room, although her face was blurred out. She was named as Woman X to hide her real identity.

Interesting. For some reason the e-newspaper had seen fit to connect a 2005 rape story to a 2021 article about transgender sexual offenders.

I went back to the latter story. It was about Police Scotland's pro-trans plan to record sexual offenders with male genitalia as female if they identified as such, even if they hadn't yet obtained official certification as trans women. It ended with quotes from four people and asked readers to comment what they thought.

One quote was from a police officer, another a politician, the third a board director of Rape Crisis Scotland. The fourth person was: 'Lizzie Roundtree – Edinburgh'.

Interesting. Three professionals/authorities on the subject, and a woman with seemingly no relevance.

I made another search after this. Facebook. Lizzie Roundtree. I found three women from Edinburgh with that name and quickly eliminated two. The remaining profile soon yielded good news. In a holiday photo album from 2007, I found a picture of Lizzie standing on a pier. I flicked between this photo and the single picture included in the 2005 rape story.

Now I was certain. The woman on the pier and the blurred-faced woman in the living room wore the same yellow trousers. Lizzie Roundtree quoted in the 2021 article because she was a rape survivor, although this fact hadn't been imparted to its readers. I knew her name and where she lived.

My interest in her? The focus of the 2005 article had been women who considered themselves at fault for their rape, and the details of Lizzie's attack had been consigned to a single line. But it was in that line I'd found the single word that had hooked me:

WOMAN X WAS RAPED DURING A *GEOCACHE* TREASURE HUNT.

Seventeen years and countries apart, yet I felt a connection. I just *knew* that Lizzie's rape and mine were related. The same monster had attacked us both. He was not lurking in dark places in hope; he was targeting women at geocaches. To know of these zones, perhaps he was a geocacher himself.

I felt a heavy weight suddenly lift from within me, like something anchored suddenly floating free. The idea of justice no longer felt ethereal. It was solid, within reach. The clues to naming, finding, convicting this bastard were out there.

It cost me a yearly subscription, but I located Lizzie Roundtree's phone number on a people-finder website. I dialled half of it before changing my mind. Instead, I made note of her address. This was not a conversation to be had across airwaves. I wanted to be face to face. I planned my trip for the next morning. I hunted out some old clothing I hadn't worn for ages and put it in my car, along with some scissors and make-up.

After breakfast on Wednesday, Ted kissed me and left. Dan got his school bag and we headed out. The neighbour, Mr Skewis, was loading his van. As usual, his car was on the street and a good portion of the front was across my driveway. When Dan was in my car, I approached the low wall between our properties and waited for the young builder to spot me. He gave a nod-greeting. He'd lived beside me for over a year and weak hellos were all we'd ever shared.

'Your car is across my driveway again.'

'What do you mean?'

I pointed at his car. He said, 'It's like a foot over. I have to be able to get my van out.'

'And I have to get my car out, and it's always a squeeze. It would be great if you could stop doing it.'

That didn't please him. 'It's on the main road. You don't own the road.'

'Move the car. Don't do it again.'

'Get lost, missus. I'll stop that when you stop those tree branches poking over my back fence.'

I just stared at him. Wow, I was fired up. And it worked. He walked out onto the road and I got in my car. He backed his vehicle up three feet. Feeling a little guilty, I gave him a thumbs up as I drove away. He didn't return it.

Joan and her kid weren't at school that morning, which was nice. After dropping Dan off, I made two calls. The first was to my sister, but it went to voicemail. I left a message: 'Maud, I need you to pick up Dan from school. I've got a doctor's appointment. I won't be home until later. I can pick him up from yours or you can bring him home. Thanks.'

The second call was to work. Carla answered. In the

background I could hear the racket of money going through the cash office coin sorter. 'Carla, it's me. I can't make it in today.'

'Really? You okay? It's just that if Alice's off again, we're doomed. Alan thinks that FC is today. He wants us all cleaning like robots.'

The last thing I cared about was a flash check, although I felt bad leaving Carla extra work. 'Sorry. Can't be helped. Dan's off school ill, no babysitter. I'll be in tomorrow. Sorry again.'

'Okay, babe, we'll manage. Kids come first. Alan's arse comes last, so for once he can get off it.'

After that call, I filled the petrol tank, then hit a McDonald's for an extra breakfast, unsure when I'd get to eat again. I used their restroom and performed yet another pregnancy test. Negative. I could relax until tomorrow.

Actually, there was no relaxation to be had. I couldn't shake the idea that the monster was following my vehicle. If he tailed me to Lizzie Roundtree's house, would he realise who she was? That I was onto him? That his best option was to kill both women, there and then?

In a quiet corner of the car park, I changed into the old clothing I'd stored. I applied a heavy amount of make-up. And I used scissors to cut my hair a lot shorter. What I had planned for today couldn't come back on me. However, seeing the final product in the mirror made me feel that I'd gone overboard. I was hardly a spy on a secret mission. But what was done was done.

And with that completed, I had only one more task. Get to Edinburgh. Before hitting the motorway, I made a number of nonsense turns, circled a few roundabouts, pulled up to park at various locations, all of it designed to expose a tail. I figured I was okay, but it was impossible to know and I couldn't delay my mission any longer.

Once I was on the motorway, anxiety faded. In fact, there was a euphoria. I was making important forward steps. Soon, no more looking over my shoulder, no more sleepless nights. I was on the path towards ending the nightmare.

CHAPTER TWENTY

Lizzie Roundtree lived in Barnton in Edinburgh in the Scottish Lowlands. A Wikipedia article on the suburb, which lay just a mile south of the Firth of Forth estuary and four miles west of the city centre, said that the author JK Rowling lived there. Dan had read a Harry Potter book and I briefly wondered about the chances of getting him an autograph. I made the journey in five hours with a single toilet stop at a service station.

Lizzie Roundtree lived on Barnton Park View, a leafy road in an estate surrounded by greenery. The houses here were detached, with double garages and backyards overlooking a golf course. Just in case there was any doubt that Lizzie Roundtree had money, a flash white BMW SUV sat in the driveway. The property had high, squared hedges and no gate.

My new appearance would be for naught if Lizzie or a neighbour noted my registration, so I parked on a side street a five-minute walk away. A camera watching the driveway must have alerted the occupant: the front door opened before I even got to it.

The woman standing there was tall, slim, black-haired, in

her late thirties, wearing jeans and a shirt and a lot of hand and wrist jewellery. She looked me up and down and didn't seem impressed. I knew I'd made a mistake with my disguise; in a wealthy estate like this, I must have looked like a tramp.

'Can I help you?'

I stopped about ten feet away. 'Yes. I'm here to see you. Lizzie Roundtree? I saw the newspaper article about you. From back in 2005.'

The tall woman's face turned from wonder to shock to outrage within a second. 'Go away.'

She shut the door. I rushed up to it. 'I'm not a reporter, Lizzie. I'm here to help.'

She hadn't gone deeper into the house; her voice came from just beyond the door. 'I don't want help. Who are you? How did you find my home?'

'My name is Mary Taylor. I looked you up. Please talk to me. You were on a geocache, weren't you? When you were attacked.'

'I'm not getting into that. That's history. I haven't cared for years.'

'I know you gave a quote on a story a couple of months ago. So it's still in your mind. Can we just talk?'

'No talking. Go away. Look, I'm not the same person anymore.'

'I've been getting that,' I said, quiet, more to myself.

The door slowly opened. Lizzie no longer looked frustrated. 'Who are you? Did something happen to you?'

'Yes. So I know how you feel. I don't know what life is like inside your head, but from the outside it seems as if you're doing okay. I hope I can be like you in years to come.'

She looked at me for a few seconds, obviously considering her choices. In the end, the relaxing of her shoulders told me she'd dropped onto my side of the fence.

'Go round the back.'

She shut the door. I walked alongside the house, into a neat back lawn with a fine view of one of the golf course fairways. The edge of the course was lined with high, thin netting to prevent balls smashing windows or skulls. Lizzie was already standing on her rear doorstep. The door was shut behind her, so I clearly wasn't welcome inside. I moved closer, stopping a few feet away.

Lizzie looked beyond me, out onto the golf course, or maybe miles beyond, or at nothing but a chilling past behind her eyes.

'I never wanted to talk about it,' she said. 'That recent article, I don't know why I agreed to participate. They wanted the opinion of someone who'd been through it. Same for the first one in 2005. That one was about women feeling the blame for getting attacked by men. I know I did. Do you?'

'I don't know. Maybe. I mean, I know I could have avoided the woods that night. In that sense, I can see how some would say that was my fault.'

'What were you wearing?'

'My clothing? I–'

'That was something a reporter asked. Word got around after I'd gone to the police. This fool turned up on my doorstep. What was I wearing? Did I not consider that provocative clothing was dangerous?'

'I got told I shouldn't be out alone in the dark. People think we should be more careful. I should have, maybe.'

Now she looked at me, and she seemed disgusted. 'Is that attitude fair? I told that reporter I should be able to wear what I want, go where I want, and have the right to not be sexually assaulted by a man. But is that right?'

'Yes,' I said. I was impatient. I felt sorry for Lizzie, but her attack had been years ago and mine was fresh, a wound that still bled. I just wanted information, not a discussion about rape culture. 'There's no justification for these offences.'

There was a table with chairs on the lawn. Lizzie walked to it and sat. Unbidden, I sat across from her. Still her eyes were far away. I held my tongue; she needed to vent.

'That reporter, he asked me a question. He said, did I have the right to walk down a crime-ridden neighbourhood at midnight with a £20 note taped to my forehead. And I do, don't I? But, he said, should I really moan if I get robbed?'

'That's not fair. Not the same. Yes, we can prevent things, or try to. But the person who mugs you for that money is still the one in the wrong. Rape is a crime. People know they shouldn't commit rape.'

Now she looked at me. 'Maybe it is fair. I go to the supermarket. There's a sign there. It tells me not to leave valuables on show in my car. If I tell the police I left a gold watch on the dashboard and someone broke a window to steal it, they'd probably warn me to be careful in future. And I wouldn't be offended by that, would I? So why should I be offended if someone tells me to cover my cleavage? To stay in groups at night?'

'It wasn't your fault, Lizzie.'

'I saw something on the news. There's a class in America that teaches women how to vomit on demand. I've heard people say we should pee our clothing. You know, do these things if someone tries to rape us.'

'It wasn't your fault,' I repeated. 'And it wasn't my fault. If a man is the sort to take a woman by force, it's already in him. Sexy women's clothing doesn't cast a spell that turns ordinary men into monsters. If that was the case, then we'd have a cure. Put every woman in the world in rags, and watch the rape numbers drop to zero. Preposterous.'

She shrugged, clearly not convinced. I wasn't sure I blamed

myself, but would that change? Was this an outlook she'd developed over the years, or had it always been there? Had I avoided feeling like her because so far nobody knew about my attack and the only opinion I'd heard was my own?

She blinked rapidly, as if coming out of a trance. 'It doesn't even matter. Long time ago. I'm past all that. I have a long-term boyfriend, we've got two kids. He knows about my past and can deal with it. Does your fiancé know?'

I looked at my engagement ring. I did not correct her. I did wonder, though, how Ted would feel if he found out I'd been raped. Long term, would he be able to get past it? Would he blame me?

'Anyway,' Lizzie continued, 'I don't care if that man who did this never gets arrested. I don't care if he lives the rest of his life a free man. In fact, that's better because I don't want to face him in a court. I don't want the police coming to talk to me. I don't want all that back in my life when I've worked so hard to push it aside. As long as he stays miles and miles away from me, I'm okay.'

I imagined how she'd feel if I told her there was a chance her attacker, if he'd followed me, could be just metres away, watching her house right now.

She seemed ready to end our conversation, so I had to move quick. 'You were on a geocache, is that right?'

'Yes. I used to do that back then. It was March 12th 2005, a Saturday. There was a gathering that night. I was planning to attend. I decided to warm up with a few hunts that afternoon. I'd gone to a webcam geocache outside the entrance to Corstorphine Hill Walled Garden. Then I went into the woods to find another. He was there... he was...'

She clearly didn't like talking about this. But I needed to know. 'What did he look like? What did he do to you?'

'I didn't see him. He grabbed me from behind. I was thrown

face down. I wore a skirt, which made it easier for him. I kind of froze until it was over. The police, they were upset that I had no description. I... Look, no more.'

She wiped a tear from her eye. I knew I'd get no more, but I already had what I needed. Confirmation that we had the same attacker: she was grabbed from behind, just like me. And my next clue: a webcam geocache at Corstorphine Hill. I was relieved that she hadn't had a description of the monster. Her recollection would have been almost seventeen years out of date and misleading, perhaps dangerously so.

I thanked her and stood up. She said, 'What happened to you? You never said.'

I sat down. 'The same.'

'When was it?'

I only told her because she lived in another country. I'd never see her again. 'Nearly two weeks ago.'

She looked shocked. 'Two weeks? And you were raped?'

I didn't like her tone: there was doubt. It was in her eyes too. I wanted to be careful. 'I don't remember most of it.'

Her shock turned to disgust. 'The same thing didn't happen to us both. You don't have the eyes of... not for two weeks ago. I was... damaged. Torn. It took me months just to get that calm back in my eyes. I mean, if you don't remember...'

I knew what she was getting at. It angered me, but I held it back. 'I was hit on the head. I blacked out. I must not have fought him. It must have been over quick. But I do remember bits. I know he raped me.'

She shook her head. 'Just go.'

She looked away. I stood and started to leave. But after three steps I paused, unable to leave her so distraught. I wanted our meeting to ease her pain, not increase it. 'I'll get justice for us, Lizzie. He won't get away with this.'

She jerked as if slapped. 'Us? Wait... are you saying you think it was the same man?'

I didn't respond. I didn't like her new vigour.

She jumped to her feet. 'Where was this? Where are you from? What else do you know?'

'Nothing. I'm sorry to bother you.'

I again made to go. I got one step and a hand latched onto my arm. Lizzie spun me to face her. 'You know who he is, don't you?'

'No. I didn't mean to get your hopes up.'

'Don't lie. You have to tell the police.'

But she planned to do that herself. She let go of my arm so she could pull out her phone. I told her, 'Stop. Don't call them. I don't know him. You said you didn't care.'

She dialled. I backed away. 'Lizzie, I will find him. Stop the call.'

'No, stay right there. You're going to tell the police everything.'

'No.'

She stepped forward, again to grab my arm. I batted her hand aside, grabbed her phone, killed the call, and dropped the device by her feet. 'I can't have the police, Lizzie. I can't be exposed like that. I've got to go.'

I turned. I ran.

At the corner of her street, I looked back just in time to see her appear outside her driveway, phone to her ear. I darted down the next street before she spotted me, and I didn't stop running until my chest was on fire and my head was dizzy.

After consulting Google Maps, I drove just over half a mile east until a right turn put me on Clermiston Road. The woods were on my left. Edinburgh was known for its seven hills, one of which was Corstorphine Hill.

It was a nature park open to the public, its large woodland popular with ramblers and birdwatchers. At the top of the hill was the 150-year-old Clermiston Tower, which offered fantastic views across the land. Nearby was the walled garden that Lizzie had mentioned. Upon the lower slopes of the hill were residential estates, hotels, a hospital, Edinburgh Zoo, and even a former nuclear bunker.

All of the above was information for the tourist pamphlets. The old geocacher in me might have been awed by such a place, but today I saw only a predator's playground.

At the entrance to the car park, I spotted the camera Lizzie had mentioned. I parked at the side of the road and wondered why I had chosen to visit this location. The information I needed was, hopefully, online; being here was a risk if Lizzie had worked out where to send the police.

Webcam caches didn't have logbooks to sign; instead, users posted a photo of themselves taken by CCTV. The procedure was to have a friend visit the website hosting the camera and take a screenshot of the live feed. The photo, saved on Paint or another piece of image editing software, could then be uploaded to the geocache page.

Webcam caches were popular in the early 2000s, but the rise of smartphones and Photoshopping had changed the guidelines and this cache type had been grandfathered. Over the years, more and more had been removed, or archived, and little more than two hundred remained active across the world. As expected, a search of Corstorphine Hill returned many hits, but no webcam cache.

However, although the pages of archived caches were hidden, they were available for viewing and could be found using a partner website called Project-GC. I soon had the cache page on my screen.

There were 282 logs, the final one an archive notice by the admin team in April of 2015. I started scrolling back the years, seeking the date Lizzie Roundtree was attacked.

Hopefully, the man who had left her for dead, seventeen years before he tried kill me, had logged a visit. If so, I could find his profile. Find him. Find justice.

CHAPTER TWENTY-ONE

Most geocaches had at most a handful of logs each week, but I was surprised to see that the webcam geocache, called DOLERITE DO-IT-RIGHT, had forty-seven entries for the date Lizzie was attacked. That meant forty-seven profiles to examine. Had there been something special about that day?

Before reviewing the profiles, I went through the logs to scrutinise the posted photos. That quickly became a bootless errand. The CCTV quality was bad and, to make things worse, the geocache description instructed users to pose by a turnstile at the back of the car park, some thirty metres from the camera.

The photo in the first log showed a couple standing arm in arm, but I couldn't make out their faces. Not even enough to tell if the couple was male-female, two males, or two women. I screen-captured the picture and zoomed in, but that decreased the quality. I doubt I would have recognised myself in a crappy black-and-white photo at that distance.

Back to the geocachers themselves. My original plan was to discard all those with either female names or female profile pictures. Some names would be sexless – like Smith747474, creator of the geocache – and some pictures would be of pets or cars or nature, and these couldn't be overlooked. After eliminating the clearly not-applicable, I could delve a little deeper into each profile and seek relevant information.

It could take a while. I doubted I'd be lucky enough to find a user called RapistScum.

But before I could start the weeding process, I kicked myself. How had I been so silly? The cache near where I had been attacked! If the monster was a geocacher and he'd logged a visit to Dolerite in Corstorphine Hill, he might have done the same back at Sword Dance in Grenoside.

All I had to do was cross-reference the names logged at both geocaches, on two certain dates seventeen years apart. If there was more than one name appearing at both sites, I'd be shocked.

Unfortunately, I quickly realised the futility of this endeavour, indeed my entire method for finding the monster. I got out of the car and started pacing in the car park, my angry face watched by the CCTV camera that had immortalised so many smiles and happy waves. I had been so optimistic, yet so stupid.

Both Lizzie and I had been attacked *before* visiting our geocaches, and our names were not logged. Perhaps the monster had also been en route on both occasions and, following the rapes, had cautiously chosen not to proceed. After all, he would have to be stupid to not know that logging geocache visits near crime scenes would be akin to leaving a trail of breadcrumbs.

It was possible he'd already visited and physically signed the logbook at Grenoside, but I wouldn't know unless I went and looked. I wasn't going back there. Besides, a smart criminal would have returned afterwards and scrubbed that name or destroyed that logbook.

I returned to the car and grabbed my phone. I would still check the online logs, just in case.

Immediately, bad news. The Sword Dance cache in

Grenoside had no logs for the date I was left for dead. Figuring it was possible the monster had been there previously or sometime after, I checked the two days bookending that fateful night. Five names.

The profile pictures gave no clue: a digital cat with impossibly green eyes; a cow in a bright coat in a field; a blank, default avatar; a portable key safe with shackle; a baby holding a toy Superman. Their profile names were sexless. None was repeated on the webcam geocache logs.

I widened the net, now checking a week either side of the day I was attacked. Four more geocachers. Two had female names and photos, but I checked them against the Dolerite cache anyway. No luck. Of the remaining two, I looked at someone called Nutmeg_Forever first. A sexless name, but this geocacher's profile picture showed a portly bearded man of about thirty.

I didn't recall a beard on my attacker, but I recalled nothing except a face seen through rippling water, didn't I? I ran the name against Dolerite and–

– stared at my phone in disbelief.

A man calling himself Nutmeg_Forever had visited the Grenoside cache two days before I got brutalised. Seventeen years earlier, he had logged at the webcam cache on the day a maniac tried to send Lizzie Roundtree to heaven.

Nutmeg's profile information page contained nothing but the standard website line about how the person was ... `probably cool, but hasn't shared any details yet`: he hadn't written anything about himself. A search of his gallery of photos taken at geocaches told me nothing except that he had a dog. A shaggy brown one was pictured by numerous found caches. But photos of the man himself, bar that profile pic? None.

He was a veteran geocacher, though, having joined the website in 2004. Since then, he'd found 6,421 geocaches, the majority across the UK and a handful in Europe. I was more interested in his hides.

Nutmeg had fifty-three hides, all in and around Llanferres, in Denbighshire, Wales. Nineteen of the hides were in woodland and fields on the north side of the A494, which ran past the village. Twenty-three were located in a place called Pot Hole Quarry, which was popular with climbers. Ten were in Llanferres Park. The remaining geocache was in the grounds of St. Berres' Church. It was called the 1830 TO DOUGLAS.

Geocachers were advised to constantly maintain their hides, making sure nothing was broken, missing, erroneous, illegal, etc. They had to monitor logs for reported problems and perform their own visits to make sure everything was in order. A cache suffering repeated or unfixed problems could end up archived and the owner banned from listing new hides.

So, the best way to make sure you could maintain your geocache was to place it close to home. Bingo. Nutmeg lived in Llanferres, a village whose population according to the census of 2011 was an easily probed 827.

Now I knew enough to sink the bastard.

CHAPTER TWENTY-TWO

A t 3.42pm, my phone rang. It was Dan's school. I knew what it was about and answered with, 'Didn't my sister pick up Dan?'

No, she hadn't. Nobody at the school knew of any such plan. Maud must not have received my voicemail.

'I'm miles away. I wouldn't make it there for hours. Try my husband's number. Call me back.'

I hung up. The receptionist called back nine minutes later, with news that Ted had been unable to leave work early but had called Maud and arranged for her to collect Dan. I thanked the receptionist and hung up before she could give me an earful.

I'd get an earful from Ted, too, but I would delay that until we were face to face. So I turned off my phone. I didn't arrive home until almost 8pm. Maud and Ted were in the living room, and I was barely in the door before they launched a tag-team attack. I told them to wait while I spoke to Dan. He was in his room and he was fine with me. While he'd waited with his teacher, she gave him orange juice and they played chess.

'So we're still friends?' I asked.

He nodded. 'Aunty and Dad aren't happy though.'

I already knew. I headed downstairs to face their wrath. My sister took control of the scolding while Ted played spectator. He'd have his turn later, I knew.

Maud said, 'That was unfair, Lisa. Leaving a message for me and not checking that I got it.'

'I know. I was in a rush.'

'Yes, for the doctor's apparently. I called them on the way to get Dan. Just to see what took so long. And they said you didn't have an appointment.'

I feigned confusion. 'Doctor's? I went to the hairdresser. Look at my hair.'

'The voicemail said the doctor.'

'Well, I meant the hairdresser.'

'And that took all day?'

'I had to go down the M1 on the way back and there was a crash. I was in a jam when the school called. It took hours. Check it out if you don't believe me. A crash near junction 37.'

I hoped they wouldn't try to confirm this story. The way my husband and sister exchanged a glance, however, screamed that they doubted every word. But I would worry about that later. 'Look, I'm tired. Four hours stuck in a car. I need to eat and sit down.'

I left the room and hid upstairs. I heard the mumble of Maud and Ted talking for a few minutes, then the click of the front door closing. At the bedroom window, I watched Maud get in her car. Before the vehicle had even left the kerb, Ted appeared at the bedroom doorway.

'Not in the mood, Ted.'

He closed the door behind him and leaned on it. Exit blocked. 'You've been off recently. Acting strange.'

I continued to stare out of the window. Maud's car pulled away. Trance-like, my eyes stared at the empty spot of road. 'I got beaten up recently, Ted. I'm sorry if it affected me a little.'

'Yeah, I know. A teenaged girl, apparently.'

I turned to him. 'Apparently?'

'Yeah. I think a man did it.'

I fought to keep calm. Did he know? How did he know? 'Oh, do explain.'

'That geocache out of the blue that night. No police. Missing wedding ring. Four hours on a motorway today? All the mood swings in between.'

'What are you saying?'

'I'm saying, are you shagging some other guy, Lisa?'

My laughter was due to a sudden dump of tension. Ted saw it another way. 'Guilty laugh there? Or trying to act like what I said was, oh, just the most stupid thing?'

'The latter, Ted. You think I'm having an affair?' Oh, it was a battle not to leap on him for that. I lifted my hair aside and tapped my head wound.

'Perhaps he did that. You didn't want the police involved.'

'Oh, I see. I sneaked away on Saturday night to see him. But he wanted to end it, said he was making another go of it with his wife and–'

'Look at the state of you now,' he cut in, shaking his head. 'You're losing your mind, Lisa.'

'But that's because I got dumped, right? I mean, I was so desperate to continue shagging this guy that I threw my wedding ring away–'

'Just stop, Lisa.'

'–and said I was leaving you for him. But no, he was done with me. I was so angry I attacked him and he had to bash my head to get me off. And I've been so depressed since. Well, Sherlock, you got me. Well done you for working it all out.'

'Your head needs looking at,' Ted said as he opened the bedroom door. His final words before leaving: 'And I don't mean that cut.'

Ted left the house not long after our argument. I got Dan downstairs and made him supper. While he played on his phone afterwards, I twice went out into the backyard with my own device to make a call. I backed out both times.

The only alternative I could think of was a letter. I headed upstairs to write it. Two pages. Comically, I started it with Dear Police, but there was little amusement to be found in the remainder of the letter.

I sealed the letter in a stamped envelope and sat with it in the living room after Dan had gone to bed. Ted's car pulled up outside shortly afterwards. I had the letter hidden up my jumper when he walked in. He froze in the doorway.

'I apologise, Ted. You're right that my head hasn't been on straight since that night. I promise I will get better, and I promise you I haven't been having an affair.'

He said nothing until he'd dumped his coat and was sat across from me. 'So you haven't had sex with another man?'

I could have cursed for his choice of words. My own were carefully selected. 'No sneaking away with a plan to have sex with another man. No boyfriend on the side. No affair. I swear on Dan's life. You're the only one I want. I feel very bad about how I've treated you recently. You've had every right to be annoyed. And I want pizza with you. Right now.'

Ted bit his lip. He rubbed his eye. He exhaled loudly. I could also see the internal struggle as he tried to absorb what I'd said and decode his feelings about it. In the end, he nodded.

'Yep. We've both been a bit off. Me as much as you. Best thing to do is sit together, eat pizza, chat, put it behind us. Deal.'

I stood up and gave him a grin. 'I'll go get the pizza. I'll use the corner minimart, and you can time me. I'll be so quick there's no way I could have had sex with some bloke.'

'Unless he's waiting outside,' Ted said, but he was grinning too. I didn't like how his words reminded me that the monster could indeed be out there, waiting for a chance to savage me again.

I got Ted to find something funny on Netflix for us to watch, then headed out.

At the minimart, young Glenn was on duty. He gave me a wary look as I took a pizza to the counter. I returned the look with a smile. It was no act: he wasn't my attacker, after all. We spoke, I apologised for my earlier behaviour, and that was another burned bridge repaired.

Outside, I approached the postbox, envelope in hand. I fed it through the slot – and there I paused.

The letter contained the whole story. My rape. Lizzie Roundtree's rape. The geocache connection between both attacks. My visit to her. The Nutmeg geocacher profile and his connection to Llanferres. My wish to remain anonymous and declaration that finding me wouldn't help the investigation because I would never testify in court or even make a statement.

With this little piece of paper, the police could find the monster, collect evidence that was surely in his home, and put him away forever. All I had to do was release my grip on the envelope and let it fall amongst the water bills and wedding invitations. Remove two little fingers, and my pain would be over.

I pulled the envelope out of the slot. I tore it into pieces. I buried them deep in a waste bin nearby. Here, at the eleventh hour, I couldn't fool myself any longer. I didn't want justice, did I? I wanted revenge.

Earlier that day, I had examined Nutmeg's geocache hides and found something fascinating in the logs of the 1830 To Douglas cache located in the ground of St. Berres' Church, Llanferres.

The last geocacher to visit the 1830 had written that the physical logbook was soaking wet, impossible to write on. That log had been posted yesterday; this morning, Nutmeg had replied that he would repair the cache on Friday – the day after tomorrow.

Forget his hometown: I knew down to an inch exactly where the monster would be, and when. And forget the police: *I* would be there to meet him.

CHAPTER TWENTY-THREE

On Thursday morning, after dropping Dan at school, I waited outside the corner minimart. A throng of parents oozed out of the gates and spread in all directions. The river became a stream, and a trickle, and Joan was nowhere to be seen. Yet I'd seen her inside the grounds. I figured she must have had a meeting with a teacher. I'd get hold of her later.

As soon as I got to work, one of the staff told me that young Alice had called in sick again. The boss, Alan, wasn't in yet so I sat on his desk and grabbed the phone. Alice answered quickly.

'Sweetie pie, hello. Sorry about—'

'It's Lisa. Listen up. You're now officially taking the piss. Get down here now, or get down the job centre.'

I hung up before she could reply. Alice waltzed in about an hour later, while I was checking emails on Alan's computer. She had smeared eye make-up that looked like an attempt to appear ill. I almost laughed.

'You're on the tills today. You should wash your face first,' I told her.

'Can I have a bucket next to me for when I'm sick?'

'Ring the bell and I'll take you off. Look, Alice, I apologise for being sharp. If you throw up today, I'll send you back home.'

Not an answer she'd expected. 'This isn't fair, you know. You're not the boss. Alan won't fire me.'

My earlier annoyance had long gone, but I didn't want to let her get away with speaking to a superior like that. I chose to sit in the middle of both emotions and simply told her to run along now and work.

'Everyone's seen how you are, you know? I've heard things. You're having a breakdown or menopause or something. Don't know why you're blaming me for it.'

Breakdown? I composed myself. 'Off you go.'

When she'd gone, I sought a piece of information and wrote it on a pink sticky note. A short while later, I roamed the shop floor and found Toby stacking shelves. I patted his back as I walked past. 'Okay?'

'Yeah, sure.'

I looked back to see he was quite shocked by my friendly attitude. I gave a thumbs up, although I did wonder if I was opening the door to more lewd flirting. It didn't matter: he wasn't my attacker.

Pregnancy test number 5 was negative. At shift end, I drove to school to grab Dan. Joan was waiting on the field. I walked past and said, 'Need a quick word.' She'd heard but made no reply.

Once I had Dan, I got him in the car and waited outside it. Joan came towards us but stopped at the shop. She jerked her head – *follow me* – and went inside. I told Dan to wait and headed over. At the back of the shop was an alcove with office supplies, and freedom to talk without being overheard or blocking foot traffic. Joan was smiling.

'New job for me?'

'Early tomorrow. I need a man's bones breaking.'

She looked impressed. 'Go you, the big girl now. Who? The guy who did you? You found him?'

I ignored that question. 'I need to be leaving at about half five in the morning. It's in Wales. It's a two-hour drive.'

'Too early for me. Any leeway on this?'

'No. The man I'm after will go to a certain place. If he's got kids, he might go on the way to or from school. He'll only be there a few minutes. I can't afford to miss him. But he could come anytime. We might be there all day.'

'Oh, mysterious. Good for TV, but not this. I need to know what I'm getting into.'

'I'll explain all when we're in the car tomorrow. I promise.'

'Fine. I can get someone to take my kid to school. But early costs more. Bones, too. £500. No haggling and no instalments. Yay or nay?'

'Yay. I want you to meet me in the car park of The Red Cavalier pub. Half five in the morning, remember.'

'Done. So this is the guy who did you? And you're certain?'

'And you throw in one extra job. Nice and easy. No hurting anyone. Just a window putting through. Just to make me feel better. No need to know who. Do it tonight.'

'Aren't you just the new ballsy one?' Joan said with a laugh. 'Why not, eh? One bonus drive-by bricking coming up. What's the address?'

I handed her a pink sticky note.

'I'm going to get my head looked at. And I don't mean the cut.'

I'd just climbed into bed. It was almost midnight. Ted was watching a martial arts video on the TV. 'You're going to the doctor?'

'Yep. But I've got to phone at eight in the morning and they might bring me straight in. Also, I need to pop by work beforehand, so I'll be up and out by the time you wake up. Take Dan to school?'

'Sure. I'll tell work I'll be a half hour late. You've got that meeting though.'

I hadn't forgotten. The appointment with the educational psychologist was at 10am. Awkward timing, but it was via Microsoft Teams, so I could attend from anyplace in the world. Including by a geocache in church grounds in Wales. 'I'll be doing it on my phone, so even if I'm with the doctor, it will be okay. Don't worry.'

'Cool. So you really want to do this? The doctor? You think you need it?'

'Can't hurt to find out, can it?'

'No. It's a good idea. I mean, if you're depressed or scared or whatever... then yeah, a good idea.'

I could sense his relief. But not as much as his naivety. He seemed to think I could be given a magical pill that would end all sadness, increase my libido, make everything good again. If that was possible, of course I would have gone to the doctor. It wasn't. So I wasn't.

I made myself stay awake until Ted was snoring, then I grabbed clothing for the new day and headed downstairs to sleep on the sofa. I didn't want my alarm to wake him at five in the morning.

Twenty minutes after it had roused me, I was dressed, fed, and in the dark back garden. On the other side of the back fence was a playing field with a full-sized football pitch and skate park. I left through the gate in the fence and stepped onto the grass. The Red Cavalier pub was on the road on the far side, one side of it poking out from behind the football pavilion. Both buildings were just black shapes in the remains of the night.

Was the monster out there, watching? I had thought long

and hard about his methods. Did he make the two-hour return journey to Llanferres every night after a day of watching me, only to drive to my house again the next morning? Or did he have a hotel room or tent or camper van or friend's house close to me? Might he be in Wales right now so he could soon repair the 1830 geocache? Was his intention to stalk me for a while and drive home tonight?

I could take no risks, hence why I was in the field. This empty, quiet patch of land was perfect for conducting sneaky surveillance of my house, but not of me. I would always exit by the front door, and he needed to know when I did this. My theory was that he had a hiding spot that allowed him to watch the front of the house, and gave quick access to his vehicle. If so, I could cross the field and be away without his knowledge.

I had no way of knowing anything for certain, but if I failed to keep today's trip secret from him, he would panic and probably disappear, and forever deny me my revenge.

Or he would kill me.

CHAPTER TWENTY-FOUR

A t a Tesco half a mile away, I asked Joan to stop the car. Her eldest brother, Buzz, pulled up and I used the cash machine. John chose to stand by my side and I had to shield my PIN number from him. I withdrew £250 to add to the cash I'd taken out last night, for a total of £500. I was now close to the limit of my overdraft, which wasn't good. Joan stuck the money in a pocket and away we went.

Only then did I give out our destination and reason for the trip. Buzz didn't seem to care and John announced he was simply happy to have some time with me. Joan jokingly called me a terrifying bitch.

By the time the car had left Sheffield, heading west, I had sent a text to Carla to say I was ill and wouldn't be at work today. After that, I rested my head on the window for almost the entire journey, for peace and quiet. We stopped at a McDonald's for Buzz, just before leaving the M67 for the M60. The siblings ate at an outdoor bench despite the cold, but I remained in the car to eat. I didn't like these people and it made the journey drag.

On the M56, my eyes were drifting closed, but fluttered wide open at the sight of an end-of-motorway sign. Shortly after, a sign announced that the motorway had become the A494, and here I sat up straight, wide awake. Llanferres, I knew, was situated just off this road, somewhere ahead.

It was another sixteen miles. The village came into view and the satnav said to take a right on Ty'n Llan. It was followed by a quick left onto a thin road running parallel to the A494. This took us past a house and then a grey stone wall with St Berres' Church behind it. My hands started to shake.

The entrance gate to the church was shut. Buzz drove past, and turned into the car park of the Druid Inn next door.

'So where's this treasure place?' Buzz said.

I had the 1830 To Douglas cache page loaded on my phone. I clicked 'navigate' and a map loaded, with an orange line strung between my location and the geocache. The line ran past the inn, through a gateless gateway, and into a small, unkempt graveyard behind the church.

It headed west and terminated by a row of trees creating a boundary between the church grounds and the playing field of Bro Famau County Primary School. Total distance: eighty-five metres. We were so close.

'Hey. Treasure place? Where?' Buzz said, a little impatient.

'Wait here,' I said, and got out. John got out, too, but I repeated my order. He stood by the car as I approached the gateway. From there, I could look fifty metres across the graveyard to the area of woods bearing the geocache. Best of all, one of the inn's garden benches was beside the gate. I returned to the car.

'Wait here. Joan, I'll call you in about five minutes.'

There was no argument. I followed the map line to the trees, while keeping an eye out for anyone entering the graveyard via some other entrance. There seemed to be only that single way in or out, and I was here alone.

Once by the trees, I consulted the cache page. The clue was 'deep dive down sky-pointing fork'. As soon as I entered the woods, I saw it: a tree stump that had been split in two, its twin prongs jabbing upwards. Inside the 'fork' was a small hollow bearing a tubular clear plastic container. I would not be signing the logbook inside. This geocache could never become one of my finds. Not given what I was about to do.

I called Joan. 'There's a bench by the gate. Wait there. Keep watch if you see someone come in, but don't do anything unless I call for you.'

'Call for us? You said bones were going to break.'

'No need today unless I call for you.'

'I hope you don't think there's gonna be a refund for this. Cos that's not happening.'

'I don't care. Just wait there, please. I'll talk to you soon.'

I hung up. Talk soon? The monster might not come for hours, if at all. It was 8.24; hopefully, if my theory about his having kids to drop at school was correct, he could be here within half an hour. But I was ready to wait all day.

I found a thick tree to hide behind and watched the entrance to the graveyard. I saw Joan and her brothers approach the bench and sit. They chatted so loudly I could hear them, but thankfully they didn't mention today's plan. I hoped they didn't scare him off.

I had no idea how I'd feel or what I'd think when he came and as he walked closer to me. But I knew what I intended to do. The monster would never end his evil thoughts, but I'd make sure he couldn't act on them for a while.

I picked up a heavy branch that I knew I could wield with one hand and do mighty damage with.

By 9.30, I knew I could be in for a long wait. Beyond the trees behind me, I had heard the arrival of noisy kids to school, then silence after the young ones entered and the parents left. But nobody came to the cache. Perhaps, if the monster had indeed dropped off his children at that school, he might visit the cache before picking them up later. I wasn't sure I could wait that long.

At 9.42, Carla replied to my text: Okay, babe, get well. Alice quit, by the way.

At 9.55, with five minutes to go before my Teams meeting, I realised I had the app on my laptop, but not my phone. I downloaded it, but hit a snag. I couldn't recall the username or password for Dan's school account. I called the school to explain. The secretary told me she'd try to get those details, and would I hold the line?

'I'll call back in five minutes,' I told her, and hung up. I had just seen someone enter the graveyard via the gateway. It was a middle-aged woman. Joan and her brothers, still sitting at the table, ignored her. She was alone.

She started to cross the graveyard, towards me. Was she a geocacher? I was about to hide when she stopped walking and turned around. She whistled loudly; moments later, a dog bounded through the gateway and to her side. A shaggy brown dog. I was shocked – it looked exactly like the dog pictured in Nutmeg's pictures.

Together, woman and dog entered the trees. She had no phone in her hand, but she walked immediately up to the split trunk and stuck a hand inside. This was no geocacher on a hunt.

'Nutmeg Forever?' I said as I stepped out from behind a tree.

The woman just about jumped out of her skin. Her dog barked at me before she shushed it. 'Who are you? Did you come for the cache?'

'Yes. I read that you were fixing it today.'

She showed me the container. 'Yes. Water inside, look. The lid is cracked. Just give me a moment.'

She extracted a replacement container from her handbag. It had a new logbook inside. She held it out to me. 'Did you want to sign this before I put it in the hidey-hole?'

'I saw your profile picture. Was that your husband?'

'Oh, that man with the beard? That was just some image I found online. I used to have one of me, but men were always messaging me and wanting to meet.'

'Does anyone else help you maintain this cache? A husband or brother? Any men?'

Nutmeg's smile faded as concern set in. 'No. Just me. I come here with my daughter. I just dropped her at school. My husband doesn't like this sort of thing. Why are you asking?'

'Do you come here at night?'

She put the new container in the trunk and the old one in her bag. She seemed in a rush suddenly. 'Sometimes. All times, really. Anyway, I need to be going.'

I stepped closer. 'Don't come at night.'

'Excuse me? I don't think you have the right to tell me what to do.'

She turned to leave. I grabbed her arm. She yanked it free. 'Don't touch me. What's wrong with you?'

Again she turned to leave, and again I latched a hand onto her arm. 'Listen to me. Don't be coming here alone at night, understand? It's dangerous.'

She tried to break free, but this time my grip was too strong. 'Get off me. I'll set my dog on you. Get off.'

She thumped my bad shoulder with her fist. I pushed her away. Moving backwards, blind, her foot got entangled and she tripped, landing hard on her butt. Her dog started barking at me. I stood over her. 'You're lucky it's me. If I was a lunatic, you'd be dead. Don't come here alone. Not even in the daytime.'

The woman scrambled to her feet and started running. Her parting words were, 'I'm calling the police. It's you who's the damn lunatic.'

Up ahead, Joan and her brothers were standing up, having surely heard the commotion. They watched the woman with the dog scuttle past and out of the graveyard. I walked over to them.

'Let's go,' I said. 'We're done. False alarm. Waste of time. Don't ask.'

'No refunds,' Joan said. 'We did our bit.'

'Let's just get the hell away before that woman calls the police.'

I was buzzing with adrenaline and anger that didn't dissipate until we were back on the road, miles from Llanferres. Only once calm was restored did I remember the Teams meeting. The time was 10.17am.

I called the school. The secretary had already been passed a message from the SENCo after my failure to attend the virtual appointment. Meeting cancelled. To be rescheduled. When the secretary started to harp on about wasted time and effort, I hung up so I didn't scream at her. I threw my phone on the floor of the car.

I didn't know how to feel. Nutmeg had been present at the sites of two rapes years apart, so I had been right to assume I had solved the puzzle. Nobody would have thought differently. Courts would have convicted on such evidence. The most intense atheist would have spat on coincidence and accepted the hand of God.

Ultimately, though, I had been tricked by outlandish bad luck. The monster had fate on his side. The ball was in his court. The itinerary was his to write. I would stand before him again, but only when he chose to emerge from the gloom with deadly intent.

CHAPTER TWENTY-FIVE

My sixth pregnancy test was performed at a service station toilet on the way back to Sheffield. The negative was good news, but I wasn't at peace. I was thinking about the argument I'd have at home with Ted.

By the time I'd been dropped off at The Red Cavalier pub, I'd decided I wouldn't tell him about the missed Teams appointment. I would pretend it went well and that we now had to play a waiting game. Hopefully, the meeting would be rescheduled soon and Ted would never know the truth.

I entered my home the back way and went immediately to my bedroom, where I looked out the window and tried to spot a strange car or pedestrian. In Wales I'd felt a measure of control and it hadn't allowed much room for worry. On the return journey following the failure at the 1830 cache, all the old paranoia had started to renew, mile by mile, and now it was back in full force. I couldn't go on like this.

I needed to get out so went shopping and from there straight to school to pick up Dan. I expected to be met by the SENCo for a telling-off, but she wasn't there. However, Dan had been told to inform me that I had been sent an email. I checked, and there it was. The SENCo regretted my missing the meeting and she would contact me soon with another date.

However, the email wasn't listed as a new message. It had already been read. Ted had access to that account. So much for hiding my error from him.

As soon as I heard his car pull up later that evening, I headed upstairs and waited in the bedroom. Dan was watching TV in the living room. When Ted entered the bedroom, I waited for him to speak first.

'Meeting go okay?'

I could see by his face that a lie would only cause more damage. I was a little annoyed that he was trying to trick me. 'I missed it, as you well know. I didn't have the app and couldn't sign in. I was out.'

'Out bloody where? How long have we got to wait now? What if we don't get Dan into a new place before the new school year?'

'That's months away. It will be fine. This is a setback, but it won't matter in the long run.'

'It will if you keep messing things up. Mistake after mistake.'

'That's not fair. You know I said I'd get some help for that. This isn't easy for me. You act like I just decided not to care one day. My head is messed up.'

'And you said you were going to get help with that.'

'Like I can do that in one day!'

'What did the doctor say?'

I wasn't the only one who could read my spouse's face. I'd forgotten about the doctor lie, and for half a second it must have showed. Long enough.

'Jesus,' Ted snapped. He threw his car keys on the floor. 'Can you do anything right?'

'Piss off,' I shouted back. 'I've been doing everything. How many meetings have you been to about Dan? Do you fill in the forms? Did you look through specialist schools? I did all of that. You did nothing.'

'I tell you what I did do. Taxed my car today.'

He waited for my reaction. It was slumped shoulders. Something else important I'd knocked to the back burner because of the monster.

'Exactly,' Ted said. 'Add that to all the other stuff. You're falling apart, Lisa. You have a think about some of this stuff and how it's affecting me and Dan. For now I need to get away from here. I'm going out for a bit.'

I fought it, I really did, but my willpower just wasn't there. Ted was halfway down the stairs when I appeared at the top. 'Out to your girlfriend, you mean?'

He froze on the steps, but didn't turn around. If I hadn't been completely, absolutely certain after following him the other night, his long pause dusted away any lingering doubt.

He eventually turned. 'What girlfriend?'

'I'm sorry, have you got more than one? The woman on Ravenscost Avenue. The house with the flowery porch.'

He rubbed his forehead, probably because he couldn't look at me. 'Is this nonsense because I accused you of the same?'

'No, it's because I followed you there. I waited outside. I saw you rub your gym pyjamas in the mud. I saw you spit mouthwash so I wouldn't smell her in your damn mouth.'

He turned. Continued down the stairs. At the bottom, before vanishing out of sight, he called back, 'It's now a priority, Lisa. Go to the doctor. Tell him you're losing your mind and getting paranoid. Do it before you split this family into pieces.'

TED: I'll sleep downstairs tonight.
LISA: Forever?

TED: If that's what you want. If you don't want to get help.

LISA: I do. It could take a long time to get cured. What happens till then?

TED: I don't know. But tonight I will sleep downstairs.

LISA: No, I will sleep in Dan's room if that's what you want.

TED: Ok.

How had it come to this, texting each other like kids from different rooms in the same house?

Ted had stayed out until after Dan had gone to bed. When he came in, he checked the living room, saw I was there, and went into the kitchen. I heard him rooting in the medicine cupboard, then a rustle I figured was the opening of one of his keto bars. A good indication that he had actually been to the gym – but sex could be a hard workout, right?

Next, I heard him grab a plate and the beep of the microwave. I waited for him to return to the living room, but the next noise was his feet on the stairs – he planned to eat in the bedroom. I didn't hear the shower, so figured he hadn't been with his mistress. That said, he knew I knew, so what was there to hide anymore?

A couple of hours later, I went upstairs to fetch a sofa throw from Dan's room. I had decided to sleep downstairs after all in the hope that I could see Ted in the morning. I was worried he'd skip out early and avoid me all day. With my current problems, I needed my husband as a friend.

If his mood was the same tomorrow, I would tell him everything. The truth. All of it. He needed to know why my head was so messed up, even if it messed his.

Not long after I'd settled on the sofa with the TV, there was a soft knock on the front door. I grabbed my dressing gown out of the tumble dryer, since I was wearing only shorts and a T-shirt. I poked a gap in the living-room curtains so I could peer out. I needed to know who was there; I'd just worry more every day if I didn't find out.

The movement of the curtains alerted the man on the step, who gave a smile and a wave and stepped up to the glass. It was John, Joan's brother. He was in jeans and a Varsity jacket adorned with the name of a university he'd never been to, and his hair was neat again.

What do you want? I mouthed, but I already feared I knew the answer. He'd shown interest in me – was he here to ask me on a date?

He made a movement suggesting I should come to the front door, which I did after tightening my dressing gown. John tried to step inside as the door opened, but I pushed him back and stepped out, and shut the door behind me.

'What do you want?' I said, eyes flicking left and right for nosey neighbours. If Ted heard about a late-night visit from a man, right after I'd confronted him about an affair, he would have every right to assume the worst.

'Any other jobs you need doing?' John said.

'What do you mean?'

'Ass-kicking. I'm in the mood. Anyone else you need messing up?'

It took me a moment to fathom what he was getting at. This was worse than being asked on a date. 'No. I don't need anything. You should go.'

'No ex-boyfriends or grumpy neighbours need a kicking?'

'No. Please don't ask again. I'll come to you if I need something, and please don't come to my house again. I'll talk to Joan if anything is needed. You can't just come knocking late at night.'

He lost his smile, and the warmth in his eyes was replaced by something much colder. This was the animal I'd glimpsed in a sex offender's living room.

'So you used us. Just for them two jobs? One and done, and now piss off?'

'No, it's not like that. You got paid. I just needed those things doing, that's all. I... please go.'

His eyes ran up and down me. I felt exposed. 'If it's about the money, you can pay other ways.'

'No. Just go.'

'That's not on, using us like that. So there needs to be other jobs. Make sure there's more jobs. You don't want your people, these snobby nice arses around here, knowing what you've been up to. Or your husband. In fact, he know about why? He know you gave it out to some other dude?'

I wanted to hit the bastard for such words. 'He already knows,' I said, but I knew I hadn't sounded convincing.

'I always get my way, sweet pie, so make it easy. Have a good think about who needs teaching a lesson, and give my sis a call. Soon.'

'Just go, please.'

He started to back off down the path. Far too slowly for my liking. At the gate, he turned and walked into the darkness.

I entered the house and locked the door. I was shaking so badly I had to sit right there in the hallway. What had he meant by *I always get my way*? I had already proved to him that a man could rape me and I wouldn't go to the police. Was he planning something terrible?

Had he already done something terrible?

CHAPTER TWENTY-SIX

My plan failed. I woke at nine thirty on Saturday morning to hear thumping from the bedroom above. When I got up there, Ted was gone – so much for my plan to tell Ted the whole, truthful story. Dan was leaping on and off the bed.

'Hey, Mum. Watch this. It's called a palm spin. I'm learning parkour.'

Another obsession? He went through phases of passion. Whatever parkour was, he'd go mad for it until the next fad. Whatever he tried failed, but he didn't get hurt and laughed about it. 'Do you know where your dad went?'

'Stuff to do at work.'

'He said that?'

'Yeah. So what we doing today?'

I tried to ignore darker thoughts about where Ted could be. My first job was to make breakfast, and while Dan ate, I performed another pregnancy test. After that, I told him we needed milk. We didn't. I'd poured the milk away. I wanted to pay a visit.

Ravenscost Avenue. The house with the flowery porch.

Ted's car wasn't there. Good news, but it didn't do much by way of relieving tension.

Milk bought, I took Dan to Jump, an inflatable park, in Rotherham. I fell numerous times and inflamed my bad shoulder, but I'd never seen Dan laugh so much. My own mirth was cut short when he said, 'Wish Dad was here.'

So did I. 'He'll come next time.' I so hoped that would come true. I wondered about his cheating though: would I be so accepting of it once I had the monster out of my mind? Maybe I'd be so hurt and mad that I left him, and made things so much worse. Perhaps it would be better to constantly worry about the murderous attack instead?

After jumping came eating. I took Dan to a café. Then the library. That took us up till just after three o'clock, and Dan announced that he wanted to go home. I could tell by his fidgeting that all the noise and people had started to get to him.

Ted was home, gardening out back despite the chilly weather. Dan went out to help him and I tidied the house to get my mind off its current, most popular subject. I did all the dirty pots, changed all the bedsheets, and hoovered. When the boys came in, Dan announced that his dad was going to buy him a mini trampoline for his parkour. Ted went upstairs to work on his computer.

I made dinner around five and got Dan to tell Ted. My son returned and took his father's plate upstairs. That was the final straw. Perhaps I'd invited this foolishness by being first to use Dan as a conduit between us, but I was annoyed. We couldn't continue like this.

Around half six, Ted called Dan upstairs. About ten minutes later, I heard the front door go and looked out the window to see Ted get in his car and leave. Dan came downstairs and said, 'Dad's gone to jijisu. He said he'll be back in a bit. Why did he want me to tell you?'

'Easier,' was my answer. I went to the toilet for a five-minute think about what to do. When I went downstairs afterwards, Dan was getting water from the kitchen. He watched in puzzlement as I headed into the backyard – carrying Ted's laptop.

'What did you do with Dad's computer?' Dan asked when I returned.

'It's in the shed.'

'Can I see?'

'No. It's locked.'

I headed upstairs and Dan followed. Ted's current library book – *The Choice* by Jake Cross – was on his bedside table. I tore out the date label.

'Won't he get in trouble for that?' Dan said, bouncing on the bed.

'Maybe.'

I put the book back on the bedside cabinet and headed downstairs, with Dan on my tail. In the kitchen, he watched me take Ted's three remaining keto bars from a cupboard.

'Dan needs them. Mum, what are you doing to all of Dad's stuff? Does he know?'

'I'll send him a text to tell him. Now, I need to pop to the corner store. You coming? And then tonight do you want to stay at your auntie's? You can stay up late.'

'Why? I mean, yes. But why? You going out somewhere?'

'Yes, son. I'm going to a hotel.'

After his grappling class, Ted checks his phone and sees a message from his wife. It reads: RUINED YOUR ENERGY BARS, NEED MORE.

Maybe he's annoyed, maybe not. But Ted is pretty strict about his workout routines. A banana thirty minutes before jiu-jitsu, and a keto snack bar within an hour afterwards. On the way home, he stops at the minimart. He's probably the only customer who buys the bars, so nobody will have touched the retail ready box. It's been turned backwards and Ted has to spin it to get at the contents. He's shocked to see something alien yet familiar.

A book date label. But not just any – the very one from his library book. He takes it, knowing his wife has done this. At home, he notices her car is gone. Inside, he restocks the medicine cupboard with his snack bars and heads upstairs. His library book is where he left it, but there's something inside it. A rusty old key.

This he recognises, too. It's the shed key. So, out he goes. Inside, sitting on his nary-used workbench and open, is his laptop. The screensaver text has been changed from the time to the words Penalty Spot. Bizarre. But intriguing.

Their back gate leads into roughly the centre of the football pitch, which means he has a choice of left or right. He goes left, or right then left. Sometimes kids play here, but today there are none and upon the painted spot he finds a second key. This one is attached to an orange band stamped with 305.

Also familiar. Magnus Leisure Centre in Rotherham is ten miles to the east. There are closer swimming pools, but Dan loves the Fun Splatter session it hosts on a Sunday. It's a common event for father and son. So Ted knows full well that the key is from one of the facility's lockers.

Ted makes the drive. Inside locker 305, he finds a scented envelope bearing a simple note: a postcode and a time – 7pm – and an instruction to give his name at reception.

Ted types the postcode into his satnav and learns it belongs to an Aves Hotel about two miles west, by a superstore and a business park. It's a straight run along Maltby High Street, no more than a five-minute drive with half-decent traffic.

At reception, he gives his name and a pre-instructed

receptionist – a woman with no job satisfaction, given the abrupt manner she displayed earlier – will hand over a spare key for room 18. Ted enters that room to discover flowers on the bed, a bottle of wine on the table, and another note...

'What does that note say?' Dan asked. We were driving to his auntie's house.

It said: *Strip, get comfy in bed, and wait for me.* Not something I could admit to my son, so I told a little white lie: *Pick something on Netflix for us to watch.*

'Sounds cool,' Dan said. 'Like one of your gecash things.'

I laughed at his butchering of the word. But he was right. The treasure hunt was like a multi-cache. I wish I'd used GPS coordinates in the clue trail.

We arrived at my sister's and I parked. 'What if something goes wrong?' Dan asked. 'What if Dad just gets his laptop out the shed and doesn't read the screensaver? What if he decides to get more snack bars tomorrow? What if his satnav's broken?'

'I'm sure it will all work just fine.' I wasn't sure, of course, but that wasn't my worry. I was more concerned that Ted would realise what I was up to and refuse to visit the hotel. But I had to try.

All I'd told my sister was that I planned a romantic night with Ted. She knew nothing about our recent arguments, or the reason for them. When I got to her door and she opened up, Dan blurted it all out. Maud was impressed. 'How cute. Are you going to renew your vows?'

'We'll see,' I replied. Renewed vows? I was hoping to escape divorce. 'There was a bit of an argument. I need to make it up to him.'

She spoke low so Dan couldn't hear. 'I'm almost jealous. You look nervous. After arguments is always the best time. It gives you those first-time-gotta-impress nerves.'

I agreed. After dropping Dan off, I headed for the hotel. My plan was to lurk in the car park and watch Ted enter. I'd give him ten minutes to settle, then head in and give him the best sex he'd ever had.

I had agreed with my sister's theory, but it had been a lie. It wasn't nervousness, it was dread, and it existed because I was about to perform an act that, even with my own husband, had become wholly disgusting to me. Perhaps for life.

CHAPTER TWENTY-SEVEN

A t just past seven, I saw three cars enter the car park of the Aves Hotel. The third was Ted's. I'd picked a far corner so he wouldn't see me, but he parked just ten metres away. I ducked low in my seat, sure the game was up, but he somehow failed to recognise the vehicle just two spaces away. As he walked towards the hotel, more cars arrived.

I gave him five minutes and got out. I left my phone behind so there would be no interruptions. I entered the hotel slowly, carefully, just in case Ted had been delayed in the lobby by the sudden influx of guests. There was a mob in the lobby, but he wasn't among it. I had to queue to see the receptionist, but thankfully only a handful of the throng was checking in while the others mingled about.

As I waited, I overheard snippets of conversations. People were being introduced to others. I noticed that some in the group milling around wore T-shirts with Kate Bush on them. Another had a Kate Bush bag. Someone had a bunch of brochures and I saw the same artist on the cover.

When it was my turn at the desk, I said, 'Hello again. Something special about today?'

'Can I help you?' she replied, not even a ghost of a smile on her face.

Bad day at the office? I almost said. 'My husband just came in. Did he collect a key for room 18?'

She checked her monitor. 'Yes, ma'am, your *husband* has gone up to the room.'

The throng began to move away, towards a function room. I noticed a free-standing sign next to the door: YORKS/HUMBER KATE BUSH MINI-CONVENTION 2022.

Had there been something special about that day?

I ran from the hotel.

Back in my car, I grabbed my phone and loaded the geocaching website. I searched for Edinburgh. It was a major city, so of course there were myriad pages of geocaches. I clicked the DATE PLACED column to sort the results into oldest-to-newest – it would be quicker to scroll forwards in time from 2001, when the website was created.

Soon I found 12th March 2005, the date that Lizzie Roundtree was attacked in Corstorphine Hill. My hands were shaking with anticipation.

I hadn't found the monster's profile name on Dolerite, the webcam geocache visited by Lizzie, or on Sword Dance, the Grenoside one I'd been raped en route to. He'd attacked a woman near both, so either he'd exercised caution by not logging his visits to those places, or he hadn't attended them at all. But with regards to Edinburgh, what if he'd been there specifically for another cache?

Lizzie Roundtree had told me, *There was a gathering that night...* I had thought she'd meant a party with close friends, but she had also said... *I decided to warm up with a few hunts that afternoon...*

What kind of party could tempt people to use geocache

hunts as a warm-up? An 'event cache', of course. These were one-off or annual get-togethers for geocachers, sometimes to hunt a special cache created just for the occasion. Popular and well-promoted events had games and stalls and could attract hundreds of die-hard treasure hunters from around the world. Just like a convention.

With that many tourists in the city, many local geocaches would see heavy traffic. It would explain why Dolerite had had so many visitors in the days around the 12th. How had I not realised this earlier?

Geocaches in the SIZE column were listed as micro, small, regular, large, virtual, or 'other' – and predominantly the latter were events. There was only one 'other' hosted on the date that would forever haunt Lizzie: KFG FUN, held at Lauriston Castle at 8pm.

A mile and a half north of the Corstorphine Hill crime scene, hours after Lizzie Roundtree met a monster. Reason enough, perhaps, for a vile rapist to think he could safely attend and log his visit?

The KFG FUN cache page had a photo of a sign welcoming people to the Kyoto Friendship Garden at the castle and the description read:

```
Three   years   ago   we   celebrated   the
joining  of  Kyoto  and  Edinburgh.  Join
Pearl  and  me  for  a  night  of  Japanese
poetry,  hunts,  and  beer.  Or  maybe  just
the hunts and beer.
```

The organisers, Elaine and Mike, had arranged a food-and-drinks tent and a multi-cache in the fields and woods surrounding the castle. The old me would have loved it.

There were sixty-seven logs. A catalogue of attendees numbered 121. I ignored both on the off-chance that the monster might have chosen to miss the event after raping a woman in the city that very day. Instead, I clicked on the WILL/MIGHT ATTEND list, which some geocachers had signed weeks in advance. 247 profiles. I started scrolling through them.

Two hundred and forty-seven was too many profiles to check in depth one at a time, so I went through page after page, each with ten entries, and hoped for a male profile picture to spark something. It was on page fifteen, geocacher entry 146, that I froze. But it wasn't because of a face.

The geocacher was called Dallas9999 and his profile picture showed a portable key safe with a shackle. Dallas's profile was locked, so I wasn't allowed to view anything other than the main page. I couldn't click on the gallery to find other images and Dallas hadn't written a mini bio, prompting the website to insert the standard: 'This person is probably cool, but hasn't shared any details yet' line.

But the main page did list 263 geocache finds, fifteen hides, a join date of December 2002, and a location of Texas. So, he lived in Dallas, Texas – or had as of 2013, when the profile was locked.

Intriguing, though, was a note at the top of the page by the website admin team. All of Dallas's geocache hides had been archived and the profile locked because of a 'guideline transgression'.

Geocaches had to be maintained, but that wasn't the only rule. They weren't permitted to promote commercial products or political ideals or charities. They couldn't instruct geocachers to make a purchase or download software, sign up to a cause or provide personal information to third-party websites. They also had to be family friendly, so no adult content or language. But as for which law Dallas had broken to get his profile locked, it didn't say.

With a shaking hand, I loaded up the Sword Dance geocache. Last time, I hadn't clicked on any of the profiles because of the Nutmeg red herring. Now I did. My focus was a user called Sunshine-and-Roses, who had been at the Grenoside site two days before I was attacked. Sunshine's profile wasn't locked, but it was bare. No pictures in the gallery, no location listed, no statistics, no mini bio. It had a few snippets of information though.

Sunshine had joined the website in 2013, the same year Dallas's profile was forever locked for breaking the rules. Big deal. People came and went all the time.

Of Sunshine's twenty-seven hides, nine were in Tulsa, Oklahoma, one was in Spain – although that had the archived detail of a red line through it – and his remaining seventeen were in Dallas. So what? Major city.

Those details, although intriguing, could be put down to coincidence. But his profile picture, which I'd remembered from that brief glance days ago?

A portable key safe with shackle.

CHAPTER TWENTY-EIGHT

When I finally spotted the time, it made me gasp. 9.03pm. I'd been lost in my own world for two hours. Ted!

I rushed into the hotel and must have looked like a woman possessed because the receptionist took a step back from her desk.

'Room 18,' I wheezed. 'My husband. Is he still here?'

Now she smiled for the first time. 'Been and gone. Guys like that don't wait around. Are you checking out now?'

Her hand was already extended for my key. I said, 'What do you mean, "guys like that"?'

'We don't approve of that sort of thing here. Key, please.'

I took the key out of my pocket. 'Did he say anything when he left?'

'No, but he'll spread the word and you'll lose business. We don't want to see you back here.'

Now it hit me. 'You think I'm a prostitute?'

She waved her hand for the key. 'You're easy to spot. Have a good night. Please don't consider us next time.'

I lobbed the key over her head and stormed out. I wondered

why Ted hadn't called or texted, but the answer was obvious. He'd been annoyed with me before this mishap, and must be fuming now. I needed to explain, but it would not be by phone. I got in my car.

I got home just before 9.30, but the entire house was dark. I went in and hurriedly slapped all the downstairs light switches on, then listened out for noises in the rooms above before going upstairs. Ted wasn't there.

Then I heard his car. I was standing in the living room when he came in. He saw me but went straight past and clumped upstairs, not a word said. I heard the shower turn on and flopped onto the sofa like a rag doll. Could he have made it any more obvious that he needed to scrub another woman's scent away?

How was this going to progress? Would he soon start telling me where he'd been? Asking me to give him a lift down to that other woman's house? Bringing her round here when I was out? Sneaking her upstairs when I was in? Fucking asking me to join in?

The bastard. But so what? I'd expected a long argument, yet now I had free time. I pulled out my phone and continued my research into the geocacher called Sunshine-and-Roses.

Sunshine had logged the Sword Dance geocache – with a simple 'Found it' and no accompanying photo – on Thursday Jan 20th. Two days earlier, he'd visited a geocache in Birmingham. Three days prior to that he was at two geocaches in Dorchester, Dorset. From the 3rd to the 9th, he'd logged one geocache a day in seven different London boroughs. None of his finds included a photo.

Eleven geocaches in less than three weeks, but preceding these there had been a large period of inactivity, all the way back to the early months of 2021. He'd been in three cities in Sweden in January, five in Poland in February, and a quartet in Pakistan in late Feb and March, logging a total of seventeen geocache finds in Cameroon, Egypt, Belarus.

Before this, another large slice of inactivity. I quickly noticed a pattern dating all the way back to 2013. Sunshine logged geocaches only in the first quarter of the year, dedicating almost a whole month to one country before moving on. His trips would begin on the first few days of January, and they would end in late March.

There was little form to be fathomed from his destinations, however; 2017 saw him spend all his time in South America, but in 2014 he'd been to Iceland, Spain and Russia.

Only one location featured more than once. He'd been to the UK in 2022, obviously, but had also travelled around England, Wales and Scotland in 2016. Then there was his Scottish trip in March 2005 to rape Lizzie Roundtree – as Dallas9999.

Did he have a connection to the UK? Did he have family here that he often visited? It would have been helpful to get a look at Dallas's profile to see where the monster had been in the years between 2002 (when he joined the website) and 2013 (when his account got locked).

'We need a sit-down talk.'

I looked up from my phone. Ted was in the living-room doorway. It was almost midnight. 'I know.'

He paused. 'Problems to iron out. Best not in front of Dan. Not when one of us is about to go to work. Best when we can sleep on it afterwards.'

'Yes. You're right.'

He sighed. 'Some other time then.'

He turned to leave. I heard his footsteps on the stairs.

The dates – the dates were more important than Sunshine's

destinations. He had travelled in Jan, Feb, March, those months only, every single time, ten years on the trot. Why? Did his job send him around the world in those months? Perhaps his timing had something to do with other commitments between April and December.

My focus, however, was not where he'd been, but where he was now. He tended to spend each month geocaching around one country. In 2016, he'd spent January in England, Feb in Scotland and March in Wales. It was January now and he'd clearly been here because he'd attacked me.

It seemed logical to assume that he was here, in the UK, until the end of March. Unfortunately, in 2016 he'd spent March in Wales, whereas his destination that month in 2005 had been Scotland.

That was the best I could guess, and despite the evidence it *was* a guess. Either he was in Wales or Scotland, or about to leave England for one of those countries. But how would I find him when he popped up? Look for a rental car driving around? Check local hotels?

I didn't know, but I had a focus now and needed to be ready. When the monster next logged a geocache, I needed to move at a moment's notice, snake-like, to sink my fangs into the bastard. If I missed him, and March slipped by, he would be gone for the rest of the year. Maybe forever. And even if I did reacquire his scent, he might next rear his ugly head thousands of miles away, out of reach.

But it wouldn't remain so. One day his obsession with me would bring him back, to satisfy the lethal intent he had been denied.

CHAPTER TWENTY-NINE

I had been lost in the desert, but I'd found a sand dune that I knew lay next to a city, and help. But upon reaching the crest, I was confronted by a continued sea of sand, stretching away into the horizon. Dismayed, I had screamed for help and sat on the top of that dune to await it.

I woke at just past 8am on Sunday and immediately grabbed my phone. I checked Sunshine's geocache profile, but was disheartened. No new finds listed. I would check again in an hour.

While performing another pregnancy test, I had a revelation. The desert dream had been a sign, I knew. It had been my brain telling me I could not sit around and wait. The monster might never again log a geocache visit, thus leaving no clue as to his location.

But there was one certainty: I was in his mind, and he would be back for me. It was unsafe to assume from geocache logs that he could and did travel only during the first quarter of the year. Obsession was a powerful driving force and distance, job or family commitments, money, whatever – none of that would obstruct him.

I needed to take action, but how? Last night, learning the name of the city my attacker called home had been like a fireworks display: loud, bright, extravagant, a cause for joy and celebration, but soon to peter out into nothing. I had shrunken the whole world to one city, and surely that was a good thing?

Of course not. Dallas was one of the ten biggest cities in the USA, with well over a million residents. It would be impossible to find him without a name or description. There was a chance he'd left a clue in his hidden geocaches, but I'd checked those and discovered nothing that helped. The Dallas angle was effectively a geocache with no coordinates.

So what could I do? I—

I heard a noise upstairs: Ted waking. He would want to talk, and we needed to, but not right now. I got my shoes on and headed out into the backyard. I shut the door behind me so he wouldn't know I was out there. I sent a text to my son.

I had no way to find Sunshine in Dallas, but perhaps I didn't need to. Before drifting off to sleep last night, I'd wondered why he had left such a long gap between Lizzie Roundtree's rape and mine. Now wide awake, I wasn't so confused. Seventeen years dormant? I doubted a monster like him could fight his evil urges for that long. I was certain he'd attacked other women. What if there were other rape news stories out there?

Finding Lizzie Roundtree had ultimately led to the monster's geocache profile. Perhaps if I found more victims, there would be further clues to this bastard's identity.

The bag!

I rushed inside, but too late. The holdall was on the armchair and Ted was standing over it, looking inside. He was dressed. He saw me in the doorway. He pulled out an item of my clothing from the bag. 'So what's this? Are you leaving me? Just like that, after ten years?'

'It's not like that. I'm not leaving.'

'Right,' he said, totally unconvinced. 'So what's the clothing for?'

I prayed he wouldn't look deeper inside the bag. 'It's for work. Just a change of clothes if I need it.'

He rubbed his head. 'Look, Dan texted me to pick him up. He wants to go to Jump. I said yes.'

I knew about Jump: I'd texted Dan, telling him to ask his dad to pick him up and take him to the inflatable park. So I could have free time in the house. 'You know what he's like. Once he gets his teeth into something, there's no stopping him. Parkour is his new obsession.'

'Yes. Cool kid. You want to come?'

'I can't. I have some stuff to do. But we can talk later. Maybe go out. You and me.'

'Right.' Again that word was loaded with scorn. 'Okay, see you later. Maybe.'

When he was gone, I took the bag out to my car. I was lucky Ted hadn't delved under the top layer of clothing, for he would have found a few more ominous items. Phone charger. Packets of food. Cash. Dan's toy binoculars. A hammer. I suddenly felt a bit silly about it. It was like a doomsday prepper's bug-out bag.

That didn't stop me putting the bag in the boot of the car.

I started with Sunshine's latest geocache visit, down in Birmingham just days before my attack. There had been a sexual assault in a car park the day after his log, just two hundred metres away, but a second newspaper article informed me that the perpetrator had been one of the victim's friends and that he'd been arrested the day before I was jumped. I moved past. Next geocache, next location, next attack.

I knew from previous rape research that it was a very

common crime, so I was ready for a long slog of dead ends. But every one needed my scrutiny. Some attacks had very little coverage, often no more than social media rumour, while others had been covered in-depth by the media and police reports. Some were easy to discard, others not so without lengthy analysis. A handful raised my hopes before further research popped these balloons.

I turned to my laptop when my phone battery needed charging. When Ted and Dan returned, I grabbed free moments when I could. I hate to say it, but the fact that Ted and I continued to ignore each other gave me additional opportunity for internet surfing.

By late evening, I was exhausted and ready to give up for the day. My head and fingers hurt. My phone was burning hot. I had checked out the locations of dozens of Sunshine's geocaches, in every corner of the world. I had read about hundreds of rapes, sexual assaults and other attacks on women. I had made eight pages of handwritten notes. I had guaranteed myself some terrible dreams that night.

But I had also found three very interesting stories.

Pakistan, 8th March 2020. There was something called the Aurat March, an annual demonstration against violence against women. It was in honour of International Women's Day and attended by various representatives of women's rights organisations. Around the same time, Pakistan's parliament had passed a resolution that child killers and rapists should be publicly hanged.

It was hard to imagine a worse day for a serious rape. Yet that had been the fate of a young woman near the grounds of the Fatima Jinnah Medical University in Lahore. I could find few details about this because all the big news was about the marches, but I learned that the crime was unsolved and the police still had virtually no clues.

Except that, according to the victim, the attacker was a white man. He had assaulted the woman from behind, throwing an arm across her throat.

The crime scene was just a hundred yards from a geocache that Sunshine had logged at the day before the attack. I couldn't believe that the police hadn't made the connection. The most likely reason was that the victim hadn't been a geocacher; I found no mention of that word anywhere.

The second story was from 2015. In that year he travelled more than ever before or since, recording 159 geocache finds, but they were all in the United States. It was the only year in which he hadn't gone abroad. Short of money, lost passport, family commitments? I had no idea, but it was clear that he didn't mind shitting on his own doorstep.

In Kalamazoo, Michigan, in Feb, a nineteen-year-old woman was attacked on the east side of Lyons Lake. She lived close to the western side of the lake, between it and Comstock High School, and liked to jog around the water. The circuit was about a mile and a half, but on that day, the victim said, she had chosen to increase her run to two miles. It meant detouring through the woods, the first time she'd ever done so. She'd never gone jogging since.

The attack was close to a track that led south to East Main Street, where police thought the perpetrator might have parked a vehicle in order to enter the woods. Despite the fact that it was mid-afternoon, police found no witnesses. Nobody saw a parked vehicle or a man, and since she was attacked from behind, the victim didn't get a good look at her assailant. There was no other evidence and the case had gone cold.

I found no mention of the word *geocache* in any of the news reports, yet there were two geocaches in those woods and Sunshine had logged at both just two days after the attack. Perhaps police had checked them before he logged. But most telling in my eyes: he subdued the jogger by throwing an arm across her throat from behind. Four rapes, same modus operandi.

It was intriguing Sunshine was logging geocache finds a couple of days removed from his attacks. In Michigan, for instance, he'd raped the woman by the lake two days after his find – had he waited for the buzz around the crime scene to die down? In Grenoside, he'd logged two days before attacking me – had he, in reverse, left a gap after his lakeside rape so no connection would be made? Both instances proved that he was being cautious, but why leave the logs at all?

I had an idea. As a geocacher myself, I understood the sense of achievement felt by locating hides, by increasing those numbers, by recording your travels. Sunshine was a veteran geocacher and was probably willing to take risks with one hobby in order to achieve success with the other.

This could provide a golden opportunity to catch him: if he posted a log here in the UK, and planned to attack in the days following, I could simply watch the geocache and await his return to the area.

The third and most important story I found was about a rape in Paris, France, in February of 2018. Late one evening a forty-year-old woman was driving along Allée de la Reine-Marguerite, a main road running northwards through the Bois de Boulogne, Paris's second largest park.

When she stopped to check her phone map, the driver's door was yanked open and a man hauled her out. Using an arm across her throat. He carried her into the woods and attempted to rape her. Luckily, she broke away from him before he could commit the monstrous act. She got back to her car and fled.

She told police she had seen her attacker's penis. She got the impression he had modified his trousers in order to easily release his manhood, which was already hard and sheathed in a condom. Clearly he had been there with the intention of rape. Unfortunately, she hadn't seen his face and could offer no other information. The victim wasn't a geocacher, so no connection was made to this world.

But a geocache lay just a hundred metres from the crime scene, and Sunshine had logged it that same evening.

However, police did find one piece of golden evidence. I had never known of Sunshine to snatch someone right out of a car and perhaps this was a first, and he broke his tried and tested methods. That might explain why he made the mistake of leaving his fingerprints on the car door handle!

My joy was short-lived. The attack was four years ago, but an article from two years later said no arrest had yet been made. Obviously, Sunshine's prints were not on file. He was a ghost.

CHAPTER THIRTY

In the black, early hours of Monday, I woke and immediately checked my phone, but Sunshine hadn't posted any new geocache finds.

Ted was snoring softly by my side. After he'd returned from Jump, Dan had wanted to show both parents some of his parkour moves. It had involved sitting Ted and I on the sofa. Awkward, but we'd had no choice other than to talk to each other. Things were very far from rosy between us, but we had agreed that it was foolish for one of us to sleep on the sofa.

So, we were back in the same bed. There hadn't been much chat between us after the parkour display and Ted had been asleep when I came, somewhat nervously, upstairs. I would make more of an effort in the morning, and hopefully we'd soon put recent arguments behind us.

Now, I quietly got up. It was barely 3am, but I knew I wouldn't sleep again. I checked out the window, watching for about ten minutes to try to discern movement on the street. Nothing. I did the same at Dan's bedroom window, but it was too hard to see anything out on the pitch-black football field.

The monster was out there, but perhaps he was taking a

break from watching my house. Or maybe he wasn't active at such an hour, figuring I would be asleep and that he'd be conspicuous to patrolling police. Plus, he also needed to sleep. He would probably be back on my tail when I went to school or to work.

Or would he? Maybe he was in some far-flung corner of the UK right now, hunting his next victim. He knew where I lived and worked, so there was no rush. He could satisfy his urges elsewhere, ruin some other woman's life, and know that when he decided to kill me, here I'd be.

I performed a pregnancy test, then checked his profile again. No new log. I looked out of the window again. No lurking man. He could be partying, sleeping, working, raping. His last log had been two days before my attack, so I had no clue what had happened in his life since.

This thought sparked another. I grabbed my phone. Sunshine's attack in Paris was four years ago. The newspaper article that had reported no arrest in the case had been from two years ago. But what if, in the two years since, things had changed?

What if Sunshine had been arrested for some other crime, his prints taken, and the French police now knew who their rapist was? Clearly he wasn't a convict because he'd attacked me two weeks ago – but he could be a wanted man.

I googled 'wanted criminals in France' and got a listing for Europol – The European Union Agency for Law Enforcement Cooperation. There I found a list of the most sought fugitives in the EU. There were about seventy on the list, so I eliminated the females and non-Caucasians and studied each face carefully. I waited for that eureka moment, but it didn't come. I had no face in my mind and eventually discarded every person. Had I just given him a free pass?

I needed to go wider. Sunshine was a veteran traveller of the whole globe, not just Europe. This led me to Interpol, the International Criminal Police Organisation – coincidentally headquartered in France, where Sunshine had left a fingerprint. It had over 190 member states. Including the USA, where the bastard lived.

Interpol had something called 'Notices'. These were, according to the website, *international requests for cooperation or alerts allowing police in member countries to share critical crime-related information*. The Notices were sectioned into colours, for instance yellow for missing people and black for unidentified bodies. I wanted the Red Notices – worldwide wanted crooks.

The people featured weren't subjects of arrest warrants; however, the Notices were more like an information board for member countries to peruse if they arrested a foreigner on their soil who might not have a criminal record. It was akin to one country simply saying to a friend, *Hey, if you see this person, let us know.*

As long as a Notice followed Interpol's guidelines, it would be published without research – apparently a cause for abuse because sometimes member states targeted people simply because of rumour, with no evidence against them. This lax attitude meant the Red Notices catalogue had a mammoth 60,000+ entries.

I was dismayed, but not by the vast number – the search criteria could be filtered. No, it was because only 7,342 files were currently available for public viewing. I was worried that Sunshine would be amongst the 53,000 profiles restricted to law enforcement eyes.

Still, I needed to check. It would have to wait, however, because by this time it was 7am and my husband and son were stirring upstairs. Ted and I exchanged a few words as I made breakfast for the boys. When Ted was dressed and about to head out the door, he pulled me aside and said, 'I'm not going to focus on why you left me at that hotel room. It was a nice idea. Shame it didn't work out. The thought put in matters most. Maybe we should have a chat tonight. Just us.'

'That would be nice. I'll see you when you get back.'

No kiss, but we swapped thumbs up and he was gone.

I got a chance to get back to the Notices while Dan washed and dressed. First, I filtered the profiles by choosing to display only males. It dropped from 7,342 to 6,299 – so, the number of wanted men was almost seven times that of women. There was no ethnicity choice, so I couldn't view only Caucasians.

There was an option to add a keyword, but I chose not to search solely for those accused of rape or sexual assault, just in case Sunshine was wanted for some other crime. I listed his nationality as USA, which returned 102 men.

'Mum, is it time?'

Dan was in the doorway, dressed, clutching his bag. I'd only checked eight of the wanted American men. 'Yes. Let's go.'

We drove fast, but got caught at a level crossing. I pulled out my phone. I discarded another six criminals before a car horn behind cut me short. The train had gone and the way ahead was clear.

As I parked outside the school, Joan and her grimy kid ambled past. I tried not to look at her, but I sensed a lack of movement and had to turn my head. She was just feet away, paused on the pavement. Staring. Obviously she'd waited for me to clock her, because the moment I did she shook her head as if I'd been foolish, gave me a sly finger behind her kid's back, and walked on. Obviously her brother, John, had been at her ear, bemoaning me.

Dan opened his bag to check everything was correct. It wasn't. 'My dinner,' he moaned.

I'd forgotten. 'I'll get you something from the shop.' Dan

started to open his door. 'Just wait a second now, honey. Just let me find my thing.' I started rooting in the driver's door pocket.

'What thing?'

'Just a thingy I need for later.'

It wasn't in the pocket, I told him, so I checked the glovebox, and after that the door pocket on his side. Then I had to check under both seats and elsewhere inside the car. Dan played on his phone and seemed okay with the delay.

And a delay it was. I watched as the mums and dads filed out of the school grounds, free for six hours. Joan was in the last third and she gave me the finger again as she waltzed past with a pair of other mums. Once she was gone, by which time the crowd had thinned to a handful of stragglers gabbing by the gates, I opened my door. We popped into the corner shop and I bought him a sandwich, crisps and a banana. I checked the time.

'Damn. Sorry, Dan, we're a little late.'

It immediately flicked a switch. Dan wasn't really one for needing to stick to routines, but breaking some norms could result in fireworks. I should have remembered that being late for school was perhaps the biggest. He threw down his phone. 'I'm not going in.'

He hated walking into class when everyone was already seated. This had happened, truly by accident, three times before. The first time, I'd had to stand in the school yard for forty minutes, winning him over. By the third, I'd learned the cure.

Now, I called the school and outlined the problem. The receptionist knew to call his teacher, who appeared on the street by the time I'd calmed Dan down. He hid his face until she was at his window, which I wound down.

'You're not late,' Mrs Cross told him. Her facial scar wrinkled when she smiled. 'Nobody's gone in yet.'

He looked at her. 'No one's in class?'

'Not yet. Everyone else went in early.'

He was a little doubtful, but was soon convinced. The last time, his teacher had asked all the other kids to step out of class as I brought Dan down, and she'd done so again today – and this time they'd been warned not to tell Dan he was late.

I watched her walk away with my boy, and when they reached the gates he ran inside. Success. I got some more time with my phone while heading back to my car. Driving away, I went past Joan, now walking alone. I was tempted to pull over and try to talk to her, because avoiding her had made Dan late and that was something I didn't want to happen ever again. If I kept avoiding the woman like a bullied kid, it would warp my mind and make Dan suffer.

But I hit the accelerator and blew by. I'd go to work, forget this place and that woman, and hopefully tomorrow would be a different story.

I managed more internet research while waiting at red lights. By the time I arrived at Meadowhall, I'd managed to run quickly through all 102 Americans. I hadn't done more than look at their faces, though – Sunshine lived in Dallas, but I couldn't really be sure he was a US citizen, could I?

While walking towards my workplace, I tried something different. The rape that had given police his fingerprints had been in France. So in the WANTED BY filter I chose that country from a drop-down list. Thirty-three males. But, again, I skimmed over the faces staring back at me. I had no idea which countries might be eager to arrest Sunshine, did I? It could be any.

The moment I got in the door at work, my boss, Alan, collared me. 'I got emailed by the manager down at Barnsley.

They just had a flash check, so we need to be on the ball. Let's get back on making that stockroom tidy. Fill the shelves with anything expensive that looks like it's been there ages.'

I got his point. Head office often sent their people to flash check a number of stores in a region on the same day. If the checker was at Barnsley, he would probably come here at some point. And one thing they hated was money tied up in backroom stock. I told Alan I'd get right on it.

'Alice quit,' he said next. I waited for him to ask what I'd said to make her jack in her job, but he didn't. She must have kept quiet about our little chat. Good.

Once in the stockroom with a cup of tea, I pulled up a box and sat down. Out came my phone and the Red Notices. I had skipped criminals whose main photo failed to give me that eureka moment, but this was a mistake. I hadn't seen Sunshine's evil face and couldn't rely on some kind of internal radar to spotlight him.

So, I would go back through the list and this time I would read up on each criminal, take a much closer look at every photo the profile contained, and carefully decide if I could eliminate the man.

I had been in the stockroom, researching, for no more than five minutes when one of the staff poked his head in. 'The Flash is here. Alan says get a move on. He'll hand over to you in a few minutes.'

Hand over to me? Alan had done this to me once before. He'd tell the head office guy that I was the stockroom guru, so that I'd have to answer all the man's questions. No way. The stockroom was still a mess, and I couldn't stop my internet research now.

I picked up a heavy box and dropped it hard on the floor, so the bottom buckled. Then I slid my leg under it and let out a yell.

As the same staff member burst in, I let him decode the scene before pushing the box away and clambering to my feet. I moaned in fake pain. He ran to get Alan.

'What happened?' the boss said when he arrived. 'The bloody Flash is here.'

'A damn box fell on me. This place is a bloody deathtrap.'

I saw his face change. Head office was terrified of staff and customer injuries on-site. Alan knew the hitman in his office would pummel him for this. He came in and shut the door behind him.

'Jesus, we can't let the Flash see this. Can you walk?'

I rubbed my not-sore-at-all calf. 'Yes. But I need to get my leg looked at. Can I go to the hospital? I can be back in an hour.'

'With NHS waiting times? I doubt it. Look, just go. But let's pretend you're ill or something. Don't limp if the Flash sees you, okay?'

'Yes. Sorry.'

'Just get out of here.'

I did. Once back in my car, I opened my phone. As well as having no clue as to Sunshine's appearance, I also couldn't rely on what I thought I knew about him, so all filters bar SEX would go. Once more in front of me I had 6,299 profiles of male killers, terrorists, fraudsters, and all manner of other bad boys.

Up first, a Russian chap, wanted by Russia for 'aggravated robbery and participation in the activity of an illegal armed formation'. It didn't sound like my guy, but I studied the three included photos hard. No eureka moment, but this time I trusted it. I eliminated him.

One down, 6,298 to go.

CHAPTER THIRTY-ONE

When I got to school to pick up Dan, his head teacher, a skinny fifty-something called Mr Wade, was standing by him and Dan's teacher. Mr Wade took me aside. I could tell by his face that this wasn't good news. 'Dan hit a teacher. I think perhaps his lateness this morning affected his mood all day.'

'Okay. I'm sorry about that. I'll have a word with him.'

'That's good. Erm, is there something important on your phone?'

I had been looking at profiles on the drive down and the walk across the field. I was still throwing glances and swiping the screen even as we spoke. I felt a little embarrassed, but time was of the essence. 'Yes, my mother just got taken into hospital,' I lied.

'I'm sorry. I didn't know. Is she okay?'

'Yes, fine. I need to take Dan down to see her. Is he ready to go?'

Of course he was. This was no time to tell me off about my son's behaviour. We were home soon afterwards.

I sent Dan to his room to do homework, telling him I'd call him down when his dinner was ready. On the drive home, I'd lamented the fact that many of Sunshine's attacks didn't have a lot of media coverage. Now, that very fact gave me optimism.

The attack Sunshine made in France had been an *attempted* rape, hardly worthy of a major task force or months of newspaper coverage. And I'd read nothing that suggested the police thought he was a foreigner. So why would the French police have uploaded his details to Interpol?

They wouldn't have. And perhaps no one else had.

But he was a still a wanted man in France. His fingerprints were on file, along with whatever else they knew about him. Perhaps many other countries had similar files on this man, but jurisdictional boundaries meant none knew about the others. Numerous police departments, each unable to decipher their piece of the jigsaw that identified Sunshine.

Maybe other countries had his fingerprints, or his DNA. Maybe the UK was one of them, and police here were just waiting for that next, vital clue that would unearth him.

I think I knew how to help achieve that.

Ted sent a message after work, claiming he was off grappling. I replied with simply OK and got on with my research. It was 9pm when he rolled in. I was on the computer in our bedroom and the first I knew of his presence was when he swore from behind me.

'What the hell is going on?'

I spun on the chair. He was in the doorway. I shut the computer off at the plug so he couldn't see what I had been up to. 'Nothing. Why? I'm just–'

'Dan's not had dinner.'

I'd forgotten. When I went downstairs, Dan was in the

living room, watching TV and still in school uniform. 'Did you get any food, Dan?'

'I was waiting for you. You said you'd do it. I'm starving.'

It was his bedtime, but I told him he could stay up until he'd eaten. I made waffles and beans. Ted was still upstairs and I knew he was waiting for me. I stayed in the kitchen to avoid a reprimand.

No such luck. Ted came down and beckoned me. We went to the bedroom and he shut the door. 'Been to the doctor yet?'

'No. And every time you ask, you might as well tell me how much of a mess-up I am.'

'You said it yourself. So what happened this time to make you forget about your son? What was so important on the computer?'

'I didn't know you'd be late. Dan wanted you to cook his dinner. I just didn't think after you sent that text.'

Ted let out a heavy sigh. He seemed to think about what to say next, but chose nothing. He left the room. I shut the door and sat on the bed.

Had he been at jiu-jitsu, or in another woman's bed? I should have fed Dan when I knew Ted would be home way after dinner time. But Ted shouldn't have been late, should he? He shouldn't have been with his bit on the side. If she didn't exist, the argument wouldn't have happened. It wasn't the first row we'd had because of her and wouldn't be the last. She was a wedge being driven deeper and deeper into our union, splitting us.

If our marriage was going to work, if our family was going to stay whole, then he had to give up that bitch. If she was an addiction for him, he might not be able to end their fling on his own. But she could do it. If there was a clean soul inside her, maybe she would dump Ted if she knew what their shagging

JANE HEAFIELD

sessions were doing to his family. She just needed proof of the damage she was causing.

When Dan was in bed half an hour later and Ted was in the shower, I grabbed my car keys. During the drive, I worked on how best to broach the subject. How would I begin such a taxing conversation?

In the end, I didn't need to. Either Ted had shown his mistress a photo of me or she had done her own research into his other half. By the time I had reached the flowery porch, she was at the inner door.

She wore a baggy dressing gown and I couldn't see her physique. She also wore a lot of make-up and her hair was a clearly dyed blonde, both of which further fogged my impression of her age. I'd hoped that Ted hadn't betrayed me for a much younger woman, but this I hadn't expected. She was easily fifty, which was twenty years my elder. That felt worse.

'Don't come closer,' she said. 'Stay that side. I know what you want.'

I remained outside the porch, a glass door and ten feet between us. 'Ted's my husband.'

'I know. I just said that, didn't I? I hope you didn't come here to start trouble.'

I hadn't, but I felt like it now. She'd stolen a husband and was now giving the shamed wife attitude? 'I just came to show my face. I figured if you knew about me, you might have second thoughts.'

'I already knew.'

'And didn't care?'

She laughed. 'I think the blame belongs elsewhere, don't you? Talk to your husband. Find out why one woman isn't enough for him.'

'Did you know about me? I mean, from the start?'

'Yes. But I always told him it would be over when you found

out. Since you're here, obviously you now know. So I'll tell him it's over. And now you can leave.'

I wanted to say more. I wanted this woman to be upset, embarrassed, but she was very far from drowning in those emotions. At least I had achieved my goal. I got out of there quickly.

CHAPTER THIRTY-TWO

O n Tuesday morning, I woke at 5am. On the sofa.

Highly unfortunate, because I'd felt things were mending between Ted and I. Last night we'd sat on the sofa, watching TV for an hour. There had been little conversation, but sharing the same room had been helpful. When he'd gone to bed, he'd even remarked that he'd see me when I came up. I hoped my empty side of the bed last night hadn't undone what little progress had been made.

After checking outside, to make sure nothing was out of order in the front or backyards, I took a tea upstairs for Ted. I gave him ten minutes to wake up before returning to ask how he was.

'Fine. Cool. Knackered. We need a lottery win.'

He sounded okay – as in, it didn't seem as if he'd heard a tale of an aggressive wife from his mistress. At some point, though, he'd learn about my visit to flowery porch woman, and I wasn't looking forward to his reaction. Hopefully she would invent a reason for ending their affair that didn't include me.

I woke Dan and said, 'Hey, king, how about I let you stay off school today? I need to make a trip down south and I need a driver's mate.'

That brightened his day. I set his phone and his iPad charging and made us both packed lunches. When Ted was ready for work and heading for the door, I got up the nerve to slap his butt. He left with a smile. Everyone in the Holten household, it seemed, was having a happy morning.

Until 9.20. Dan and I were driving when the call from school came. As soon as I saw the name on the screen, I realised I'd forgotten to call in sick for him. After taking that call and lying about a bellyache, I phoned work. Yesterday I'd received word from Carla that the flash check had been a disaster, with our store being put on an assessment plan.

This meant another check in fourteen days and if things hadn't been turned around, the store would be fined. Bonuses would evaporate. Alan was in work early to start getting things shipshape, and it was he who answered my call. I'd hoped to pass my message to him via a cleaner.

I basically told him my ankle was sprained and the hospital had suggested I take at least today off. He wasn't over the moon about this, but he kept his frustration to himself and wished me a speedy recovery. Those words probably burned his tongue.

After that call, I turned off the phone. I would not reactivate it until we were at our destination.

The trip took well over five hours because of three service station toilet stops, a petrol fill-up and a wrong turn. But finally we found Fryent Country Park, in Brent, north-west London.

Our destination was three hundred metres north-west of the car park, close to where a trail led through a gap in a row of trees. Once parked, Dan looked up from his iPad. 'A park? What's here?' Is this it?'

'This is it. You always wanted to come on a geocache.'

His eyes lit up. I'd never taken him on a treasure hunt before. I showed him my phone. 'This is the map. See these green circles? They're all geocaches. This is the one we want. So, if I click on it, it brings up this page, which is all about it. Look, it's called HANGING FREEMAN. A freeman is someone honoured by a town or city. You might have heard of someone having the key to the city.'

'So they can open all doors?'

'Not quite. There are privileges. Some don't really apply, but freemen still have the right. For instance, here in London, if the police are called to a drunken freeman, he won't, or shouldn't, be arrested. They'll just send him home in a taxi. This clue here, look. Read it.'

'"Comfortable Hanging Freeman"? What does that mean?'

'Well, that's the puzzle. We can click here to decipher it or–'

Dan immediately clicked the button. He said, 'Silk noose. If you're hanged with a silk noose, is that comfortable? Do you die?'

I laughed. Soon, we were walking across the field. When we stepped onto the trail through the woods, following the map as it counted down the metres to the geocache, I became aware of noise nearby. I saw a woman and two young girls in the trees. I cursed loudly enough for Dan to hear and reprimand me. I knew the three in the woods were after the same geocache. I told Dan to hustle.

We got ahead of them and veered into the trees. When the map told me we were just four metres from the geocache, I cast my eyes around.

'Noose,' Dan said, pointing. I saw it hanging from a high branch: a white rope with a noose. Dan ran to the tree. 'How can we get up there?'

I heard the girls behind us, closing in. One said something about the distance. 'We don't. The rope is only up there to stop muggles taking it. Look, in here.'

The trunk had a basketball-sized hollow. Dan poked his hand in, and his face lit up. He extracted the geocache. My eyes widened. I took the geocache from Dan, shocked. I could now be holding the key to the monster's demise.

None of Sunshine's geocache-find logs contained photos of the event and ninety-nine per cent of the time he'd also withheld the fanfare, writing only 'Found it' or some simple variation. The remaining one per cent was reserved for geocaches at which he'd displayed his benevolence.

Some hunters reported faulty geocaches, and some performed their own maintenance. I'd replaced a few damaged ones in my time. I had read dozens of Sunshine's logs, stretching back years, and had found at least ten instances where he'd swapped a busted container for his own. Curiously, instead of employing a standard plastic tube, Sunshine had used the item featured in his profile picture: a small key safe with shackle and combination lock.

On January 12th, 2016, halfway through a jaunt around England, Sunshine had written a log: *Found it. Container waterlogged. Replaced. Code is scratched into rear.*

While staring at the key safe in my gloved hand, I heard voices behind me. It was the woman and her two girls. The woman said, 'They've found it, look. Let's just wait back here for our turn.'

'Can we open it, Mum?' Dan said. 'What's the code?'

I held the key safe carefully, but tightly, and grabbed Dan's hand with my free one. 'We'll open it back in the car. Let's go.'

'Excuse me,' the woman said, 'but what are you doing?'

I ignored her and dragged Dan towards the woodland track.

'Hey,, excuse me, but that's stealing. You can't do that.'

JANE HEAFIELD

'Auntie, is that lady taking the treasure?'

'Mum, are we allowed to take it home?'

'Yes, Dan, so let's go.'

'Hey, you thief. Bring that back. That's for everyone. You're going to get banned.'

I increased speed, almost dragging Dan. The woman continued yelling, but did not give chase. We got back to the car and I locked the doors. The woman and her nieces were nowhere to be seen. I extracted a small plastic freezer bag from the glovebox and secured the key safe inside it. I saw a code scratched into the metal on the back.

'Are we not opening it?' Dan said.

'No, we can't. I need this to help me find someone. It will only have paper inside it for people to sign.'

'Who are you finding? How?'

I looked at him for a long time, silent. He might not understand, but he was my son and I was not going to lie yet again. There had been too much deceit.

'A man hurt me, Dan. He did this to my head.'

'Why?'

'Because he's a bad man. I don't want other people to get hurt, so I'm going to use this little safe to stop him. He planted it in that tree. It's been six years, but I'm hoping his fingerprints are still on it. For the police.'

'Are you going to tell them he hurt you?'

'No. I don't want anyone to know. Including your dad, okay? You have to make this our secret. Can you promise that?'

'Yes!' he yelled. His clenched his fists and shouted, 'So why will the police look for him if they don't know he hurt you? How will they know to look for his fingerprints?'

I stroked his hair, which could often soothe his angry impatience. 'Calm down, honey, just calm. The police don't know the bad man's name or address or anything. And they

186

don't know he's a geocacher. But when they open the safe and read the logs inside, they'll know it belonged to him. They'll be able to arrest him, or tell some other police to. At least, they will if they match the prints on the safe to some already in their files for a bad crime. That's what I'm relying on, unfortunately. Now, in order to get them to dust the safe for fingerprints, I have to do something stupid. Something else you can't tell your dad, or anyone. Promise me that and I'll let you watch me do it.'

'I promise. Properly promise. What are you going to do?'

I explained and we started driving to find what I needed. A short way north, just past a roundabout called Kingsbury Circle, there was an Iceland supermarket. There, in the car park, was what I sought. I parked and got out. Nobody seemed to be watching.

I approached the empty police car, pulled back my arm, and lobbed the key safe, no longer bagged, through the driver's side window. The impact of smashing glass was a dull thump that barely carried. Nobody even looked my way. Nice and casual, I got back in my vehicle and eased it away.

'What if the police don't already have his fingers?' Dan said.

'Fingerprints. Well, if that's the case, this will all have been a waste of time.'

CHAPTER THIRTY-THREE

There was a police car outside the house when we got home at close to 9pm. I parked a short way down the street and turned my phone back on. Sure enough, there were missed calls. Ted had rung a bunch of times and there were two unknown numbers, which I guessed belonged to the police. I also had two voicemails, one from Ted and one from one of the unknowns. I didn't listen to either. I knew I was in trouble.

Ted came to the front door before Dan and I got there. He took our son's hand and said to me, 'You, living room.'

Ted took Dan upstairs while I entered the living room, where two officers sat. 'This is about London, isn't it? I admit it. I was silly.'

The pair were very nice. I was arrested for criminal damage and booked into a police station, but there were no cuffs and they let me use the toilet before we left the house. I wanted to admit everything and get it over with, but they had procedures and told me to say nothing until interview. That, I was told by the desk sergeant, would probably be tomorrow morning.

Years ago, when I had been a less than stellar personality, I'd known many people who'd fallen foul of the law. I'd picked up a few tips that I was a little ashamed to still know.

'It's probably too late to bring in a solicitor tonight, is that why? I just want to tell my story. Can you get one in early tomorrow? I mean, I'd prefer to tell my story tonight.'

They told me it was indeed too late to bring in a duty solicitor. I had my photograph taken and DNA extracted by mouth swab, then got escorted to a cell. I kept my ear open for footsteps, hopeful that I wouldn't be here all night.

It took only minutes. A pretty lady in blue trousers and a blouse came for me. 'We can interview you now if you're willing to waive your right to a solicitor. We'd like to get you back to your son tonight.'

They weren't worried about my son. The police liked their suspects to talk, and solicitors liked them to say little. I agreed to a chat without legal representation. The lady went away to prepare and half an hour later I was walking with her to another room. She was very pleasant and we chatted about our children – her daughter, like Dan, was on the autism spectrum – before getting down to business.

As I expected, they knew I'd damaged a police car. The vehicle in question had had running dashcam and the officer played the video for me. I watched my car park in front of the police vehicle, my registration plate clearly visible. I watched myself approach that vehicle and vanish off-screen as I walked down the driver's side. I heard the thump of the window caving in, then saw myself walking away. It was very embarrassing.

The Metropolitan police officers using the car had returned with a bag of snacks three minutes later. Four minutes after that, they had my name and address from the DVLA. Six further minutes down the line, South Yorkshire Police got a phone call. Officers had been at my house before I'd even hit the motorway for the journey home.

After getting no answer at the door, they'd left a note for me to hand myself in at a police station. Ted got in around 8pm, after going to the gym, saw the note, and called the station. It had been his idea to allow the police to wait in the house.

When the lady shut off the video, I said, 'Yes, that was me. Yes, I was stupid. But I just want you to know I picked the first car I came across. I wasn't trying to upset the police. And I didn't try to steal anything from the car.'

She laid a photograph bag on the table. It showed the key safe, in two pieces. A card lay by the safe marked with numbers and RELIABLE PROTECTION KEY SAFE.

'Tough product. They had to take an angle grinder to it. Want to explain what happened? Why you threw this through the window? Where you got it? Why you were in London?'

I told her the safe was from a geocache and I'd gone to London with Dan because he had never been on a hunt before. Once we'd found it, I'd tried to log the visit but had been unable to get an internet connection on my phone. I'd driven around to try to find a signal and had ended up at the Iceland store.

By that point, I said I had been angry and I foolishly wanted to break something. The anger had built up over a number of days because I had missed an appointment with Dan's educational psychologist. I said I was very sorry. Would I go to prison?

The officer ended the interview, then said, 'No, you won't get prison. No one got hurt, I accept your explanation, the window can be fixed. And I can see you're scared, but don't worry. If you agree to pay for the busted window, I can tell you now I won't pass this along. No charge.'

'Thank you so much. And I will pay. Of course I will.'

I was released soon afterwards. While waiting outside for a taxi, I had to thump my chest to get my breathing back to normal. I had had a lucky escape. If the police had checked the key safe for fingerprints, I could have been in a world of trouble. They would have tied me into a vicious and prolific rapist.

The whole story would have emerged. I would have forever been known as Woman Raped. I had tried to keep my name hidden, but my silly actions had instead almost screamed it from the rooftops.

However, when I was riding home, something occurred to me and my sunken mood took a massive leap skyward. My arrest hadn't nearly foiled me at all – in fact, it might have just given me the key to finding my attacker and ending this nightmare.

When I walked in the house, Ted was waiting in the living room. I stopped in the doorway. 'Tomorrow. Not now. We talk about this tomorrow. I need a shower. I know you want answers, but please give me some time alone.'

I didn't wait for a response and rushed upstairs.

'Lisa, what the hell? You have to tell me what's going on. Come back here, Lisa!'

'Not now,' I yelled back. I locked myself in the bathroom and started the shower. But I didn't bathe. I sat on the closed toilet lid, opened my phone, and delved into cyberspace.

I'd shrunken the world down to a portion just shy of 1,000 square kilometres, but knowing Sunshine lived in Dallas, Texas, had warranted no joy. Now, I believed I'd decreased my target area substantially again.

Sunshine's profile picture was of a padlock-style key safe. Nine years ago, when he was Dallas9999, he'd also used a key safe picture. Sunshine had replaced many damaged geocaches on his travels, and in every instance the cheap original container had been swapped for a key safe. Why the interest in these items?

In 2013, Dallas got his profile on the geocaching website locked for a rule transgression. An advertising rule? Had Dallas been banned for trying to sell a product? Had he, under his new guise of Sunshine, undertaken a sneakier sales campaign involving placing key safes in geocaches so that myriad users could see how handy they were? Hadn't a police officer just told me how impressed she was by the resilience of the key safe I'd stolen?

The research was easy. *Key safe manufacturers in Dallas, Texas.* There were various hits, but one immediately leaped out at me. It was a company at 2241 Irving Boulevard, just under two miles west of Dealey Plaza, where President John Fitzgerald Kennedy was gunned down in 1963.

When I loaded the address into the geocaching website, the map displayed numerous nearby geocaches by the Trinity River and in the Dallas Floodway and all over Trammell Crow Park. Over three quarters of them had been hidden by Sunshine-and-Roses.

And in the centre was a building marked with the same two words that had been written on a piece of card by a police officer: RELIABLE PROTECTION.

Bingo. I still didn't have his name, but I now knew where the man who raped me spent his working week.

'You're fucked now,' I yelled at the phone.

CHAPTER THIRTY-FOUR

The 'About Us' section of Reliable Protection's website said the company had been founded as Reliable in the 1970s, with a single travelling salesman selling padlocks out of a suitcase. Today, Reliable had over 400 employees and manufactured key safes, home safes, security alarms, and window and door locks. They sold products worldwide.

The 'Our Family' section covered staff, but was nothing more than a self back-pat about commitment to training and professionalism. It boasted that Reliable's employees included engineers, salespeople, production line workers and staff in a showroom attached to the factory, but no individual was named.

The 'Contact Us' section was the only place I found a name. It was the admin coordinator to whom all sales enquiries should be directed, and it was a she.

'I'm going to bed,' Ted called out from the other side of the door. I checked the time: I'd been locked in the bathroom for over an hour. I shut off the shower, which had run cold. Then I opened the door.

Ted looked me up and down. 'You didn't shower at all.'

'And you said you were going to bed. I don't want to have this conversation right now.'

He shook his head and turned away. I followed him into the bedroom. He'd just entered the en suite, which meant we again spoke through a bathroom door, this time reversing our positions. 'Ted. Look, I'm sorry. You know my head hasn't been on straight. What do you know about where I was today?'

'Next to nothing. You didn't take Dan into school. You didn't tell anyone where you were going and turned your phone off. If I had to have a million guesses where and what – in stone-dead last place would have been London and tossing rocks at cop cars in some field.'

Rocks? So, the police hadn't shared with him the exact details of why they sought me, leaving him to fill in the gaps. 'Come out.'

I sat at my dressing table. Ted exited the bathroom and sat on the bed. I told him I'd taken Dan on a geocache. I needed to get over the fear of the woods that I'd developed since my attack. I wanted to effectively jump in at the deep end by visiting a new, faraway site, although in contrast I chose daytime and to have a partner.

I'd been spooked by a repeat of my attack: a thuggish girl had given me abuse at the geocache. Annoyed at myself for being so scared of nothing, I'd thrown a rock, which had struck a nearby police car window.

Ted believed my story, but he was far from pleased by my behaviour. We spoke for a few minutes and I repeated decayed promises to try to get help. It was not a lie, but I was in no rush to start calling doctors when I was so close to exposing my attacker. The pledge was enough to placate Ted and he asked if I was coming to bed – 'to sleep', he was careful to add.

I really wanted to read more about Reliable Security and

Dallas, but someone other than the faceless monster had to take priority at least some of the time.

Once in bed, we wished each other goodnight and Ted turned off the light. In the dark, I said, 'Oh, good news. Profits are up. The company is holding some prize draws. My store won. I've got a chance for a prize.'

'Top notch,' Ted replied. His voice was already raspy with tiredness. A few minutes later, he put a hand on my hip. He didn't try anything sexual, for which I mentally thanked him.

However, he soon started snoring, and I moved his hand off my skin.

———

Breaking news: I got a full night's sleep. I woke refreshed for the first time in ages and was almost bouncing around the house. Ted loved my buoyant demeanour and left for work with a smile. Dan wanted to know if I'd had good news.

'Sort of, sort of.' I had a way forward. No more treading water for me. Nightmare end in sight. Was this, rather than the sleep, the reason for my upbeat mood? 'Anyway, I also got time to do your homework before you got up.'

'Aren't I supposed to do it?'

'Yes, but it's the act of learning that matters. I've got something I want you to learn about. Do you recognise this man?'

I showed him a photo on my phone. Dan shook his head. I said, 'He's known as JFK. Can you remember that?'

'JFK. Who is he?'

'Well, that's your homework, little man. Ask a few teachers. Use your phone on the way to school. I want to see what you can tell me about him by the time I pick you up from school. If you impress me, there might be some money for you.'

Dan was silent on the drive to school, engrossed in his phone. I got the odd glance and saw he was researching. Good. When I parked outside school, Joan walked past with her kid and gave me a long look. She stared as I waited with Dan at the inner gate. Her glare was on me from outside the corner shop as I made for my car after the kids had gone.

When I got behind the wheel, she approached and rapped the passenger side window. I took two seconds to choose between winding it down or blasting out of there.

'Heard the police arrested you,' she said.

How did she know that? There was no point asking. 'Yes.'

'Heard they let you go without charge.'

'Yes.'

'Might that be because you sang like a canary?'

'No. About what? You? What we did? I'd be in handcuffs if I told them that. If you're worried about that, don't be.'

'But I am. So whether you think you know the score or not, here's a reminder. You just keep your damn mouth shut about it, okay? Or things could turn bad for you. I'm not your business. We're not friends. We just did that thing together and that's the end of it. I'm sure you know the rules about snitching. It's not just a prison thing. Even out here you can get messed up for it.'

'You're right, we did that thing and that's the end of it. So I'd appreciate it if you could ask your brother to stop coming to my house. There's no more money.'

Joan hawked and spat onto my passenger seat. 'Just watch how you open that mouth and take care of your family. Say sorry for your damn mouth, right now.'

'I'm sorry. Look, I don't want trouble.'

'That damn gob will get you lots, and I've got all you can ever need. Now piss off.'

Joan sauntered back to her friends outside the shop. I drove, fast.

CHAPTER THIRTY-FIVE

Before heading into work, I visited a bank in Meadowhall and then a travel agent. The detours made me a little late, but Alan wasn't in and nobody else complained. I lurked in the office all morning and afternoon to work on my plan.

I wanted to avoid Joan that afternoon so called the school and said I needed Dan ready ten minutes early. They obliged and I got him to the car just in time to avoid the influx of parents. I didn't see Joan until we were driving away.

'JFK was the 35th American president,' Dan said. 'He was born near Boston in 1917.'

'Very good. Tell me more.'

He did. I was very impressed by how much Dan knew. What pleased me more was his desire to continue reading about the assassinated president. At home, he asked if he could use the internet and I let him. I took his dinner upstairs so he wouldn't have to pause his studying.

When Ted came home, I kissed his cheek. I didn't miss the surprise it created on his face. 'Good day?' he asked.

'Getting there. I owe it to you and Dan.'

'And you. You owe it to yourself.'

'Yes. Oh, I told you about the prize draw at work, remember?'

'No.'

He'd been asleep. I filled him in. After a year of healthy sales figures, Heaven Homestore wanted to reward its staff. They'd done a draw and my store had won. Soon we'd have the in-house draw to see which staff member got the top prize.

'What's the prize?'

'A holiday somewhere. We could do with that.'

Before Ted could respond, Dan bounded downstairs and assaulted his ears with facts about November 22nd, 1963. He only stopped when Ted picked him up and spun around with him.

'If only you had this much enthusiasm for jiu-jitsu, I'd have a world champ on my hands.'

'JFK is sooooo better. Jijisu is for wimps.'

Ted mock-chased Dan away. I got to making my husband's dinner.

Later, Dan called me to his room and pointed out his computer screen. He'd found two books about JFK on Amazon. 'Please?'

I used my phone to find them and made the purchases. Also on the page was a book about Dallas itself and a wall map of the city, both of which joined them in the shopping basket. I paid for premium delivery. Shortly after, Dan went to bed. Normally he wasn't allowed his phone, but tonight I broke that rule. He was looking at famous Dallas landmarks on Google Earth.

Next, I ran Ted a bath he wasn't expecting. When I called him upstairs for it, he was pleasantly surprised. More so when I helped him undress and soaped his back and shoulders. When I moved the sponge under the surface, to his groin, he softly grabbed my arm.

'You don't need to do this. I mean, not if you're doing it for my sake.'

I kissed his lips. 'It's for my sake as well. I'll be in the bedroom. Now hurry the hell up.'

Ted dunked his entire body under so fast that a wave splashed over the side and soaked my socks. He jumped up like a jack-in-the-box, dripping bubbly water. 'Done.'

I led him into the bedroom, laid a towel on the quilt, and pushed him backwards onto it. I undressed and threw each item of clothing at his face. He waited until there was no more before tossing the garments aside. Then he dragged my naked body on top of his.

'I'm only doing this for your sake too,' he said.

'My hero,' I joked.

Ted rolled us over and pinned me beneath his wet body. He pushed my hands above my head and pinned them there. My breath caught as I tried to move my arms and couldn't. A wave of fear coursed through me.

'No,' I moaned before I could stop myself. I quickly regretted it when Ted adopted a look of horror. As his muscles relaxed, I freed my arms, circled them around his back, and reversed the flip to put myself once again on top. 'I meant, no, not like that. Like this.'

I forced Ted's hands above his head. He grinned. We kissed.

He tried to flip me again, but this time I was prepared and thwarted it. I reached down to insert him into me. 'Take me like this.'

Afterwards, I showered while Ted went to the backyard for a smoke. Sitting under the spray, I cried. What I had done had been necessary for our marriage and for Dan's sake, but it had been about more than that.

My period was approaching and, despite a battery of negative tests, I could still be pregnant. If there was a demon seed inside me, Ted might find out somehow. I could not hope to hide that fact from him forever. He could discover the truth a month or ten years from now.

He could not know of another man, even one who took me by force, for it would destroy our already brittle marriage, and that meant I had only one option. I would have to tell Ted he was the father. Now that he'd ejaculated inside me, I could run with this lie. I felt like a real monster for tricking him like this.

But the shame would be nothing compared to if I had to tell my husband I would be aborting his child.

When Dan and I left the house to go to school, I spotted a flat tyre. Dan started kicking it. 'Does this mean the day off school?'

Mr Skewis, the neighbour, had stopped blocking my driveway. He was also willing to make amends in other ways. When he came out of his house to go to work, he spotted the tyre and offered to swap it for my spare. When it was done, he showed me a slit in the original tyre.

'Looks like a stab to me,' he said. 'Piss anyone off? Hey, I hope you don't think it was me?'

'No, of course not. Just vandals, probably.' I doubted it. I had a suspicion who was behind the popped tyre and soon got confirmation:

'I feel *flat* today, how about you?' Joan said. The tyre change had made Dan and I a couple of minutes late, although Dan had taken it well this time. When I left, Joan was with her cronies outside the corner shop yet again.

'Look, I've got this for you. As an apology for my cheek the other day.'

It was a £20 note from my purse. Joan snatched it. 'I forgive you. Things are no longer *smashing* between us though. A few more of these might make things better.'

Smashing. Obviously a busted car or house window would be next, perhaps even if I paid her off. I made no reply bar another apology and got in my car.

I was back in the same spot six hours later. Joan was around but completely ignored me this time. When Dan came out, I saw he had a big tear in the knee of his trousers. Dan said he'd fallen at playtime. I asked his teacher, Mrs Cross, to confirm this.

'Yes, that's what he told us. Can I just ask you something? Dan's been allowed to read about the JFK assassination, right?'

'Yes. Well, everything about JFK. You know what he's like when he gets interested in something.'

'For sure. It's just that we really need him to do his homework. He was set a task for last night to identify kitchen dangers, but he said you told him he could study JFK instead.'

'Well, I said both. Homework first and JFK afterwards. I thought he'd done the work. I'm sorry.'

'Okay. I'm just not sure it's decent material for a child. The conspiracies as well as the killing act.'

'Like I said, it's everything about JFK. I can't stop him reading about what he's interested in. He can't do nothing but homework and it beats watching TV.'

'For sure, for sure. How did he suddenly get a fixation on the death of President Kennedy?'

I shrugged.

In the car, Dan pulled me up. 'Why did you tell my teacher you said to do both? You told me I could do JFK.'

'I meant both,' I lied.

CHAPTER THIRTY-SIX

Ted called after work and said he was going to his jiu-jitsu class. He was back by nine, just as Dan was brushing his teeth in preparation for bed. I said, 'I won the draw at work. We won a holiday.'

'For real? All-inclusive?' Ted walked past me and I followed him into the kitchen. He was wearing his Gi. He dumped his bag by the washing machine.

'No, we have to pay for our food. But we got the flights and the hotel.'

'Where can we go? Brazil?'

I laughed. 'For your jiu-jitsu? Maybe. There's a list of places, but I haven't seen it yet. I'll get that tomorrow.'

'A list of places? Never heard of that. What if there's nowhere we like?'

'It's free. We'll like. We're hardly going to be given a choice of war-torn countries.'

Ted unloaded his clothing from the bag and stuffed it into the washer. 'Does it have to be a holiday? They must know some people can't get away. Can we have hard cash?'

'No. Besides, I want a holiday. We need one. It's only for three days.'

'Three days? No point in Australia then. We'd end up on planes for that long.' He went to a cupboard for washing powder, but I got there first and told him I'd do his laundry if he fetched Dan so we could get his opinion.

A mere thirty seconds after Ted went upstairs, Dan's thunderous footsteps rang out. He burst into the kitchen, yelling, 'Dallas, Dallas, Dallas, JFK, JFK, JFK.'

Ted entered behind him. 'Apparently he wants Dallas. The JFK obsession is taking over him. It's a big city, Dan, super crowded.'

'I want to see where Kennedy was shot. I need to.'

I laughed. 'He needs to, Daddy. So let's vote. If all three places are on the list—' Dan cut in here, demanding to know what list I was talking about. I quickly explained everything. 'If all three are on the list, we pick out of a hat. I want to go to Italy. Rome. The Colosseum for me.'

'Brazil,' Ted said. 'But not for sport. It's got hot beaches.'

'Dallas,' Dan said. 'Not just JFK. It's got the Cowboys Stadium. World Aquarium. Museum of Art. Come see, Dad. On my computer.'

Dan dragged his father away. I shouted out that I needed to pop to the minimart. I was going nowhere of the sort though.

I had sent Ted upstairs to fetch his son so I could check his work uniform, which he'd been very eager to wash immediately. I had found no other-woman smells, but a wet stain on the sleeve had the unmistakable stench of mouthwash.

So, despite our intimacy last night and all my other attempts to rekindle our love, Ted had not given up his bitch. And she had lied to the face of his distraught wife.

Perhaps the problem had started with a lack of sex, but Ted had now developed an emotional attachment to his other woman. Wasn't that every wife's fear – not that a husband would sleep with another woman, but that he'd fall in love with her? I had shown Ted I was still carnally interested in him, but this ploy had failed to strike down his love affair with another. Was it now too late for any action to save our marriage?

Perhaps. But that did not mean I had to lose him to that bitch. And it would not happen anytime soon. I needed him, especially right now.

I parked at the kerb and walked up the garden path, to the flowery porch. This time the woman didn't appear to block me. Once inside, I was hidden by walls of flora. Nobody beyond saw what I slipped out of my trousers. I rapped on the door.

The woman answered in jeans and a T-shirt, and I could see she was quite athletic. Trim. She might have been older, but I didn't doubt that an unarmed tussle between us would go her way.

Unarmed, that was.

'I don't want to use this,' I said, raising the hammer. The woman had answered the door with zero fear on her face, but that changed in a clock-tick. She tried to slam the door, but I whacked it with the hammer and she abandoned that ploy. She backed into the house. I pushed the door fully open, but didn't step over the threshold.

'What do you want?' she moaned.

'Me and Ted, we're going on holiday. It's something I have to do and if he leaves me, it will ruin everything. We need to be a loving couple again so we can go away, but that won't happen while he's hypnotised by your tits and pussy. So, end it with him. Do it tomorrow morning while he's at work. Send a text. Tell him you met someone else. You never want to see him again. Warn him that if he contacts you ever again, you'll tell me. You stay away from him forever, and this is your last ever warning. If I lose this holiday, I'll hurt you.'

I thumped the door one more time – an exclamation mark – and casually walked away.

CHAPTER THIRTY-SEVEN

I had a new dream, and like the last, the desert vision, it was borne of consuming worry. In the dream, I stood at a cliff edge with a roiling ocean far below, and in my arms were two babies. The little humans were identical in appearance, but I knew vast differences lay within. One baby belonged to the man who'd married me. The other was the offspring of the man who'd raped me.

I was supposed to keep just one, and condemn the other to the ocean. But I had no idea which man had fathered which baby. I woke before I could make that choice.

It was obvious what the dream meant. I had allowed Ted to ejaculate his seed into me as camouflage, so I could pretend my rapist's child was his. But I had overlooked something mammoth. I might now be pregnant with Ted's child, even though my fertile window had been right around the time Sunshine raped me.

In a few days I would either have my period or be able to perform a legitimate pregnancy test, but until then I had no idea if I was carrying new life or who the father was. The thought immediately loaded me up on anxiety.

Ted noticed my low mood when he woke. Even Dan didn't miss it. I blamed a lack of sleep, which was partly true as I had woken at 4am. I barely said a word to Dan as we drove to school. Dan, though, made up for it by chattering ceaselessly about all things JFK. He was very eager to go to Dallas and asked me to promise I would pick that city if it was amongst the ones on the holiday list.

'I can't believe we won a holiday,' he said perhaps fifty times between waking and getting to school.

And he shouldn't. There had been no prize draw at work.

As we strolled into the school grounds, lagging behind Joan and her kid, I said, 'No more parkour on the playground, please. I don't want another pair of trousers ruined.'

Dan said nothing at first, which immediately raised my suspicions. When I stopped him and bent down so we were at eye level, his voice was a whisper. 'Not parkour. Didn't fall. A boy threw me to the ground.'

'Someone in your class?'

'No, a year above. Someone called Dale. Him. Look.'

He pointed ahead. I knew before I'd looked, really. Joan's kid.

'What was it over?' I asked. 'What did you do?'

'Nothing. I was playing. He came over. He said he'll break my legs today. Not supposed to come into our section of the yard, but he just came over. Should I fight him? Dad says that's the best way to beat bullies.'

'No fighting. If you get picked on, you do what you just did. Tell your parents. Or the teachers. The adults will sort it out.'

'By fighting?'

'No, Dan. By talking. I'll talk the problem out of existence and that boy won't pick on you again. Okay?'

'Okay.'

After the kids had been dropped off, I paused and

pretended to take a phone call so that Joan could get ahead. She was, again, in a group at the corner shop when I exited the school grounds. She watched me close the distance. At one point the whole group looked my way and laughed, so Joan had obviously said something unsweet about me.

I headed towards the shop. At the door, watched by all, I waved my purse at Joan and entered the building. She got the message and pushed through the door seconds later.

I moved along the centre aisle, to the office supplies alcove, where I plucked something off a hook. I gave Joan my back and continued to even when she spoke from right behind me.

'It's hot in here. I'm just *burning* up. I might need cash for a few thousand ice creams.'

'My boy can't go on holiday with broken legs.'

Joan laughed. 'No clue what you're talking about. Maybe I can help with that problem. Hey, face me so I–'

It was the last order of hers I'd ever obey. In a single motion, I turned and jabbed the compass under her chin, hard enough for both miniature spikes to sink a couple of millimetres into the skin. Joan yelped and tried to yank her head back. My other hand, fisted in her hair, negated that.

'How dare I?' I said. 'Don't I know who you are? Aren't I aware that you're surrounded by bloodthirsty lunatics who'll do whatever you ask? I mean, I've seen that with my own eyes, so I must be stupid. Risking my health, my kid's, my husband's, the house, the car, everything? That's right, isn't it?'

Scared, in pain, locked tight, Joan said nothing. I pulled her closer. 'This is what you do the next time you plan something against me. First, call those bloodthirsty lunatics. Tell one that you need him to get a fire extinguisher and set up camp outside your house, twenty-four seven. Order another one to stick by your side every single time you go out, anywhere, no matter how big a group you're in. Get a third. His job is to stick next to your kid, all day long. I just paid three psychos including you to do something bad. I can do it again. Understand?'

I loosened the fist in her hair slightly. Just so she could nod, which she did.

'I'm going on holiday and I need everything to be okay, and it better stay that way. If you do anything that costs me this holiday, I swear I'll put this thing in both your eyes right outside the school gates in front of a hundred kids.'

I let her go. I dropped my arms, which gave her the chance to strike back. I needed to know if the threat had worked. A good sign was the way Joan backed off and then scarpered. It didn't mean she wouldn't plot bloody retribution, but I was free to leave.

I went to the counter, where I showed the shopkeeper the compass. 'I broke the packaging. It's only fair to buy this now.'

Outside the shop, Joan and her crew were some distance away. Nobody looked back. I figured she was too embarrassed to tell the tale.

———

The travel agency emailed me around 11am, so at lunchtime I left work and paid a visit. They had found exactly what I needed. All told: £1,835. I paid, returned to work, and found Alan still in his office.

'I need next week off.'

'And I need a full-body massage from Katy Perry. Welcome to the shit-out-of-luck club.'

'Tell Perry your sister's just got terminal cancer and maybe you'll get that massage. Meanwhile, cut being a tosser, Alan.'

'Okay, look, sorry about your sister. If you need to see her, can't it be in the evenings or–'

'I'm not coming in next week. You can put the holiday in

last minute or I'll take it as authorised unpaid leave. But if you try to put me down as absent, I'll tell your wife you've been shagging Alice.'

Alan kicked his desk somewhere out of sight. 'And you would. Because you're losing your damn mind. What's wrong with you the last few weeks?'

'I'll be off from Monday. One week. Thanks.'

Next to learn of my short-notice jaunt was school. With Dan waiting out of earshot, I gave his teacher, Mrs Cross, the same bullshit about my sister. Maud's phone number was on their files and some of the teachers knew her because she sometimes picked up Dan, but I doubted they were on condolence-call terms. Mrs Cross said she would pass the news to the head teacher and I should expect a call.

'Do you think there's a chance Dan could still attend the play?'

I'd forgotten all about Dan's play. The teachers had made the odd mention and I'd seen the posters, but Dan hadn't brought it up in weeks. He was a little embarrassed about having his parents there and my plan had been to turn up in secret. The show was next Tuesday. No chance. 'I'm sorry, no. I plan to take my sister and family away for that week.'

'Oh. Okay. A shame since he rehearsed so hard. Anyway, I'll get Mr Wade to call you in a little while.'

I told Dan all about the upcoming trip on the way back to the car. He bounced with excitement. 'We're going to JFK, we're going to JFK!'

I told him to keep his voice down. When we got in the car, Dan suddenly lost his giddiness. 'Aw, my play. Tuesday.'

'I know. But there will be other plays.'

'I know. I wanted this. Bad timing.'

'But we'll be in Dallas, Dan. You'll stand right on the corner where JFK was shot. This is the only chance you'll ever get to go to Dallas. But we don't have to go. You can always look at Dallas in books and on the internet.'

'No, we're going.'

'For deffo?'

The smile returned in spades. And the bouncing. 'We're going to JFK, we're going to JFK.'

CHAPTER THIRTY-EIGHT

'Monday? As in four days from now? What have you been smoking?'

Ted had just walked into the kitchen, Dan with him. His son had raced to the front door when Ted got home from work, eager to tell him all about their upcoming holiday.

'Spur of the moment,' I said. 'You've told me before that you like the spontaneous.'

'I meant the cinema or... you know what. Not flying across the ocean. They can't do this to us.'

'They didn't. The only holiday choices we had were Barcelona or Paris. I don't care about those places. Someone at another club-winning store chose Dallas but had to back out. They offered it to me. I mean, what were the odds? Dan's mad on Dallas and we suddenly get a chance to go.'

Ted sat at the table and stole a piece of Dan's dinner. 'It's too quick. I can't get time off work.'

'Bet you could. Just lie. Family emergency.'

'What? I'd get found out. Is this all-inclusive?'

'No, we have to buy our own food. Flights and hotel. It's just three days. Deathbed memories, Ted. Something else you said you wanted.'

'I meant seeing a volcano erupt or flying to space. Or a threesome.'

'What's a threesome?' Dan asked.

'Hasn't Dan got a play on Tuesday?'

I stroked Dan's hair while he ate. 'He knows this is a once-in-a-lifetime thing.'

Dan nodded. Ted sat back and sighed. 'Dan's never been on a plane. Can he sit there for so long?'

'He'll have his phone and books. He's already said he'll be fine. I know he will be.'

Ted thought some more, but I knew this was a sign he'd soon be won over.

An hour later, while in the bath, he called me to him. He lay in the water, eyes on the ceiling, and said, 'I've never had sex abroad.'

'Or outdoors. But if you say that to me this time next week, you'll be a dirty liar.'

'Sold,' he said, and we high-fived each other.

There was one more person to tell: Maud, my sister. Like Ted, she was surprised by the short notice, but also enthused. 'I think this will be so good for you. You've only ever been overseas that one time. What was that, eight years ago? You need to de-stress. I'm so jealous. My Donald never wants to go anywhere.'

The boys spent the remainder of the evening looking at Dallas travel guides and it was beautiful to see them so eager for the holiday. An hour after Dan went to bed, though, Ted's mood changed. Earlier he'd sent a text message – to a work colleague, he'd claimed – and now got a reply. It put a painful look on his face.

'What's wrong?' I asked.

He seemed to snap out of a trance and put the phone away.

'Nothing. Work thing. Delivery problem. I just need to call the boss.'

I'd seen him call his boss many times – and by 'seen' I meant he'd made those calls right in front of me. This time he went out into the dark backyard and shut the door behind him. I saw him pacing as he spoke into the phone. Afterwards, he was distant and a little snappy.

Good. I knew he'd just talked to his bitch about why she'd dumped him by text, and it hadn't gone well. So, it was over between them. We could get back to being a tight family. And the Dallas mission could go ahead.

Ted retired to the bedroom soon afterwards to watch TV. I went up a little later and as I undressed, I noticed blood spotting in my underwear. I felt a chill. It could be a prelude to my period, which would be great news.

But it could also be implantation bleeding, which meant a fertilised egg had attached to my uterus. If so, it was far too early for Ted's sperm to have fertilised the egg. I rushed into the bathroom, sat on the toilet, and tried to calm my erratic breathing.

It had been well over two weeks since my rape and a pregnancy test should have been able to detect hCG by now. Yesterday's had been negative, but today I had been worried about taking one. I tried to convince myself that late at night wasn't the optimum time, but who was I attempting to fool? I could have performed the test earlier, yet hadn't. I'd almost put off yesterday's. It was clear why.

Early on, those negatives results had been soothing. But as the days passed and test accuracy increased, I had become more and more scared of the outcome. Now, as I sat on the toilet in the dead of night, that fear peaked. Ignorance was comfort. No more peeing on a cheap superstore piece of kit.

I would pay for a superior pregnancy test and know once

and for all, but Dallas came first. It was a mission whose results meant far more to me.

———

After an hour on the tills at work, my face was long enough for customers to remark about it. I ignored most comments, but following one man's heard-a-million-times wisecrack, 'Cheer up, it might never happen', I froze with a tin of his corned beef in my hand. Then I dropped it onto the barcode scanner.

'Just a joke, love, take it easy.'

I must have looked like a deflating doll as I let my head sink forward. From the other till, Carla called out, 'Babes, you okay?'

Everyone in my queue was staring. It became both queues when I erupted into laughter. When I stood up and ran, Carla called out for till cover for me.

In the staffroom toilet, I shoved a hand down my trousers and felt the hot wetness. On my fingers: blood.

On my face: tears of happiness.

CHAPTER THIRTY-NINE

When Ted came home that evening, he had a face of thunder. As soon as I saw it, I said, 'Dan, go put your headphones on in your room.'

Dan left the living room without question. Ted threw down his coat and flopped into the armchair. I turned the TV off.

'I just checked my emails,' Ted said. 'The bank. Want to have a guess?'

I knew he knew, so lies were no good. 'Dan's child saver account.'

'The money we're not allowed to touch. The money for when Dan turns eighteen. Yeah, that. Suddenly short by two thousand pounds, Lisa. Why do I suddenly suspect there was no free holiday.'

I also knew I wouldn't be able to swing Ted round. My best option, although a little sinful, was to make him feel guilty. 'You're right, I used it to buy a holiday for Dan. He needs it, but we can't afford one. I can replace the money.'

'You told me—'

'That it wasn't to be touched. I know. That was then.

Things are different now. I've been distant from Dan, and this is to say sorry.'

'Dallas? Two grand on a bloody trip to nowhere?'

'It's not nowhere, it's a place he wants to go. Ask him. There's nowhere else on earth he wants to go. This will make his whole year. And mine, and yours. We've all been through the wringer recently. I don't want to fight you on this. You work and socialise a lot and you haven't seen what I see in Dan. He's not happy. I want this for him. I don't see why he has to suffer now so he can be happy at eighteen. I'm doing this for my son. End of argument.'

He stood up. 'No, it's not the end. A free holiday I could take. Get a refund. We can make Dan happy in other ways. We're low on money and we could do a lot with two grand, if you insist on spending it. Cancel the holiday.'

I stood too. We faced each other like gunslingers. 'No. Okay? No. We all need to get away, Dan especially. It'll do you good, too, Ted. It'll stop you moping about now you've been dumped by that bitch.'

'What? Piss off.'

He grabbed his coat and started to walk away. I got to him as he opened the front door, and I kicked it shut. 'Don't lie to me again, Ted.'

He said nothing and returned to the living room. He threw down his coat one more time and stood by the window, staring out.

'No more lies, Ted. You were sleeping with some other woman. I know she just ended it. I told her to.'

He didn't look round at me, but I saw his body tense.

'Yes, I confronted her. Right there at her house. I ended it for you. And why? Because I want to give this another chance. Do you hear what I'm saying? Another chance.'

He looked at me. He seemed shocked, and of course, this wasn't playing out how he'd expected.

'I'm going to move on from it, Ted, and so are you. You had some fun, had your little break, and now it's back to work. We're going to work to make this marriage awesome again. We're going to do that for Dan, because he needs two parents. If we're lucky, we get a nice little bonus of actually falling in love again. It all starts now, clean slate. And it begins with this holiday. De-stress, clear the cobwebs, watch our boy have a blast. If that sounds good, come here.'

I held out my arms. He seemed suspicious at first, like a rescued beaten puppy.

'Come on,' I prompted him. He came with a smile: no longer a smacked pet, but more like a criminal who'd just had all charges dropped. He crushed me in his arms. And I hugged that cheating bastard right back.

Ted had spotted the email about Dan's account before he'd had a chance to try to book holiday time, and afterwards had had no intention of making the Dallas trip. Having left it so late, he was unable to take paid leave. However, he'd managed to swap some shifts with a colleague, and we were good to go.

On Saturday, Dan and I packed our gear. We only needed enough for three days, but the task took a good portion of the day because Dan found it hard to decide what to leave behind.

On Sunday, he loaded Google Earth to map the journeys he had planned for us once in Dallas. After that, he used 'street view' to walk the routes real-time. I left him to it and gave the house a real good clean, so we wouldn't be returning to a mess. I was just burning impatient energy though. By 11pm, all three Holtens were in bed.

I was the last to sleep and I lay in bed for what seemed like hours. There was no urge to get up and check locks or look out windows, though, and all creaks and groans of the house settling failed to convince me there was an intruder inside. My impending mission had given me a new confidence. Besides, Sunshine hadn't come at me since the rape and it was easier now to believe he was somewhere far from here.

It wasn't wise to disrupt Dan's hours, so I had booked a flight for 10am on Monday morning from Birmingham International Airport, with a single two-hour stop in Frankfurt before arriving at Dallas/Fort Worth International Airport. We made it from house to plane without a single hitch.

The flight touched down at what was midnight on Tuesday – back home. In Dallas it was just after 6pm on Monday. This was just the coolest thing to Dan, who thought planes were time machines. Ted tried to be funny with faux moaning: 'I hate Monday mornings, and now I've done two in one day.' Delays getting through customs and finding a taxi didn't help his mood.

Our hotel, the Tiara Plaza on Elm Street, was fifteen miles west-south-west in downtown Dallas. I used my own phone satnav to watch the journey unfold. Three miles out from the hotel, there was a turn-off at US Route 77 and onto Wycliff Avenue. It wasn't part of our route to the hotel, but I eagerly waited for the taxi to pass it.

As the taxi passed the turn, I stared out of the window. Because just half a mile up Wycliff Avenue was the junction where it met Irving Boulevard. From that junction, I would be able to see Reliable Security, just a hundred or so metres away. I'd shrunken the whole world to one point, and now I was just minutes away. It was hard to sit there as the taxi drove past, away. But I would be back.

We checked into the hotel, and that was when the boys' moods deflated. The room was on the second floor and the view from the windows was all busy roads and tower blocks. Highly frustrating for Dan because Dealey Plaza was just half a mile away. The Human Rights Museum and World Aquarium were even closer. Yet he couldn't see them.

He begged to go out, but it was now 8pm and far too late. He then pleaded for a top-floor room, but I again had to give him bad news. Ted was just unhappy that we'd spent so long travelling and still had nothing to do.

'Two grand to be stuck in a hotel room. Wow.'

The time difference between here and home meant everyone had been awake for much longer than normal. Dan and Ted soon fell asleep. I, too, was tired, but only in body. My mind was vibrant. I stood at the window, staring out. By chance it faced north-west and this made me wish, like Dan, that we'd booked a top-floor room. Because just two miles in that direction lay Reliable Security.

I knew from Sunshine's travelling habits that he was far, far away until the end of March. Hell, he could even be in my home right now, playing with my underwear or stroking pictures of me. But I imagined he wasn't. I pictured myself turning up at Reliable as the staff filed out. I approached him and…

I'd played out this scene in my head many times, in various locations, and it always hit a dead zone in the same spot. I stand before Sunshine, he with a look of recognition and horror on his face, but before a word is spoken by either of us, the vision freezes and fades to black. I knew what it meant: I had no idea what I would do when finally attacker was confronted by victim.

But that meeting would happen one day. I knew it.

CHAPTER FORTY

'Dallas was the anti-Kennedy base in the early sixties,' Dan said. 'Did you know the people living here didn't want the book depository to be a shrine? They thought it tainted Dallas. Did you know that, Dad?'

'I know it's bleeding cold out here,' was Ted's reply.

It was midday on Tuesday and we'd been out for two hours, and for the duration I'd watched the same routine: Dan would try to surprise us with facts about the Kennedy assassination, while Ted moaned about everything.

Dan was a little deflated by our arrival at Dealey Plaza. He didn't like how the area was 'just a street', with very little to advertise that long-ago event. He didn't like that the Texas School Book Depository was now the Dallas County Administration Building. He didn't like how locals just went about their business, as if they should still be in awe of what happened almost sixty years prior.

However, his mind was soon blown by our visit to the Sixth Floor Museum and a walking tour. Ted, however, wasn't impressed. He hated the queue to see the spot from which Lee Harvey Oswald fired bullets at JFK's motorcade. He moaned about the crowds clogging up the Grassy Knoll on Elm Street. When I told him to quit sulking because this was what we'd come for, he said, 'Not me. We're on the tip of Tornado Alley. I came to see cows flying around in the air.'

The high numbers of tourists soon wore on Dan and we left the area. After food at a McDonald's, Dan felt ready to face people again and we hit the Dallas World Aquarium.

Dan loved the animals, especially the snakes, but overall he didn't like the crowds and the slow pace because too many people were blocking small passageways in order to take selfies. Ted moaned that it was more like a jungle than an aquarium and hated the big queue at the café. Here, as earlier in Dealey Plaza, I felt little emotion beyond impatience. I was not here for JFK memorabilia or to see tornados ripping away houses.

By 3.30pm, the boys were worn out and we headed back to our room before rush hour got too bad. The hotel had supplied a Dallas version of Monopoly, which I played with Dan on his foldaway bed under the window, while Ted headed out to fetch a hire car. He even moaned that he couldn't get one with a manual gearbox.

'It's got a handbrake, although God knows why. The whole place is flat as a pancake.'

Despite his moaning, Ted was eager to try Texan beers and steaks, so we agreed to visit a restaurant. We chose 7pm, which gave us over two hours to wait. I said I'd go scout local ones so I could try out the hire car.

I was out the door within minutes. I was not going to find an eatery though. I was going to Reliable Security.

Raymond Mirasol was a handsome forty-two-year-old, born in Mexico. He worked full-time at Reliable Security and was divorced with two daughters. In his spare time he played the sport of axe throwing and was ranked in the top twenty in the world, having come fifth in the World Championship last December.

According to his Facebook posts, he was in the quarter-final of the Queen of the Hearts Club Classic and was the current 'killshot' leader with ninety-three per cent. During tournaments, Mirasol liked to practise for a couple of hours every day after work.

Next door to Reliable Security was a credit union with parking spaces for customers. It was here I waited for the daytime shift at Reliable to end. I applied make-up I'd bought that afternoon. When the staff filed out of the warehouse, I didn't bother trying to locate Mirasol. I just watched his motorbike.

There were three axe-throwing establishments in Dallas and I didn't know which one Mirasol would visit. The closest was Awful Axe Throwing, about five miles east of Reliable, and it was indeed this establishment I followed his bike to. There was diagonal parking outside and a spare spot right next to his bike. A sign out front said the walk-in price was twenty-six dollars.

The place was quite busy and popular with families. The music was thumping. There was a bar and a food counter and a ball pit for kids too small for lobbing axes. The throwing lanes were split by chain-link fencing and each had two targets painted on the wooden back wall. The floors of the lanes were littered with wood chips from the targets and even the chopped-up wooden ceiling.

As I joined the queue to pay, I scanned the lanes and found Mirasol, already lobbing axes. Luckily, the lane next to his was free and I managed to secure it.

Once in my lane, I lobbed my first axe. It hit the target, but handle-first. I yelped when it bounced back and landed near my feet. Eight feet away, Mirasol smiled at me. Then he stuck an axe close to his bullseye.

'How do you do that so well?' I said, approaching the fence.

His eyes ran me up and down. I'd suffered in skinny jeans and a tight blouse all day because I knew Mirasol liked such a look on women. 'Practice. I'm a tournament player. I came third in the World Championship last year.'

I pretended to be impressed. 'Wow. Was that on TV?'

'It sure was. Axe throwing is the easiest way to get on ESPN. You're Irish, right? UK?'

I gave a giggle. 'English. Any chance you could help a girl out with her technique? I'll buy you a drink. Or do you need a clear head?'

'I'd say half the guys who do this sport threw their first few hundred axes after a beer or two. Come on over.'

I moved into his lane and we swapped names. Of course, I already knew his. A trawl through Facebook posts containing the words Reliable Security had led me to a woman who'd posted a photograph from a Christmas party at the firm. I searched through her posts and friends. Then their friends and posts. Rinse and repeat.

After a lengthy slog, I had fifty-one names of males working at the security firm. Every face got intense scrutiny, but there was no eureka moment. And none of their profiles mentioned geocaching.

Mirasol had grabbed my attention though. He posted a lot about his axe throwing and about his love of women. When I learned that he was currently practising his sport every night, a plan formed: flirt, chat, and extract information.

It took no time at all. He watched me throw an axe, then decided to get hands-on with his guidance. He stood right behind me, our bodies touching, and physically altered my stance. I pretended to like it. 'So what else do you like to do on nights off?' he asked.

'I like geocaching. You ever heard of it?'

'Oh, the treasure-hunting thing? We've got a guy at work into that. Okay, when you throw, follow it through, like you're throwing a dart.'

He stepped away so I could lob the axe. I was so tense with anticipation that I kept hold of the weapon and almost arced it into my knee. Mirasol laughed. I raised the axe again. 'What guy at work? I might know of him.'

'The night-shift janitor. Guy called Steve Albany.'

The axe dropped from my hand, bounced off my shoulder and thunked on the ground.

CHAPTER FORTY-ONE

S teve Albany was forty-nine years old and a bit of a joke amongst the staff. Only one other person had been at Reliable for over twenty years, and that guy had risen through the ranks from janitor to shift boss. But Albany had started as a janitor on nights, still worked nights and hadn't had a single promotion.

Despite this, Albany loved the company and was always trying to help it succeed, even going so far as to advertise key safes online and sometimes man a Saturday market stall selling them. The brass said thanks, but there ended their appreciation.

He had a wife and a grown daughter, but none of his colleagues had ever met either because he never attended work parties. He was very quiet, shy, never liked to talk about himself. He didn't have any social media accounts as far as anyone knew. People only knew about his geocaching hobby because he liked to slink off and do it during lunch breaks.

'I'd like to meet him,' I said. 'I've got a few more days here.'

'Am I not good enough for you?'

I laughed. 'Of course you are. But I love any excuse to chat to a fellow treasure hunter.'

'You might have a pretty face, but also bad timing. The guy's away on holiday.'

'Shame. Where?'

'He goes to his uncle's farm. Only place he ever goes, I think. He looks after the place. Oklahoma. Okay, let's change that stance a little.'

Bingo. Nine of Sunshine's twenty-seven hides were in Tulsa, Oklahoma. I had to hide my growing excitement. 'When will he be back?'

'You got a hankering for sure. Unfortunately, you're out of luck.'

I was. Because every year, religiously, Albany took three months off to go work on the farm, all unpaid. January, Feb, March.

Mirasol didn't have a full address, but he knew Albany lived in north-west Dallas. I would get no more, needed no more, so told Mirasol I had to use the toilet and skipped out of there. It was dark out, but the significance of this didn't hit me until I had driven and parked round the corner and turned on my phone.

I was shocked to see it was 7.35pm. I'd been gone from the hotel for way over two hours, and of course, I had missed calls and a message from Ted. I sent a return text claiming I'd broken down and would be back soon.

I accessed Spokeo, a people-search website, and found a pair of Albanys living on a street off something called Loop 12, a short way past the western end of Bachman Lake. It was seven miles north-west and only two miles from my hotel. I considered dropping by to explain to Ted, but it was too risky in case he prevented me from going out again.

Ted called as I was driving west, which interrupted the

satnav. Killing the call would upset him more, so I waited for him to hang up. It happened again a few minutes later. When I reached Albany's street, I turned off the phone.

Commercial establishments soon gave way to traditional single-family homes. I slowed down as I approached Albany's and parked just before, on the other side of the road. It was closing on 8pm and the sun had set two hours ago. There was no car in the driveway and the windows were dark. It appeared that no one was home.

I'd read that Northwest Dallas was the most crime-ridden part of the city, and I'd expected this street to be run-down. But it wasn't. The homes were worth roughly $495,000 and the median income was $80k. I didn't doubt that a lowly night janitor could afford such a house, but I was puzzled by Albany's ability to jet around the world for three months every year. It made me think his wife could be the main breadwinner.

I'd figured Albany had been lying to her, claiming he was in Oklahoma while he zipped around the world, but seeing the dark house made me reassess. Was she with him overseas right now? Just how much did she know about his secret life? Much as I had left Ted behind tonight, did Albany dump his wife in hotels while he went geocaching and raping?

Or did she know everything and accept it all in the name of warped love? For all I knew, she could endorse or even partake in his rapes – the true crime annals were loaded with bizarre criminal couples.

Both scenarios seemed possible and impossible at the same time. I had shrunken the world to a city and now a single house, and the truth, the end to the nightmare, lay just feet away. No more guesswork, and no more delay. I walked over and knocked on the door.

No answer. There was an attached garage with a door cut into it, which I tried and found unlocked. I was so pumped with adrenaline that I entered the garage without even a glance back to see if the coast was clear. It wouldn't have mattered anyway, even if a police car had been cruising past. I hadn't come all this way to stop now. I wasn't going back home to continue a life of fear and paranoia.

The interior door to the house was locked, but it was thin wood with a simple bolt lock that easily broke under the impact of my good shoulder. I moved quickly through the dark. Simple living room. Simple kitchen. If Albany had proof of his crimes in this house, it wouldn't be on show for visitors or burglars. I wanted a computer, or a safe, or the attic, so I hit the stairs. I was not scared. Albany was time zones away.

All the top-floor doors were shut. I opened the one I figured led to the main bedroom. And froze. There was a shape standing against the far wall. Moonlight spearing through the window illuminated someone in a dressing gown. With a black gun in their hand.

CHAPTER FORTY-TWO

Seeing another female standing before her, and not a hooded thug, the woman with the gun swapped her fear for puzzlement.

Before she could ask the question, I answered it. I didn't fear the gun, even though it was the first I'd ever seen live. 'I'm one of the women your husband has been raping across the world over the last two decades.'

Another change in her face, but I did not see the disbelief or anger that I expected. Instead, she looked like someone who'd suddenly found herself on the gallows – but had long been expecting it.

The woman said nothing. The gun lowered. And, right then, the last wisps of doubt vanished. I was in the home of the man who had raped and tried to murder me.

'So you know?' I said. 'You know your husband is a monster.'

'No, I don't know anything,' she spat, and the gun raised again. But her anger was a flash, and as it subsided, the weapon sank in time. 'I certainly don't know you. How did you find this house?'

'But you know something, that's obvious.'

She paused. 'I know my husband has been lying to me.'

'For years.'

'Maybe. I don't know you and I don't know what happened between you, and I don't want to. Maybe he raped you and maybe it was consensual, just like with all the others.'

I started to object, but she ordered me to shut up and the gun came up again, fast. Like before, it instantly began to lower. This time I let a few seconds pass in silence, until the gun was aimed fully at the carpet.

'He goes to his uncle's property,' I said. 'Every year. January to March. Like clockwork.'

'Yes.'

'And you never go with him. But you know he doesn't stay there during those months. You know he jets off around the world.'

'I never go anywhere. But... I saw his passport one time. All those places. I never knew. So, yes, I know he lies. I confronted him and he said he was geocaching. Him and his uncle. His uncle got him into it after he retired. I believed him. I mean, I know he likes geocaching, so why would I doubt this? He... he won't be at his uncle's now, will he?'

I felt a stab of worry. 'Are you telling me you don't know where he is?'

The gun jerked up. 'You think I'm lying? You think I need to, with this gun and the police just a phone call away? I don't know anything, okay?' The gun again began its sink towards her knee. 'You're British. Is... is that where he went?'

'He was there a few weeks ago, when he... came across me. Will he go back to Oklahoma before he comes home? Is there a chance he'll go there soon?'

The woman slowly moved to her right, towards the wall, where she flicked a switch to turn on the bedroom light. We both squinted against the brightness. She took a long look at me, and I her. She was close to sixty, with short, dyed-brown hair and age spots on her jawline and cheeks.

'You've been talking to his work,' she said. 'They don't know about Oklahoma. He pretends his uncle still owns a farm there. Hasn't done for over twenty years.'

'I don't understand. Is there no uncle? So what... I mean why...?' My head started to spin.

'The farm was sold. This was in 2001. His uncle, Johan, he bought a big retirement mansion out in Monaco. That's where Steve goes. Johan retired because he couldn't work the farm anymore. He didn't need to because he inherited a lot of money. The farm was just a pet project. So, when he was too infirm to do it anymore, he moved away. But he was too ill to take care of the mansion and the grounds, and so that's what Steve does for him. He flies out to fix and tidy, stocking the cupboards and doing the gardening, that sort of thing. And they do the geocaching thing together. That's Johan's new hobby.'

She gave a wry laugh. 'Listen to me, pretending I know a damn thing about any of this. I've never been out there, so maybe there's no mansion at all. I mean, Steve has been lying to me all these years. So I don't know anything. Except that he flies around the world, meeting these women.'

'Attacking,' I said. 'He's not having affairs or one-night stands. He's going out and raping women, then hopping on planes to escape.'

I expected the gun to jump towards me again. It remained pointing at the floor. 'What did he do to you?'

Not a question I was going to answer. 'I don't understand. How could you not know he was flying around the world? Why did it take your finding his passport to know this? Are you not in contact with him when he goes away? For three months?'

'No. That's a rule. I have him for nine months. When he goes to Monaco, that's it. I don't call him, he doesn't call me. I don't ask about his time away when he comes back, and he doesn't offer any information. You think that's bizarre. Too bizarre to be true, maybe.'

It was not a question. She was right. 'I think you're his wife and you're loyal to him. I think some strange woman just came in here with a wild claim and you've got no reason to believe me over him, even though he lies about being at his uncle's place for three months.'

'That's right. But what I'm telling you is no lie to protect him. If you don't believe that, let's see how you feel about this. I don't have an address in Monaco. Twenty years his uncle has lived there, and I haven't got a clue where.'

Something about her tone was off. I got the feeling she was not bluffing, but... leading me somewhere... that she had something to prove...

And then I knew. 'What did he do to you?'

Her answer was instant. 'Tried to strangle me. Years ago. I saw something in him that night. And afterwards, he was different. Changed.'

She explained that way back in 2001, just after his uncle moved to Monaco, Steve once got rough during sex. She complained and he stopped, but she knew he was upset. The next time it happened, some months later, she decided to let him run with it. She wasn't sure why, but it was a big mistake.

She was face down, he lying on her back, and he put an arm across her throat, his other in her hair, pushing down on the back of her head. I could picture it. I could almost remember the feel of that same forearm across my own throat.

'After that night, he never tried again. I don't mean rough sex, I mean sex itself. He never again came onto me. We haven't slept together since that night, over twenty years ago. I got over what happened, I really did. I even told him that. But it changed nothing.'

The gun jerked up halfway towards me and immediately fell, even though she continued to look at the bed. It was as if the muscles in her arm were attached to her frustration and anger.

'Now I know why,' she continued. 'He's been having other women. Forcing them. Raping them. Because that night with me, something changed in him. Or something hidden came out. Out forever. Did he stop sleeping with me because he could only get aroused by rape? Or did he not trust himself to not hurt me?'

I didn't know. I didn't really care. I wasn't here to ease this woman's torment. 'Is there a way for you to contact him? To bring him home?'

'No. That's the way it is with us. I just wait. I always just wait. So I can't help you. I'm not sure I want to help you put him away for life. Are you going to call the police?'

'I don't know,' I said, and it wasn't a lie. 'I don't want to... to expose myself. All I know is I want to stand in front of him and look him in the eyes. After that, I just don't know.'

She looked up at me. 'Well, I can't help you with that. I wish you hadn't come here. You've ruined my life. So you have to leave now. There's nothing else I can do for you.'

'Yes there is. I need to see his face. I want a photograph of him.'

It was close to 10pm when I got back to the hotel. Dan was asleep. Ted was far from it. As soon as the door opened, he was there, blocking entry. I stepped back and he came out. He stormed to the end of the corridor and through the door into the stairwell. I followed, knowing we were about to have an argument he didn't want Dan or the other guests to hear.

'No more, okay?' he said. His voice was calm, but there was rage on his face.

'I'm sorry, the car broke–'

'Stop. I don't believe you. I can't believe anything you say now. I want action, not words. You need to get help. You're going to get it as soon as we are home. You're messing up this family. Are you on drugs?'

'What?'

'Drugs, Lisa. Like way back. You messed up back then and this is no different. Is it a relapse? Or a new-found way to kill boredom? What?'

'It was a man,' I said before I could really stop myself.

'What? You went to see a man? What are you talking about?'

I took a breath. In for a penny, as Joan would have said. 'In the woods that night. It wasn't a girl who robbed me. I got attacked by a man.'

Ted took a few seconds to digest this. I watched him and assessed my next move. Ted would, of course, ask if I was touched inappropriately. How much should I admit? Should I continue to claim the attack had been just a mugging, but a little more violent? Take a further step and claim there was a ghost of a sexual assault attempt? Or cut the duplicity and use that terrible word: rape?

'Stop the damn bullshit, Lisa. You're killing this family.'

I was knocked for six. As Ted tried to leave, I stepped into his path. 'I'm trying to admit the truth here.'

'I don't want to hear it.'

He tried to get past; I pushed him back. 'I'm trying to find him. Before he hurts us. He's stalking me. He took my ring.'

He gave a slow shake of the head. Words couldn't have better conveyed the absolute doubt and disgust he felt. 'Stalking? Jesus, Lisa. I actually hope you're still lying. This whole thing is a lot scarier than I thought if you actually believe that.'

I grabbed his shoulders. 'I'm telling you the truth, Ted. That's why we're here. I came to Dallas because he's here. I'm trying to find him. It's the only way to stop him before he kills me. Maybe all of us.'

Ted pushed my hands away. 'You've got PTSD or something. From all that drug-taking you did. Finally it's all catching up on you. Or the drugs you're on now. Please, this has to stop. We have to get you that help.'

Again he tried to get past, and again I stopped him. But this time he pushed me aside. That changed everything. I had bared my soul, admitted my darkest secret, and he'd shot me down. I saw red. My left hand lashed out and snapped over his throat. I shoved him against the wall, teeth bared.

'Listen to me, you wanker. I'm trying to save your life, and you take the piss? Maybe I shouldn't even fucking bother.'

Ted's hands latched onto mine, trying to prise it away. He was taller, beefier, but I had fury power.

'I know who the bastard is. I'm going to stop him, and now that you know, you're either going to help or you're going to get out of my damn way, okay?'

He made a gurgling sound and his nails dug into the back of my hand. It was in that moment I realised I was, indeed, out of control. I relaxed my grip. Ted slapped my hand away and rushed for the door, out, away.

CHAPTER FORTY-THREE

I'd bought a last-minute flight to Dallas and given myself three nights to find Sunshine. For the return journey, I'd managed to find premium economy open-ended tickets. I wanted no fixed return date for one of two reasons. The first: in case I was close to finding my attacker when the journey home was due. The second: leaving if I completed my mission quickly.

Luckily the latter applied, which gave me no cause for argument when Ted, once we were back in the hotel room, announced that he wanted to go home. While Ted shifted Dan into our bed, without waking him, I made some phone calls and got lucky: a flight from Dallas Love Field Airport at 10.28am tomorrow.

Including a short layover in Atlanta, the flight was over thirteen and a half hours, but the time zone difference would see us touch down at Manchester Airport at 6.10am on Thursday.

That Tuesday evening, Ted slept in Dan's bed. I lay next to our son and read about someone called CometBoy. It gave me goosebumps. The next morning was taken up by packing and a white lie to Dan – we told him various tourist attractions he still wished to see were closed due to city-wide electrical problems –

which meant Ted and I were able to avoid speaking to each other. Dan didn't seem to notice.

Once on the plane, we put Dan between us. Whenever we did have to talk, it was all short sentences and no eye contact.

Because of emotional turmoil and the rush to get out of Dallas, none of us realised an error had been made until we were literally leaving the plane. It was Dan who pointed out that we'd left my car in Doncaster. He was the only one who laughed.

Doncaster was over east and home sat in the middle, so Ted and Dan got dropped off with the luggage and I took the taxi onward. I needed the thinking time. En route, I called school and work to say Dan and I would be back to business tomorrow.

Once in my own car, I opened my phone and accessed its most recent photos. I had taken pictures of pictures inside Steve Albany's house.

There had been many photographs of the man, but I'd settled on two. One was a wedding photo, in which the monster was with his wife and friends and held a toddler in one arm. He wore a tailored suit and gave a beaming smile. In it he was chubby and brown-haired with a smooth face, but his wife had assured me that the passage of three decades had changed him considerably.

I'd chosen it in part for exactly this misrepresentation. The photo portrayed a happy time, but today it was a sham. The Albany pictured was a disguise to mask the blackness inside him. To me, that photo was evidence that he was a chameleonic beast among us.

Of course, I wanted to know the man's true appearance, so the second photograph was just a couple of years old. There was no social media profile for the man; this was all I had.

Posing by a new shed he'd built in their backyard, Albany wore long shorts and a T-shirt advertising the Texas State Fair, which he'd attended every year in September and October since he was twelve. He looked closer to forty than sixty-one. I hated to admit it, but he was also quite handsome.

I had stared at this picture many times since acquiring it. Now, I felt nothing but hate. When I had first laid eyes on it, I'd felt that buzz, the eureka moment, and then joy. I'd found him, I was absolute on that.

Steven William Albany, born 12/07/60 in Junius Heights, Dallas, was the man who had caused me interminable suffering, and I was determined to return the favour.

Dan needed to tell someone all about his adventures, so I took him to visit my sister at her Meadowhall stall that afternoon. In the evening, Ted went to jiu-jitsu – or his bitch, not that I cared anymore – and I left Dan to his own devices while I did some computer research. By 7pm, jet lag knocked him out. I got a blanket for the sofa downstairs.

When Ted came home about nine, he figured my plan and headed upstairs without a word. But I got a text soon after:

Called work, going back in tomorrow.

I replied with:

Same here and Dan school.

I then settled down for the night. But not for sleep. Not yet. I still had work to do. And next on the list: finding a high-class female escort.

At just past midnight, as I was drifting off, I heard a scraping sound outside.

Things were different now. There was a void in my gut where paranoia had once been rooted. The noise was probably a cat. I closed my eyes again.

The next morning, my alarm woke me at seven and I noticed Ted's car was gone. The bedroom was empty. Normally he'd never leave for work so early, so he'd probably slipped out to avoid me. I got Dan up, gave him his phone and breakfast, and pulled down the ladder to the attic.

My mother's jewellery was in a taped-up freezer bag in a dusty corner. I put it, and my engagement ring, into my coat pocket.

Next, a call to Ted. Thankfully it went to voicemail, so I avoided an awkward conversation. 'Ted, I will be viewing flats all day, so you'll have to pick Dan up. Don't try to call me today. Perhaps we'll chat this evening.'

I hung up and turned off my phone, only in part to save the battery. I had a moment of guilt about what I was planning to do. Ted had done nothing wrong, and he didn't deserve my recent treatment of him. I promised myself I'd make it right with him. But not yet. Not until this was over.

I made sure my phone was fully charged when we left the house. We set off half an hour early for school so I could take a detour. Dan was engrossed in his phone so didn't even notice when I pulled up alongside a vehicle in a private residential car park. We were on the move again a few seconds later.

When we pulled up at school, Joan was walking past with her kid. I got out and stared at her. She gave a thumbs up. Even better, her boy, Dale, ran over to Dan. I heard him apologise and ask if they could hang out at playtime, then both boys ran off ahead. I walked towards the school with Joan just ten feet ahead. She never looked back.

A throng was already waiting at the gates. I pushed through to find Dan, who was one of four kids pressed up against the gate to be first inside. I took him aside. 'Your dad is picking you up today.'

'Okay. Good. Whatever. Why can't you?'

I bent to his level and looked into his eyes. 'I have to go away for a few days. I can't tell you where, but I have a very important job to do. I want you to be strong and wait for me and don't worry about me, okay? I love you and can't wait to see you again. Please don't worry. I'll bring you a big present back.'

He seemed fine with this, for now. Time might tell a different story. 'Okay. Why? If I can't know where, then why?'

He had a slight grin, as if he'd found a loophole in my defence. This was information I was happy to impart. 'You probably noticed that Mummy and Daddy haven't been the best of friends recently. Well, I know how to change that. To make everything better. I'm going to a place where I can find peace. When I do, Mummy will be all better afterwards. Better for you and Dad and me. Mummy will be the best mum in the world afterwards.'

The gate started to open and kids began filing through. Dan looked, but then turned back to me. 'You already are,' he said, and hugged me. I didn't let him go until he was the last kid standing.

CHAPTER FORTY-FOUR

As soon as I got to work, Carla had news.

'Alan's phoned in. He won't be in today. Someone slashed two of his car tyres. He's going to do Sunday instead. So you're the boss.'

I feigned shock and got to work. I gathered two old posters I'd found in the stockroom the other day. One was for a discontinued product and said EVERYTHING MUST GO. The other was for a HALF PRICE TODAY sale on another item. I cut them together to make a sign saying EVERYTHING HALF PRICE TODAY and put it on the main window. Some staff questioned this offer, but I told them I'd had orders from head office.

Next, I informed the staff that the card reader software was down. I removed the card scanners from all four tills. We had an old CASH ONLY sign that also went on the window and some smaller ones for each till. The storewide discount worked a treat. A steady influx of customers turned into a torrent. The staff were run off their feet.

At 2pm, the end of my shift, I asked the cashiers to swap

their full tills for fresh ones. Carla, the treasurer, wanted cover on the shop floor so she could bank the money, but I said I'd handle it. The large safe in the cash office was on a time lock and not due to open until 6pm, when we'd normally close and tally up. But the half-price sale had filled the tills, with easily £2,500 between them. A nice haul.

Even though I was watched by a CCTV camera, I dumped the contents of both tills into a canvas cash bag, which then went into my satchel.

Then I slipped out the rear fire exit.

My next stop was a pawn shop a mile from Meadowhall, where I got a tidy price for all my mother's jewellery and my engagement ring. They had new pre-payment phones, so I got one, then drove to Yeadon in West Yorkshire. Once parked, I turned on my main device to check for contact. It was almost 4pm.

I'd expected messages and missed calls from Ted, especially about my plan to find a flat, but there was nothing. I called school to make sure he'd picked up Dan, and he had. Ted was probably intending to have it out with me face to face.

That wouldn't happen.

Dan was home, so I could move on to the next stage in my plan. I destroyed my main phone by taking it apart and dumping the pieces down a drain. Then I visited a post office to exchange most of my cash for euros. I had just over €3,300. Finally, I checked into a Premier Inn.

It killed me to ignore Dan, especially if he was worried, but I couldn't risk contacting him. I already missed Ted too. I kept telling myself I would see them both soon. Real soon. As soon as my mission was over. And when I returned to them, it would be as a new, better woman, wife, and mother.

I settled down for the night, reading all about a novel called *The Fall of Prince Florestan of Monaco*. I set my alarm for 04.30 the next morning. My flight out of the country was at 06.10.

CHAPTER FORTY-FIVE

It was an Air France flight from Leeds/Bradford airport to Nice, in south-western France, with one stop of just under two hours in Amsterdam. Arrival time in Nice was 12.15pm, which would be 11.15am UK time.

The limit for taking undeclared cash out of the UK was £10,000, but smaller amounts could be seized if customs considered it to be proceeds of or intended for criminal enterprise. I was worried about having my money confiscated, but it got through without a second glance. Perhaps that was because my destination was one that could burn through cash in no time: Monaco.

At Nice Côte d'Azur Airport, I hired a car for the twenty-mile drive east. The man who brought the vehicle asked why I was visiting Monaco; my answer was 'Geocaching.' It wasn't a lie.

Apart from a queue to pay the €2.20 toll on the A8, it was smooth sailing through the beautiful French Riviera. I tried to relax and enjoy the view, but it was impossible to forget why I was here. Above me, helicopters made the same journey, bearing the rich on missions to party. My mission was to find a monster.

I'd read that only about a quarter of the residents of Monaco were born here, with the remainder composed of dozens of nationalities, and that thirty per cent were millionaires. If you want Monégasque citizenship, it's a ten-year wait, the sovereign prince has to okay it, and you need to prove you can lay your hands on half a million in cash at any time. All told, I expected this world-renowned playboy playground to be a Disney-esque fairyland.

I didn't anticipate so many run-of-the-mill tourists or normal little shops, or the heavy amount of roadworks. I saw many heavy vehicles, even getting stuck behind a stinking refuse truck at one point, but nary a flash of sublime supercars. Nor did I see the point of such vehicles in streets that were thin, winding, clogged with small hatchbacks, and limited to 50kph.

For every suit jacket there were three T-shirts. I saw not a single face recognisable from movies. Many of the buildings had been erected during a property boom beginning in the 1950s and their aged condition was evident. I was reminded of video games whose fantastic graphics became pixelated when viewed close-up.

Monaco was loaded with money but otherwise no different to any other place in the world. The rich came to be seen and Joe Ordinary came to see the rich, but behind every tourist hotspot were the people who had to live there and oil the gears. For damn sure it wasn't a playboy driving that refuse truck.

However, vast swathes of this tiny nation's massive wealth exposed itself as I drove deep in. I swung a left onto a road with the bizarre name of *Boulevard Albert 1er,* and Port Hercule opened up on my right. In the water were dozens of flash yachts, some as tall as my house, all berthed at a cost of a couple of thousand euros a night. Glitzy Lamborghinis and graceful Bentleys were parked all over the place.

Facing the harbour to the west and curving around the

north were tall white apartment buildings that would bestow a magnificent view of the Monaco Grand Prix come May. I'd read that people here didn't pay income tax, which wouldn't exactly annoy the well-heeled, but Monaco soaked up somewhere around a hundred million when that famous race visited.

I turned right, onto the Avenue Président J F Kennedy. A short way along was a side street. Using a series of thin roads, I weaved my way between clusters of buildings, to my destination just a couple of hundred yards north of the port.

I soon reached Boulevard de Suisse, which was overlooked again by large apartment blocks, between two of which I could see a backdrop of green, mountainous land. A set of buildings created a pincer shape inside which was a grassy park. I parked close, in a spot reserved for scooters, and entered through a gateway. In my mind was the clue from the geocache I sought:

'Mentioned in *The Fall of Prince Florestan of Monaco.*'

Throughout this country were pictures of the actress Grace Kelly, who became Princess of Monaco through marriage to Prince Rainer III in the 1950s. The park wasn't spared. There were nine framed photographs, each attached to a sculpture. In a copse, I found a small statue of a bearded man in a red military hussar jacket.

I knew the sculpture depicted Charles III, Prince of Monaco and founder of the Casino de Monte Carlo. He was referred to as Charles Honoré Grimaldi in the book by Charles Wentworth Dilke.

Behind the sculpture, attached to an exposed tree root, was a plastic container. I had found the geocache called THOROUGHLY ENGLISH IN ITS WAYS, laid by a user called CometBoy. I broke the container and took a photograph.

CometBoy had been a registered geocacher since 2001. His profile picture was a rollercoaster called the Comet Coaster. I had found him via a search of geocaches in Monaco. He had finds all across the world, but he listed the microstate as his home location and all of his seventeen active hides were here and in nearby cities and towns.

After some research, I had discovered that the Comet Coaster had been shut after almost forty years of service. It had been a very popular ride and there must be many grown men out there who had fond memories of their time aboard it as kids. And the location of that ride?

Fair Park in Dallas, where the Texas State Fair was held every year. As advertised on a T-shirt worn by Steve Albany in a photo taken just two years ago.

CometBoy was my attacker.

Using my new, fake geocacher profile of a man, I created a log of my find and included the photo of the busted container.

'Found this broken. Should be archived unless repaired.'

I had to restrain myself from writing, *Come step into my trap, asshole.*

I waited forty minutes, to the dot of 4pm, before ringing an apartment bell in a building across the road from the park. The woman who answered the intercom had a deep drawl I knew would please some males. She also sounded Russian. We'd arranged this appointment by email.

'Look up, chica.'

I had to step back to do this. At a second-floor window was a pale face with curly black hair. Even at that distance I could see the woman wasn't watching me, but the street. She then said a number – nine – and vanished, and I heard the door lock disengage.

I entered the lobby, climbed the stairs, and knocked on door nine. The woman who'd advertised herself as Olesya answered in a long black dress that matched her hair, with pale, bare feet that complemented her white face. She was just as pretty as her profile picture, which I hadn't expected, and matched the age of twenty-five.

I entered her flat. Olesya shut the door, and leaned against it, as if barring my exit. I'd read that organised prostitution was illegal here, but selling sex itself wasn't. Olesya had advertised herself as an independent escort, but of course she would. It didn't mean she didn't have a pimp, or that she wasn't averse to robbing potential clients. 'A full night, was that right, darling?'

I nodded. €130 got you half an hour with this woman, but it was €1,500 for an overnight stay. I extracted the cash and let her see it. 'But I might need two nights, or even three. I have the money for it. But I also don't want your body. I'm not into women. I just want use of this flat. I'll stay out of your way. You can even take more clients. I just want that front window that overlooks the park.'

'Why?' She didn't sound puzzled or worried, and I figured her job had bombarded her with a plethora of personalities, myriad bizarre requests.

'I'm looking for someone. I'm expecting him to go into the park. If we're both lucky, he'll appear in the next five minutes and I'll be gone in six.'

'So a maximum of three days and probably a lot less?' The question seemed more directed at herself, to understand the set-up, because she grabbed my money without awaiting an answer and walked past me.

I followed her down the hallway, past two bedrooms and a bathroom, into a large living room with two plush purple sofas and a computer desk with a wall-mounted TV above the monitor. A large window offered a sea view, albeit only a slice between other apartment blocks. The room lacked the personal touch of pictures and ornaments, giving it a showroom air. Olesya pointed at a doorway with batwing doors.

'Kitchen with balcony. Go take a look.'

I did. The kitchen was clean, yellow and white. The window above the sink and the exterior door in a corner gave a perfect view of the park. Even better, outside the door was a tiny, railed balcony, where someone could stand and stare without arousing suspicion. It was deep enough for one of the kitchen table chairs, so I put one out there and returned to the living room.

Olesya was on her computer. 'I'm going to update my status,' she said. 'Like you said, I can entertain other clients. But I can leave the next hour free if you want me after all.'

'No. But I wouldn't say no to a cup of tea.'

'Tea? You're British then? That accent confused me.'

'Yorkshire. It throws off people in Britain, too.'

'Throws off?'

'Confuses. Anyway, good to meet you, Olesya. And thank you. You said in the email that you have bondage equipment?'

'Yes. What do you need? I won't ask why.'

She fetched what I needed. I returned to the kitchen balcony and sat, to watch the park. When Olesya brought tea, she said, 'This man you are waiting for. It is obvious he does not know you are here. Is he someone you have had falling out with?'

'I'll say yes, and we'll leave it at that. Thank you for the tea. Now you can go about your business.'

Olesya gave a neutral nod, and asked no further questions. As a woman who probably entertained all manner of foreigners, many doubtless married, she was adept at keeping secrets.

CHAPTER FORTY-SIX

A car stopped on the street below about an hour later. I perked up, then deflated when I saw black hair – it wasn't Albany. The man approached the building. I heard the bell in the flat ring and watched her poke her head out of a window to one side of the kitchen. I sat back, out of sight, as she called down to him. She unlocked the main door moments later.

I heard her greet the man at her door. They were in the bedroom soon afterwards. I heard no sounds of her hard at work. They emerged around an hour later. He sounded flush and awestruck, as if he'd just met his movie idol. Olesya's tone was flat and it was clear she just wanted him gone.

Once he'd left, I headed into the flat to use the bathroom. Olesya was in the living room, watching TV. She looked at me and opened her mouth to speak.

'Not yet,' I said before she could ask the question.

A while later, about half six, Olesya appeared behind me on the balcony. I was watching the sun set and didn't look round. 'I am making dinner. My next client is not until ten. Do you want some food?'

I did. I remained on the balcony while she cooked. She

talked a lot, but I said little other than one-word acknowledgements to show I wasn't ignoring her. My attention was minimal, however, because I was reading scary facts about CometBoy.

She told me she had been born in Russia in the late 1990s. Her father had been a banking oligarch who made millions in the 1990s, before losing it all when he refused to co-operate with the new Russian president. Her mother then abandoned him and took Olesya to live in France, where there was fragmented family.

By the time Olesya was eighteen, her mother had died, the family had kicked her out, and she had been forced to fend for herself on the streets. Monaco, holiday destination of the rich, was just an hour away and Olesya was determined to get away from the bad people around her and make herself enough money to retire with.

Retirement and happiness were words I heard her utter often, and it seemed she was determined to convince me that she was not defined by her job. It was obvious she didn't often get time with people who didn't want her body, or didn't belittle her. I felt a little sorry for her. But not enough to accept her offer to sit with me on the balcony for dinner.

She had hers in front of the living-room TV and I ate while watching the darkening park, both together but alone. Both awaiting strange men.

Olesya approached and told me her next client was due. I was shocked to see how much time had flown past: it was 9.50pm. I simply nodded. A few minutes later a white van with a logo on the side entered the street below. It slid out of my line of sight and parked outside the building. The buzzer rang. Olesya spoke out of the bedroom window to a man with good English but an unplaceable accent.

When she opened the front door to him a minute later, the sweetness in her voice was gone. 'You did not say you were bringing a friend. Did he hide in the van?'

'You should be happy,' a different voice replied, in a similar accent to his pal's. 'Both holes plugged. We should get a discount.'

'The price is per person, not per hour.'

'Double? You're playing games. Think of the heroin you'll be missing out on.'

'I don't do drugs. For the insult, I am cancelling. Go and find a slut on the prom in Nice. Please leave.'

The two men refused. I stood up as voices got raised. When the front door slammed, I thought they'd gone, but I heard scuffling feet. I rushed to the living-room door just in time to see a jeans-clad leg vanish into the bedroom. The bedroom door slammed shut.

I threw it open to see two young white men with Olesya. She was on the bed, being held down by one, his hand clamped over her mouth. The other man was undressing. Both men turned to look at me. Or rather, at the big kitchen knife I held.

Olesya scrambled off the bed and towards me. I stepped aside so she could pass. She stood behind me, in the hallway, her breathing a ragged stutter.

'And what do you think you're going to do with that?' the undressing male said. He'd gotten one arm out of a pullover and now replaced it. The guy on the bed moved to his side.

I said, 'Get out. Get back in your Red Hare Carpet Cleaning Ltd van and piss off.'

That got their attention. I added: 'Yes, I know where you work. Calling 17 here is so much quicker than 999 where I'm from.'

'And what if I cave in both your heads before you get near a phone?' the other guy snapped. Fists clenched by his sides, chest heaving, eyes wild, he seemed likely to do just as threatened.

'You think you can kill me before I get at least one nice slice with this knife? Fail and that's your blood and DNA at a crime scene.'

Redressed man laughed. But neither man made a move forward. 'What crime scene? I'll roll you bitches up in carpets and you'll never be seen again.'

'You have no idea who we might know. It only takes one to file a missing persons report. The police will check her internet activity. They'll check CCTV. Good job you didn't book her online or come here in a van with your workplace written on the side.'

Both men paused, silent. They might as well have said, *Aw shucks, you got us.*

'You paid this woman for an hour. You messed up that hour, not her. Leave without paying her and that's rape. Break or steal anything on the way out and its home invasion. So, make your choice. Money or double murder. We'll be waiting in the living room.'

I took Olesya's arm and rushed her into the living room. I shut the door, stepped back, and stared at it. Waiting. It would open or it wouldn't. Olesya was shaking beside me.

I hadn't warned the duo against verbal abuse, so they seized an opportunity. Various derogatory words were aimed at us both, but the door remained shut. Soon after, the front door slammed.

I waited a minute before investigating. The hallway was untouched and the bedroom was exactly as I'd last seen it, except for one detail. Paper money scattered everywhere.

CHAPTER FORTY-SEVEN

When Olesya had finished in the bathroom, she emerged sans make-up and wrapped in a dressing gown. She stood behind me as I sat on the balcony chair. She asked my name. I gave her it. My real name.

'Thank you, Lisa.'

'No problem.'

'That doesn't happen often. I don't do the group sex. I don't do drugs, despite what those men said.'

'I heard you deny it,' I said, but I didn't care one way or the other. It was very dark out now and I was worried that I would miss a lone male walking into the park.

Olesya pottered about in the kitchen for a few minutes, but I knew she still wanted to talk. Eventually, she said, 'You came into my bedroom quickly. You had a look in your eyes. What those men were going to do to me... you hate that.'

'Who wouldn't? No means no.'

'I think it might be... what's the saying – closer to home than that?'

Still staring at the black world, I opened my mouth to... tell her not to be silly? Reprimand her for such an assumption?

Something in between? I don't know what I had planned in that moment, because everything changed in the next.

'I was raped,' I said.

The sounds of kitchen activity ceased. Why was it that I hid the truth from those closest to me, yet was eager to bare all to strangers?

'This is why you sit here, hour after hour,' Olesya continued.

'Yes. He was the one.'

'You tracked him here.'

'Yes.'

I didn't want to give much more, but when I felt Olesya's hands on my shoulders, a lock disengaged inside me. A door burst open. The entire story flowed out as if a dam had been breached. I gave her everything. Almost.

Afterwards, she excused herself and left the kitchen. She was back quickly with a box of tissues. She took one and offered the box to me. I refused. She was the only one crying.

She said, 'I am glad you came here. You saved me. I would do anything to help you. But why are you here?'

I understood her confusion. Steve Albany, as Sunshine, had shown a habit of dedicating a whole month to one country. He'd last logged a geocache in the UK not long before he attacked me.

However, I had found a pot of gold back in that Dallas hotel room. I told her this new twist in the tale.

Albany discovered geocaching through his uncle in 2001, when he created the CometBoy profile. Late in 2002, Albany got a job back in Dallas at Reliable Security, and he created the user called Dallas9999. In 2013, Dallas9999 got banned and Albany did a phoenix-from-the-ashes under the new identity of Sunshine-and-Roses. Pretty straightforward.

But why had Albany dumped the CometBoy profile? By choice, he'd archived all his hides in 2002, which made sense because his new job had restricted his travelling, and his ability to maintain those geocaches, to the months of Jan, Feb, and March.

But Steve Albany still logged *finds* around the world. Why not continue to travel as CometBoy and increase his numbers instead of starting over with a new profile? It hadn't been his choice to restart from zero as Sunshine, after all.

I had soon worked it out. Albany's wife. If she knew about and had access to the CometBoy profile, he'd have serious questions to answer if she discovered he wasn't in Monaco, but was instead hopping around the globe. The solution: create Dallas9999, and later Sunshine, so he could tour in secret.

This explained strange movement on the CometBoy profile. Because he was back. He'd fallen silent in 2002, but he'd resurfaced in 2017 and had been active ever since. That must have been when Albany's wife got hold of his passport and realised he'd long been lying to her. In response, Albany had started to use the CometBoy profile again.

He had logged finds, but now they were restricted to Monaco and its immediate surrounds. No more international travels for CometBoy, not if he was under surveillance from the Mrs. There were logs throughout the year, suggesting Albany had had to make urgent journeys to help maintain his uncle's mansion.

But most significant of all were the logs made during those important first three months of the year. Jan, Feb and March each contained a handful of finds. Albany was touching base to keep his wife under the illusion that he was safe and sound in Monaco and in no way abusing innocent women across the planet.

One of CometBoy's logs was at a brand-new geocache near Heli Air Monaco in the southern ward of Fontvieille. It was on Sunday 13th Feb, the day before I flew out to Dallas. Learning of this in that Big D hotel room had created the impetus to fly to

Monaco. I'd been worried about missing him, but fate appeared to be on my side:

Last night, while sitting in a hotel room in West Yorkshire, I'd spotted a brand-new log from him. He'd literally just found a geocache on a beach in the north of Monaco. He'd touched base again just twenty-four hours ago. He was here, he was close.

He was mine.

The above-mentioned detective work had brought me to Monaco. But that was not what Olesya had meant by *why are you here?*

She said, 'No, Lisa. I wish to know why you came here for him. Do you plan to have him arrested?'

'No. I can't expose myself. I won't. Rape convictions are low. Little better than one in a hundred of reported rapes, at least in my country. It's been too long. Lawyers will ask why I waited. They'll say I consented. If he walks out of court a free man, I'll be the bad guy. No. No way.'

'Then what? I saw how you were with those two men. You were ready to hurt them. Do you plan to kill him?'

Now I stood, turned from that kitchen balcony view of the dark park, and stared at her. She had asked a question I had put to myself many times. I gave her the truth: 'I don't know. All I do know is I refuse to run again.'

'Again? Do you mean when you moved to a new city as a teenager? After your overdose? That is hardly the same, Lisa.'

I had held some details from Olesya, but now it was time to cut the deception.

'I was raped. Before. Back then.'

Her eyes widened. 'As a teenager?'

'I lied about a young thug in the park, didn't I? I learned

how from lying about what happened way back.'

I told her another, more shocking story. That long-ago weekend back in Nottingham, I'd been whacked out of my head on my sedative of choice, Zaleplon. There was a city-centre five-storey office block that my crew and I used to hang out in.

Abandoned years before, it had been falling apart and had become a haunt for those shunned by society, like something out of a dystopian sci-fi movie. It had started to collapse from the roof down, too, and the condition of successive floors got worse. Most people congregated on the first three levels, while the fourth floor was little more than a communal toilet and graveyard, and the fifth was a wreck open to the elements.

I did not have more than islands of memory of that entire weekend. But one island contained fragments of when I climbed the rotten stairs to use the fourth floor to defecate. The fourth level was a disgusting cesspool after being used for nothing but bathroom breaks for years.

I remember going through a doorless doorway. Stepping past the carcasses and skeletons of dead dogs and cats once called pets by the homeless. Finding a clear spot to squat in. Rain was seeping through the ceiling, dropping here and there.

Next, seeing a man in the room. I remember the word *munchkin*. I think he called me munchkin. But I can't remember his face, age, clothing, anything else. Except for a bone in his hand. A rib or leg from a dead thing, sharpened into a weapon and brandished at me.

The next thing I knew, I was on external fire exit stairs, stumbling down. Memory skipped ahead to a rainy street. Next, waking in a bus shelter, asleep under my coat. There was pain between my legs. Blood dried around my nose, which felt broken but wasn't. I had more Zaleplon and took it. I recalled more walking the next morning. More of the Z-drug. Blood from a small tear on the outside of my vagina.

I was alone all of that Sunday. I slept most of it away in a shell of a house under construction on a building site. That night, I got word that the man was coming for me again, although I didn't recall how I learned this. But I knew he was after me. He knew me, but I didn't know him. If I didn't recall his face, how could I ever hope to stop him attacking me again?

'I couldn't,' I told Olesya. 'I never did remember his face or anything else he said. The drugs repressed everything. I was in a state of panic, and what happens when someone gets like that? Fight or flight. I ran. I woke up Monday morning and left the city. I never looked back.'

Olesya was staring at me in shock, with perhaps some pity in there. I turned back to the night sky. No movement on the street below. It was late. Albany wasn't coming tonight, I knew. I would have to hope that tomorrow paid out a jackpot. Or the day after. Or the day after that.

'And now it's happened again,' I said. 'Last time it was the drugs. This time I got a head injury. Last time, I abandoned my life to get away from a dangerous man. I could, so easily. I was young and I could run from it all, start over. But now I have the life I want. Husband. Child. Job. Fight or flight? Well, I can't run this time. I won't. That only leaves the fight. So, to answer your question, Olesya, I don't know what I will do when I find this man. Except that I plan to stop him stalking me. He won't ruin my life. I will do whatever it takes to keep me and my family safe.'

When I turned to look at Olesya again, pity seemed to have the monopoly on her emotions. I grew annoyed as I suddenly read it in a new light. I had seen the same look in Lizzie Roundtree's eyes.

'You doubt me, don't you?'

Unbelievably, she said, 'I think you are delusional.'

CHAPTER FORTY-EIGHT

I walked past Olesya to get a glass of water. I drank it fast. 'You sound just like my husband. He thinks I have PTSD.'

'He could be right. I know about PTSD. I have seen friends with it. For the same reason as you, drugs. I have seen memory lost and I have seen false memories.'

I put my glass down and returned to the balcony. I took my seat. Olesya hovered behind me. I said, 'I'm fine. I'm not paranoid.'

'Have you seen evidence of this man stalking you? Think hard.'

'He's careful.'

'And last time? Back in – did you say Nottingham? Was there evidence of a man stalking you?'

I turned to her. 'You think I had PTSD back then? I had a drug overdose. I got dissociative amnesia. See, we can all use fancy terms. Please stop talking about this.'

'Drugs can cause PTSD. They can cause dissociative amnesia. Or a psychotic episode.'

I almost laughed. A psychotic episode? 'I got hit on the head this time. I got raped. The stress caused my blackout.'

'Relapse. I know PTSD can lie dormant. All those years ago, the drugs or the trauma caused it. It lay dormant until you were attacked again. Do you know what a major symptom of PTSD is?'

I didn't answer. I got up and moved through the kitchen. Olesya followed me, so I went into the bathroom and locked the door. While I peed, she was out there, still talking. More of the same. Paranoia, hypervigilance, substance anxiety. She knew her stuff, I'd give her that. But she didn't know my situation. She didn't know me.

Finished on the toilet, I yanked open the door fast enough to make Olesya jump. 'I didn't pay for therapy. I paid for the use of this flat. Stop talking about this.'

She left me alone after that. She sat in the living room with the TV. I sat on the balcony with only my thoughts.

Olesya retired to bed around midnight, which allowed me to turn off the living-room light to plunge the entire flat into darkness. It aided my night vision, but it also permitted my mind to wander back home.

I had to know what was happening with Dan and Ted and work and all my friends. It was still day one, so maybe nobody outside of my family knew I'd gone missing. I'd promised Dan that I'd be back soon and he'd probably informed Ted by now, so I doubted they were worried yet. Certainly not enough to involve the police. Work, though, was a different matter.

My theft of money from the store would have been reported. The police would have gone to my house. They would know I'd run off somewhere, but what would their response have been? I was hardly a crime baron, so I doubted there was a task force after me. But how deep would they have delved? Surely not far, day one and all.

I was in for a shock.

Dan is standing in his bedroom, staring at his computer's webcam. He's in pyjamas. He says, *'Mum, come on home. We miss you. I know Dad does. When it got dark, he started to worry. He said you would be fine and I know you are. But I want to talk to you. Your phone is dead. Contact me on Messenger.'*

This Facebook video had been posted last night at 10.35pm UK time. I had created a fake profile for the social media site in order to check on Dan, and seeing this had brought a tear to my eye. By then, thirty-six people had seen, liked and commented on it. I had been consumed by worry for him, and angry that I couldn't reach out to him with a reply.

The reason for this had been because I couldn't give away my location – if Albany was watching, he would know I was on the hunt for him. But one thing I hadn't been was shocked. That had come later.

I'd drifted off on Olesya's sofa and woken at 6.12, which was 5.12 in the UK. I had immediately loaded up Dan's profile to see if he'd posted more. He hadn't. But others had.

By that time his video had had thousands of views and two hundred shares, no doubt as people told friends about it. I had checked my own profile and discovered dozens of messages from strangers. Some wished me well. Others didn't. Ted, my sister, neighbours, and some work colleagues had all sent pleas for me to get in touch, to stay safe, to come home. Dan had posted many. It had burned my heart.

One of the posts had been from Alice, formerly of Heaven Homestore: *She ran off with thousands from the safe at work.* The bitch. Even Alan had held his tongue about this.

Then I'd seen one from South Yorkshire Police, who had asked me to call them and had included a link to their Facebook page. There, I saw a post from just a few hours ago. It began with: *APPEAL – have you seen Lisa Holten*? It had my passport photo from two years ago and listed when I'd last been seen and what I'd been wearing. It said I had last been seen on Friday at work.

Sleep had been impossible after seeing the increased interest in my disappearance. I had made food and watched the park from the balcony. Olesya had woken around 9am and gone out.

Now, I was still on the balcony, washed in sunlight and staring at my phone. It was 12.21pm. I only knew Olesya was back when she spoke from directly behind me.

'Is that your family? My God.'

I didn't reply. Couldn't. I didn't resist when she took my phone. For about the tenth time, I heard Dan's voice as Olesya replayed a news video I'd found.

'Mum, please come home. We all miss you. I just want you back.'

And Ted's: *'Lisa, Dan misses you so much. I hope you're safe. Call us, please.'*

My sister: *'Lisa, I know you wouldn't run off like this. Whatever the problem is, call me. Call one of us or call the police.'*

Once England woke up, the story of my disappearance had spread like wildfire. Dan's video of him pleading for my return had touched heartstrings and many had sought further news. Upon realising that the police hadn't started a major missing persons investigation, they'd been bombarded with requests to do so.

But many had reprimanded them for a lax approach, and it had been this that kicked them into gear. Even the local media had gotten involved, believing that poor little Dan had had to post videos begging for my return because the police didn't care.

Dan, Ted and Maud had been interviewed for newspapers,

radio and TV. The piece I'd just watched had shown Dan and Ted standing outside my house, talking to reporters. It had even featured a detective superintendent telling what he knew so far: I was not the sort to run away like this. He also stated that I had 'removed some extra' money from work.

Clearly the police knew of the theft from Heaven, but were being careful not to paint me as a criminal. I had suffered a mugging recently that had affected my mood and behaviour, they said.

I was suddenly high profile. The police were obligated to put real effort into finding me. Of course, they would have checked my phone records, but there was no clue there because I'd ditched that number. Social media activity – useless because I hadn't logged in under my profile. Passport and bank account?

Now I had a problem.

Olesya stepped in front of me and looked out over the balcony, her back to me. 'Lisa. I did not realise you left your family. I guess I did not think about that.'

'You can't tell anyone where I am.'

'They know. That news report. That policeman. They know you flew to Nice.'

'They don't know I'm in Monaco.'

'Your hire car will give you away. You told me you stole money from work. You are wanted. I know they did not say this, but it is so. Monaco takes its security very seriously. A lot of police. A lot of CCTV cameras. They can lock the whole country down very easily. If they think you are here, they will search.'

'I haven't got a Red Notice.'

'Pardon?'

I couldn't be bothered to explain. 'Don't worry about me.'

She paused. I thought she was worried about being outed as a call girl and was going to tell me to leave her flat. But she turned to me and said, 'You should go home. You have a nice husband. A beautiful son. They miss you.'

'They miss the old Lisa. That woman can't return until she has...'

'Killed a man?'

I didn't reply to that question. 'I will be gone soon. You won't have to worry about me.'

'The police will soon know you are in Monaco. So there is no need to hide it. You should call your family and let them know you are okay. So they know you are not dead.'

She was right. I had no right to hurt my son and husband like this. Dan I especially felt sorry for, and not just because of his age. I had kept Ted in the dark about my obsession with finding my attacker, which was bad enough. But by taking Dan to London to find a geocache, I had involved him. That had been wrong whatever way it was sliced.

Knowing I owed him at least an explanation, I had already decided to call Dan before Olesya had returned. And I had failed.

I had typed his phone number into my device, but my finger had hovered over the call button. Call it a sense of self-preservation, but something hadn't allowed me to make that call. It would have soothed his soul to hear from his mother, and it had been with a heavy heart that I'd put the phone down. I could not risk capture until the monster was... no longer a problem.

Finding him, it seemed, was more important than my son's mental well-being.

CHAPTER FORTY-NINE

Olesya reserved Sundays for her only regular client, a wealthy Italian restaurateur who made a three-hour drive from Alba to see her and often brought white truffles.

At 2pm, his sleek convertible Ferrari parked behind my hire car. A handsome black man in a suit was at the wheel. Olesya had changed into a glitzy, blue, off-shoulder dress that would probably pull more stares than the supercar, at least in a place like Monaco. There was a flower in her hair and jewellery around her neck.

'I won't be back until evening. If your man turns up and you have to leave, it was nice knowing you, Lisa Holten. Please take care.'

She left. I watched the couple kiss on the pavement. He helped her into the passenger seat and away they went. It was remarkable how different people's lives could be.

Once the Ferrari was gone, I grabbed some food and returned to the balcony. I'd had so little sleep the night before that the inactivity of sitting and watching tried to pull my eyelids down. I fought it by standing occasionally. Soon, the chair started to hurt and I sat, squatted, knelt and lay on the floor of the balcony.

Three times I felt myself tense as a man entered the park from the street, one of them with a woman. Three times I deflated. At just after 5pm, as the sky was losing light and the sun was dipping out of sight to my left, I chose to shut my eyes just for a moment.

The next thing I knew, it was dark. I was sitting with my back propped against the balcony door. Olesya was sitting on the chair, now out of her dress and wearing tracksuit bottoms and a jumper. She turned as she heard my panic to find my phone and check the time. It was 8.12pm.

'Are you okay?' she said.

I punched the door frame. 'I fell asleep. I could have missed him. What time did you get back?'

'Seven. Haroun got called back home. Relax. I was watching the park for you. Nobody came. You needed the sleep. I would have woken you if I had to.'

I stood up so fast my leg throbbed because it had been folded under me while I slept. I needed the toilet so limped there. While sitting in the bathroom, I checked for updates from CometBoy. If he'd already posted a maintenance log at the geocache under surveillance, I would have exploded. He hadn't. There had been no activity on his profile. I went back to Olesya. She was still watching the park. I stood behind her.

'Thank you,' I said.

She didn't reply.

'You okay?'

She stood up, but kept her back to me and said nothing.

'Olesya? Look, I'm sorry for shouting at–'

'Is that him?'

She pointed. I stood by her side and looked. A small blue car was at the kerb outside the entrance to the park. A man in jeans and a thick jacket had just gotten out, alone. He was tall enough to be Albany, but he wore a beanie cap and I couldn't see if he had the same hair as Albany. When he walked into the park, his back was to us and I was unable to see his face.

He walked along one of the concrete paths, but then veered into the trees. Hampered by the dark and branches, I saw only slight movement. But he was in the general area of the geocache.

I rushed into the kitchen to grab my jacket and stomp into my shoes. Then I headed for the front door. I had to make sure I was on the street when the man left, or I'd be unable to follow him.

As I turned to shut the door, I saw Olesya standing at the end of the hall. 'Don't worry about goodbyes,' she said. 'You get going. And please be careful. I hope you get peace. You were never here.'

'I hope you stay happy,' I replied, and shut the door.

Outside, I got in my hire car and turned it in the road, so it was facing in the same direction as the blue car. And I waited. About three minutes later, the man in the beanie returned. He was typing something on his phone. He was about thirty metres away, and now I saw his face in profile, slightly lit by the glow from his screen. But I couldn't determine if he was Albany based on the single recent photo I'd seen.

He got in his car and it started up, headlights blazing. I followed suit, but the vehicle didn't move. Figuring he was still on his phone, I pulled mine and loaded the Thoroughly English in its Ways geocache. It was a long shot.

But it paid off. As I watched, a new log appeared. It was from CometBoy.

Hey everyone just fixed the container so happy hunting.

Albany drove north, out of Monaco and into the neighbouring commune of Beausoleil in France. When the park was a mile behind us, we were on part of Moyenne Corniche, a world-famous scenic road made eerie by the darkness. My eyes were locked on the tail lights of the car, some fifty metres ahead.

Soon we turned onto a road that weaved like a snake up a hill. Then we were on a straight, with a steep slope and a pine forest on my right, while the left side offered a magnificent view of Monaco and the Mediterranean Sea. I barely looked.

Given Albany's ability to thwart police forces around the world, anyone would have assumed he was, to use one of Olesya's words, hypervigilant. We were the only two drivers out here this late and he should have realised that he'd had the same shadow for his entire journey.

I wasn't so sure. Twenty years of slipping into countries, raping its women and scuttling out again – surely this would have given him the confidence of an immortal god. This man would be certain nobody could ever track him.

I was so confident that I closed the distance.

There didn't seem to be a building or pedestrian anywhere and it seemed we were boring deeper into the back of beyond. The hill had levelled out and on the right side was a stone wall ten feet high. Then we passed a sign that said COMPLEXE SPORTIF ET DE LOISIRS DU DEVENS and an arrow pointing ahead.

I wondered if that was our destination and quickly googled it without crashing into the stone wall or plummeting off the cliff. It was a sports complex: not Albany's home then, but it meant an urban area was close–

I yelped as Albany's brake lights came on and the car

seemed to fly towards me. I swerved to the left, the offside flank almost scraping a useless wooden fence. I flew past Albany's rear as he seemed to turn right, directly into the wall. There was a blast of his horn as he caught the near smash.

Once I'd regained the centre of the road, I looked in my rear-view mirror, and just in time to see the last inches of Albany's vehicle apparently vanish into the stone wall. I stopped. Pointing my headlights back the way I'd come involved a seven-point turn. I cut the lights and moved slowly forwards, until I saw what I expected. A gateway in the stone wall. Beside it was a plaque that said a street number and *La Nouvelle Ferme*.

In that moment, I bit my bottom lip in anger. Albany's wife hadn't had an address for his uncle, but I realised I hadn't even requested his name. Another in a long line of mistakes. How much quicker I might have found this place if I hadn't been so stupid.

It didn't matter. Albany's luck was always destined to run out, and here I was. I got out of the car and peeked through the open gateway. In the blackness beyond was a driveway cutting through the trees. At its end, some twenty metres away, were the twin tail lights of Albany's car.

In a large, open area ahead of it, lit by the headlights, was a large double-gabled house of white timber. It had a dormer window in the roof and a covered deck running the entire width. It looked very expensive, just like the sole other vehicle out front: a Rolls Royce.

Albany exited his car and I watched his black shape step onto the porch and open the big front door. The only light on was in the dormer window, until a downstairs pane of glass covered by blinds lit up moments later.

Right there, in the gateway, I dropped to my knees on loose

gravel that had spilled out of the driveway. I barely felt the pain. I started to cry.

This was it. Finally. The house of Albany's uncle. Where my rapist called home for three months of the year. He was cornered. Trapped. In the cross hairs.

And now he would pay.

CHAPTER FIFTY

I guided my car into the driveway, lights off, and sat there to see if anyone in the house noticed. They didn't. I got out and walked towards the building, and stopped before the porch. It had a wheelchair ramp at each end, probably for Albany's infirm uncle. A wheelchair sat beside the porch. Again I waited to be confronted. Nobody came. Nobody had seen me. I slipped into the trees to watch and wait.

Nineteen minutes later, the downstairs light went off. Twelve minutes after that the light in the dormer window between the gable roofs was extinguished. I decided to wait half an hour to let the monster drift into sleep.

Alone, in the silent gloom, I had time to think. Olesya had asked me what I planned to do when I confronted Albany – if I intended to kill him. I had and I hadn't, in crashing waves of indecision. If I thought about his attack on me or what it had done to my mind, if I remembered the pain or some instance when my paranoia had upset my son or husband, then I had been determined that the penalty had to be... his end.

But those thoughts had been wispy and dreamlike because

Albany was still out of reach. I had been like a lottery player waiting for her numbers to drop and thinking about flash yachts and blinged watches and hot holidays. Now, the numbers were in, I had won the jackpot, and I needed to give the future serious thought.

I could not kill the man or even seriously harm him. The hot flush of satisfaction would be extinguished the moment I was arrested. I had blamed Albany for ruining my life, but killing him would damage it far more. Dan would forever be tied to that murder. He'd be the kid, then the teenager, then the adult with a killer for a mother. He'd be judged and condemned for the rest of his life. Ted. My sister. The rest of my family. They'd all suffer.

And me? I was not evil like Albany, and the guilt, which would come as I rotted in prison, would wreck me. Albany, too, had family and friends. I had hunted Albany in order to end his threat and reassemble my fractured life. Why do something that would explode that cracked shell into pieces?

When the half-hour was up, I moved on to the porch. There was no security light and I didn't see a CCTV camera. Maybe this part of town was crime-free and its residents naïve.

The door was locked. I left the porch and went round the back, where there were three outhouses, a covered swimming pool, a walled vegetable garden, and a square of ropes creating a boxing ring under a portable gazebo. Here the house had another porch, squeezed in between a lean-to conservatory and a greenhouse.

I didn't need to try the back door. The square conservatory had a centre-pivot window on each side and one was wide open. The door inside the conservatory led into the house and it was also open. There were a pair of varnished tree-stump ornaments beside the outer door and I dragged one under the window, which allowed me to step right into the conservatory. I unlocked and opened the outer door, in case I needed a quick exit.

The interior door led to a kitchen whose worktops and cupboards were slightly lower to the ground than standard, probably for use by someone in a wheelchair. The green END readout of a washing machine blinked at me through the darkness. Two microwave ovens told the time in orange, although they differed by a minute. The fridge had a digital display with a dimmed bubbles screensaver.

I stopped here briefly to select an item I needed.

A door ahead led to a wide hallway running left and right, with stairs ahead of me and a lift beside them. To my right were four doors. To my left, the hallway opened up into a dining room beside the kitchen and a family room, which was where Albany had turned on the downstairs light. I had a brief glance around before turning back, to walk past the kitchen entrance and approach the four doors.

All but one was wide open. I passed a spare bedroom, a laundry room and a bathroom, and stopped at the closed door. There was a barely perceptible noise from beyond. A voice? I turned the handle.

The double bed was against the far wall. One wall was composed of wardrobes with mirrored doors, which helped to increase the faint moonlight oozing around thin blinds over the window opposite. I could see a wheelchair beside the bed and a shape under the covers.

It was not a man.

Despite being a double bed, it had only one pillow in the centre. The woman was on her back, stretched straight. Brown hair was splayed across the pillow. Her hands were on her chest and one clutched a mobile phone. It trailed a wire to earphones that played what I realised was an audiobook. Who was this woman?

I approached her. Closer, I saw she was about forty and handsome. I took the mobile. She didn't respond. It was locked by a password, but I didn't need it to pause the audiobook. I disconnected it from the earphones and laid it on her chest.

Then I shook her awake. When her eyes opened, I clamped a hand over her mouth and showed her the large knife I'd taken from her own kitchen. Her eyes went wide.

'Don't make a noise. I'm not here to hurt you. How many people in the house?'

I released her mouth. In a French accent, she said, 'Two.'

'Call him. He's upstairs. Tell that bastard to get down here. But don't warn him. Just tell him you need to see him.'

She took her phone. With shaking hands, she unlocked the device. And paused. She said, 'Are you going to hurt him? Why do you want him? What has he done?'

'He's an evil rapist and he's going to pay.'

'No, no, never,' she moaned, shaking her head. 'Not my son, never–'

'Son? What do you mean, son? Who's upstairs? What's his name?'

'Lucas. My boy would never rape. You are wrong. Please leave my house.'

'Where is Steve Albany?'

I saw something come across her eyes. It was relief. 'Steve? He is not here. Steve is away. He has not been here for weeks.'

My mind was spinning. The man at the geocache – that wasn't Steve Albany? But he had been at the geocache. Hadn't he? He was CometBoy. Wasn't he?

She had to be lying. 'Call him down here. Put it on speakerphone. Be careful not to warn him. I'll hurt you if you try to trick me.'

'He will not answer. Not in the house. He will know I need something and he will just come.'

She was right. She made the call, but it wasn't answered. After two rings, I heard the thump of feet above. Then on the stairs. In the hallway.

He called out in French. I understood only one word: *mère*. Mother. I was confused. Did Albany call this younger woman mother as a term of endearment?

The man who froze in the doorway had shed his jacket and shoes, but he still wore the beanie I'd seen earlier. It was the same man who'd fixed the geocache in Monaco. The same one I'd followed here. The man who'd used the CometBoy profile.

But he was barely a man at all. He looked about twenty years old. I couldn't deny the truth any longer. This was not Steve Albany. He couldn't be my attacker. Could he?

———

He was young and fit, but also a ball of nerves. Terrified of the knife at his mother's neck, he did everything I asked of him. He lay on the bed beside her. He secured himself to the disabled woman using the handcuffs Olesya had given me, and clasped his mother's hand. Even when I put down the knife and paced at the foot of the bed, trying to get my head around this, he didn't once look as if he might try to attack me.

Bizarrely, they were my captors but I became the interviewee. They had questions, and I answered them all. In disarranged pieces, like a muddled jigsaw, they got my whole story.

Except for one aspect. I was vague about some of the clues that had led me here. I did not mention Lizzie Roundtree or the other rapes I had connected Albany to. I allowed this woman, Avril, to believe I was his sole victim. She needed to be convinced of his evil in order to be truthful with me, but I couldn't risk shocking her into a mental shutdown. Not yet.

When my tale was told, I sought acceptance on their faces. I saw it on the woman. The boy just looked overwhelmed and confused. He said something to his mother in French, but I demanded to know what it was.

She said, 'He is upset that you claim his father has a wife in America. He did not know this. I did. I always told him his father was in the army.' She looked at her son. 'I am sorry, Lucas. I will tell you everything one day.'

'No, tonight. Right now.' I went to the wall and turned on the light. It stung our eyes. 'It's my turn to ask the questions. I want to know everything. Let's start with why Albany seems to have a whole new family in France.'

She told it all. Unlike when my tale was given, she needed no questions to prompt her. I paced, silent. She lay there, talking.

Albany's uncle, Johan, did indeed once own and live in this house outside Monaco, back in 2001. Needing a new hobby, Johan had found the brand-new outdoor activity of geocaching, and Albany had created the CometBoy profile in order to join him. It was at a geocache one day that Albany had bumped into Avril. She was twenty and he was twice her age, but they hit it off.

Within three months, she was pregnant and Albany's uncle was dead. Albany inherited the house and enough wealth to retire on, if he'd so chosen. He moved Avril into the property, but he himself spent little time there because he was married and had a wife overseas.

Avril knew that Albany had hidden his uncle's death from his wife, which also meant she knew nothing of his riches. He was fearful she would want to move here or sell the house. He was so committed to this deception that – and even Avril found this bizarre – he even took on a job back in Dallas, Texas, in late 2002, a few months after Lucas was born.

Avril had no doubt that he loved and would always care for his new son, but she knew Albany could not commit much by way of time. He even gave up geocaching, something she knew he loved with all his heart. In 2019, Lucas turned seventeen and was legal to drive under supervision, and he wanted to hunt geocaches like his father had done. Albany allowed him to reactivate the old CometBoy profile.

The plan, which she stuck to for two decades, was to tell her son that his father was a high-ranking army man who was based overseas and committed to his career all-year round. Ever since Lucas was born, Albany had visited a number of times a year. He always made sure he came for the new year to bring Christmas presents. He would arrive on January 1st, but be gone again the next day, back to his wife and his job.

And so it had been. For twenty years.

Here I got a glass of water. When I returned, mother and son were still on the bed. They asked for water and I shared mine. It seemed to give Avril a new confidence, perhaps because I'd shown sympathy.

'Now you know everything. You know Steve is not here. You must leave.'

'I need to know where he is.'

'Why? What do you intend to do?'

If she had asked me that an hour ago, the answer would have been very different. I said, 'Get this foulness out of my mind. Get my son and husband back. Have a long and happy life. To do that, I need to put your man in prison for the rest of his life.'

I thought she might ask, *What about my life and my son's?* I was ready to tell her that Albany should have thought about them, not just his own sexual gratification.

Instead, she said, 'He's in America. His phone is off. He always calls me, I am not permitted to call him.'

'I've heard that before.'

'He is in America, working. He is not here. So you must leave, please.'

I was not leaving. I needed her help. And she needed an incentive to give it.

CHAPTER FIFTY-ONE

'Steve Albany's wife does not know his uncle is dead, did you know that? He pretends his uncle is still alive. Every January, February, and March, year-in, year-out, his wife thinks he's in Monaco. During those same months, you think he's in Dallas. He's been lying to you both for twenty years. Do you understand?'

Her puzzled frown said, she absolutely did not.

'Steve Albany did not give up geocaching, Avril. He gave up the username your son now uses, CometBoy, and became someone called Dallas9999 instead. He did this so neither you nor his wife could track him. Know what he's been doing in those three months every year for the last two decades? Hopping on planes, flying around the world, and raping women.'

She shook her head. She told me I was wrong. Next to her, Lucas played copycat. I had to show them the knife again to elicit silence. Then I pulled out my phone. I knelt by her side and showed her the geocaching website. I showed her the international geocache logs of Albany, now known as Sunshine-and-Roses. From memory, I told her about rapes in those countries. It was unfortunate that I'd been unable to access the locked Dallas9999 profile.

I could see she was not convinced. Despite the key safe profile pictures, there was no proof that these usernames belonged to the man who'd fathered her child. I tried again. The CometBoy profile. I had memorised more than just rapes committed after Sunshine's inception in 2013.

I pointed out geocache log dates and locations in 2001 and part of 2002, before he abandoned that identity. I pointed out crimes committed in those locations, right around the time CometBoy was there.

'What do you notice about these CometBoy logs, Avril? Every single country here could be considered Third World in terms of poverty, repressed civil liberties, income, human development. Why has he picked such places?'

She could only stare.

'Rape is very rarely reported in some of these countries. If rape is not proven, a woman could be considered to have committed adultery. That can legally be a death sentence. They could be considered impure and shunned. They could face retribution by honour killing for bringing shame. Now look at this one... highest rape rate in the world. Then some of these poorer countries... here, look... are these the kinds of places where the police have the technology to investigate complex crimes? Why geocache in these places? Could it be because of the higher chance of not being caught?'

Still she could only stare. But there was a level of horror upon her face that my knife had been incapable of achieving.

'He got confident and clever pretty quickly. Now no country is better than him. England isn't. That's where he raped me just weeks ago. I'm here for him. And you're going to bring him to me. I want you to call him. It doesn't matter if I have to stay here for a week. We'll all wait together.'

'I don't know where he is. I thought he was in America. I cannot call him. I told you that. He calls me.'

'You must know when he will do this. There must be some arrangement. Every night, once a week, every second Wednesday. Something.'

'No. I swear. No. Please. I have not heard from him in a month. That was the last time.'

I stepped away with her phone and accessed the call logs. He was in her phone book as STEVE. There were no outgoing calls to his number, just like she'd said. His last call to her had been the 18th of Jan.

That was the date he'd logged a geocache in Birmingham, back in England.

'Please don't hurt us,' Avril pleaded. 'We cannot help you. We have done nothing.'

The previous call had been on the 15th Jan. On that date, Albany logged at a geocache in Dorset. Before that, the 8th, when he visited a cache in the London Borough of Lewisham.

'I know you are a good person,' she continued. 'My son, he does not know, he is scared, but you will not hurt us. You are not bad. I know this. Please, you cannot stay here. We cannot help.'

I went back further to confirm it: on or close to every date he'd called Avril, he'd also signed at a geocache. Had he raped too? Was he calling the woman who loved him after destroying the life of one who absolutely didn't?

But why hadn't he called her around the date of my attack?

'I don't believe it. Not you. My son does not see what I see in you. Please.'

I was standing at the foot of the bed, facing them, and with speed I didn't expect, she sat up and grabbed my wrist in both of hers, and pulled my arm towards her. The cuff on her left wrist yanked her son's right arm from the bed, and it dangled from the chain as she rested her forehead against the back of my hand. I didn't resist.

'Please,' she begged, 'my son doesn't know, but I see good. The good is in you. You don't want to hurt anyone. I know it.'

Before I could reply, Lucas made his move.

With my wrist just inches from his cuffed hand, he snatched it in his fingers in the blink of an eye. The next thing I knew, he yanked with serious strength and I was hauled over the foot of the bed, to land on top of him.

Avril started yelling, but whether it was for her son to let me go or hurt me, I couldn't tell because he was also shouting. When I tried to rise, he locked up my hair in his fist and pulled. His cuffed hand was thumping into my head, and there seemed to be no resistance from his mother's arm, as if they were coordinating their strikes. I put a hand on his chest and pushed, to try to raise my head, but that turned the pain of my hair being pulled from bad to terrible.

'*Bite her eyes out*,' Avril screamed.

Fear that he intended to haul my head down in order to do just that, I shifted my hand from his chest and locked it around his throat, and squeezed. Blows from Avril's free arm pattered on the back of my head, but I barely felt them. Lucas stared up and I stared right back. My eyes were rage-filled, and his had turned terrified once his air shut off.

'*Leave him you bitch*,' Avril hissed at me.

Lucas released my hair and grabbed the hand around his throat. But it was locked, tight, immovable. Fury power. His cuffed hand joined the fight, while both of Avril's hands grabbed my wrist and tried to prise me off him. But I held tight, even against the stabbing pain of his nails into the flesh of my fingers.

While mother and son were occupied, I dropped a leg off the bed, then the other, and then yanked my hand away and staggered back, out of their reach.

And then froze. Lucas was coughing, Avril was cursing me, but I ignored them both. My attention was focused on something else. I looked at my hand and saw a line of blood along all four fingers, one travelling the entire length and unbroken by my engagement ring.

Which wasn't there. It lay beside Lucas on the bed. His nails had dragged it off.

I staggered from the room, suddenly nauseous, captives forgotten. I burst into the bathroom and turned the cold tap to fill the sink. But when I bent over to splash my face, I let out a gasp. It wasn't my reflection the water cast back.

Albany's shimmering face stared up at me.

I looked to my hand, where no engagement ring sat, and remembered the words of a prostitute: *I have seen memory lost and I have seen false memories.*

Albany hadn't called Avril on or around the night he attacked me. And he hadn't called her or logged a geocache since.

As if they had been sitting on a trapdoor that suddenly collapsed under the weight, they came back. The memories. All of them.

CHAPTER FIFTY-TWO

*B*ut before my head even moves an inch, a thick iron pole whips across my throat. It pulls me back, sucking me against flesh and bone. Now I understand: not an iron pole at all, but an arm, an arm as thick and solid as the Terminator's. A man had grabbed me from behind. Because of the pressure constricting my throat, I can't yell for help. Hell, I can barely breathe...

I instinctively threw my left hand to my throat, as if to remove the arm that was no longer there. So violently did I do this, fingernails caught my chin hard enough to cause stabbing pain.

I swing my arm down, hard, like a pendulum, and the phone in my right fist connects with his groin. The grip on my throat is released. I spin and the pendulum swings again, this time horizontally. There's fire in my hand as the phone connects with his nose. The screen shatters under the collision.

I looked at my hand, those bruised fingers.

The tall man wears a surgical face mask. As my blow sends him staggering backwards into the stream, I see the white cloth awash with blood. He trips and falls, landing flat on his butt in the water.

I am there in a nanosecond, driving a knee into that already crushed nose. He topples onto his back. I drop onto him, sitting astride his hips, and feel the chill of water soaking my jeans. My hands lock onto his throat, forcing his head under the surface. His hands clamp onto mine, trying to tear them away. He can't. I have fury power. Our eyes meet through the rippling water.

I pawed at the air before my face, as if I could touch his, just inches away.

His left hand drops away from my right, but too late I realise why... a rock from the stream bed... like a meteor toward my face... cracking hard against bone. The world flashes white for a moment, and I feel the blood immediately course down my forehead, into my eyes.

The blow knocks me back slightly, easing the weight forced down through my locked arms and into the hands around his throat. His head bursts from the water, and his voice is a spluttering cry.

'Please, no, I'm sorry.'

His right hand is still locked on my left. I yank my hand from his throat, and his fingers scour across mine. I see a fragment of moonlight glint on my wedding ring before it hits the water and sinks. I stab my fingers into the cold, and snatch a rock of my own.

One blow, and his face sinks beneath the water again, and it stays there even after I release my right hand from his throat... consciousness stepping aside, making way for death...

I stagger from the water, still clutching that rock. On the bank, I turn my head to look. His body is clearly visible through the water, so I kick the nearby hollow log into the stream. It rolls against him. I know he will be visible from the other side of the *stream, but it blocks my view of his body and that is enough. Hopefully nobody will find him until he's just bones.*

The rock is still in my hand, smeared with his blood. I swing my arm to launch it backhand, far away. I feel an agonising wrench in my shoulder, and I drop to my knees with a scream of pain.

I touched my still-tender left shoulder.

I was supposed to be dead, but the nightmare was far from over. My scream of pain would bring running feet. I had to escape. So I wiped blood from my eyes and crawled away from the stream.

THE END

ACKNOWLEDGEMENTS

Obsessed is a work of science fiction, so I apologise if you didn't expect this. I was inspired to tackle that genre after watching the long-running British soap opera *EastEnders*. The TV show also convinced me to similarly do away with poetic licence (which the Cambridge Dictionary describes as 'the act by a writer or poet of changing facts or rules to make a story or poem more interesting or effective') and make the story faultlessly correct.

Wait. I should back up and explain. EastEnders? Science fiction? Well, I watched the show's New Year's Eve episode at 8pm, yet witnessed midnight celebrations – four hours in the future! The only explanation, according to a barfly down at my local: it's set on a parallel world. I created such a place for *Obsessed*. On my alternative Earth, everything is the same as on the planet we inhabit, except that Covid hits in 2025. Hope that relaxes those wondering why a story that covers events in 2020 doesn't mention the pandemic.

Actually, there are other differences between the two worlds. Those geographical, scientific, legislative or other errors you spotted that seem to negate my 'faultlessly correct' claim? There you go.

Thanks go to the usual mob: Betsy Reavley, Tara Lyons, Ian Skewis, and everyone else at Bloodhound Books who helped turn my ideas into the book in your hands.

A NOTE FROM THE PUBLISHER

Thank you for reading this book. If you enjoyed it please do consider leaving a review on Amazon to help others find it too.

We hate typos. All of our books have been rigorously edited and proofread, but sometimes mistakes do slip through. If you have spotted a typo, please do let us know and we can get it amended within hours.

info@bloodhoundbooks.com

www.ingramcontent.com/pod-product-compliance
Lightning Source LLC
Chambersburg PA
CBHW050030120726
47903CB00006B/1975